The Enormous Tiny Experiment

Written by Anna Tikvah

Cover Illustration by Hannah Young

2nd Edition

Dedicated to my son, Abel,
who imagined the plot line,
and asked me to write the book ☺

The cascading water splashed down against the rocky cliff, gurgled eagerly through the soft farmland and plunged merrily into the lake. For a few minutes the two scientists stood in absolute bliss, admiring how well their glorious new world was functioning. Neither one had anticipated that a rainbow would stretch across the hills and valleys on opening day!

"Take pictures, Evan," he called out. "This is a day to remember. One day we'll be telling the whole world about our Tiny experiment."

First Printing: May 2020
Second Printing: May 2021
Kindle Direct. Sold by Amazon online.

ISBN: 979-8-51-175193-1

Scripture references are from the ESV or the KJV

Preface to the Series

Why write a series about an atheistic Professor who tries to create his own Paradise in a 'science-fiction' genre? Will these books provide suitable reading material for your children?

In the last eight years we have tragically witnessed loved ones explore New Atheism and other anti-God theories and become swayed by these arguments to turn against their Creator. Since we were unfamiliar at the time with many of the concepts promoted online, we didn't always have the best arguments to counter those ideas and weren't effective to help. We wish our loved ones had something like this series to read when they were younger, to provoke discussions and prepare them for the challenging attacks that this world is launching through social media, the education system and even sometimes from fellow Christians.

About four years ago our youngest son made some inspiring suggestions and this plotline began to develop. Sometimes it's best to begin a difficult discussion standing on the same side as one's opponent... hence beside the Atheist Professor. We also hoped this rather zany, impossible scenario of a miniature creation might provide a lighter framework to explore God's experiences with humans - *'standing in his shoes,'* in a very small way, so to speak. It gives a basis to empathize with the dilemmas and decisions that our Father in Heaven faces daily, such as what happens when some don't appreciate His amazing world and think they would be better off somewhere else? Or rant against natural occurrences that benefit the planet? Or see helpful rules as unfair restrictions? Or when free will leads to harmful actions? Or the gift of knowledge is used to destroy rather than to benefit the community?

This series was purposely written to give humanism a 'best-case' scenario in order to make it palatable to Christians and non-

Christians, alike. The leader is a wonderful man. The Tinys are for the most part, very innocent and kind, with a few exceptions on the 'normal' human scale just to balance it all out ☺. There is a rather idealistic feel to the stories, but even in this 'nearly perfect' world, with good people, minimal suffering, no natural catastrophes or any harmful social media, human nature is still active in every one of them. On top of that, there is one problem the Professor can't overcome, which causes great pain for everyone. While the Professor initially maintains his thesis that *"Humans will thrive in a world with minimal suffering,"* he and his assistant have the most to learn.

Greenville University is close by and tightly associated with the large Biosphere in which the Paradise dome has been carefully hidden from all but the Professor and his assistant Evan. In the classroom and on campus, the Professor and Evan encounter Seth, a bold Christian student, who challenges them to reconsider their philosophy. Throughout this set of three novels, there are two stories happening simultaneously, one in the 'real' world of the Greenville University, and the other inside the beautiful, glass dome of Tinys. Occasionally the two stories overlap, especially when unforeseen events threaten the peace and safety of those in the highly protected, idealistic miniature world.

This series is actually one big story divided into three convenient sections that are very closely connected. Many of the conclusions aren't fully reached until the end of the third book. We recommend it for ages twelve and up, and hope that everyone will enjoy the journey.

With love,

Anna Tikvah

THE BIG PEOPLE

PROFESSOR
LEMANS

EVAN

SETH

THE FIRST TINY

UNCLE LOUIS

The Forest Girls

AIMEE

GEORGIA

SANAA

LILY

DIYA

Rainbow Hill Boys

ZAHIR AND
FREDDO

MILAN

THE ORCHARD GIRLS

VINITHA

ROSA

TINA

YU YAN

THE FARMER BOYS

CHARLEY AND
MAXI

KENZIE

VAHID

THE STOREKEEPER

NANCY AND
RIPPLE

THE BEACH BOYS

DAMIEN

LEMA

FRANZ

NORTH FOREST BOYS

ODIN

PONCE

Chapters

Three Messages

Chapter One

*E*van quickly scanned the mirrored hallway. No one was in sight. It was still early in the morning. Quickly he pressed the green icon on his cell phone and immediately the tile floor dropped away below his feet. In a flash, the tall, blond scientist was in the secret tunnel and the floor was back in place. It was the quickest way to get down to the underground laboratory.

It was hard to see in the dark tunnel with only tiny lights along the ceiling to guide his way. With two long strides he reached the door. Hearing a series of beeps, he checked his messages. He had received three from Professor Lemans:

"Check the kids."

"Ask Louis to replace the Wonderdrink."

"Bring up all the rest of the trees. We'll plant them today."

"Will do," Evan texted in reply.

Using the flashlight on his cell phone, Evan lit up the number pad. He stooped over to punch in the secret code, 'Osuffering66.' A heavy metal door creaked open and the young scientist entered the secret chambers. As of yet, no one knew about the hidden laboratory and what went on below the floors of the Rainforest Biosphere, except himself and the Professor. On his left-hand side were high-tech computers, a Gamma Ray irradiator, incubators, hospital apparatus, test tubes and much more. On his right were a series of nurseries set up high at shoulder level. Nearest to him was the human nursery with four separate rooms, then the animal section with ten compartments, and finally the greenhouse was positioned under a long, deep skylight.

Stopping at the human nursery first, Evan looked through the glass. There, in three visible rooms, each about the length of one of his arms and three hands high, twenty miniaturised children played happily. The 'Tinys', as they called them, had been brought into existence only ten months ago, yet they were already functioning at the level of ten-year-old children. While the Professor did not fully understand the reason for this rapid development, he and Evan had various theories.

For a few minutes Evan observed the activities. Four girls and one boy were reading a book about going to a farm. The book was much bigger than they were. Evan had tried to find the smallest books possible to fill their library stand, but even the smallest books were taller than the children. Sitting on the corners of the book to keep it open, the children read and admired the pictures.

Ponce, Odin and several other boys were busy building forts out of toothpicks and Blu-tack. The rest of the Tinys were drawing pictures with 'Pipsqueak' markers that rose above their heads. Standing up with a marker tucked under their arms, they were able to walk around the piece of paper and make large drawings. On the wall behind them many pictures were on display. Scribble drawings had come first, then crude shapes, and now Evan was often amazed by their ability.

Knocking on the glass to catch their attention, all of the children, except Odin and Ponce, eagerly looked up and waved when they saw Evan's smiling face. Ponce and Odin glanced over, but they didn't see the need to acknowledge his presence.

Stooping over to speak into the microphone, Evan called out, "How's it going, kids? Are you having a good day in there?" The Microphone was positioned under the window. Evan always had to stoop.

Sanaa showed him the picture she was colouring. She put it right up against the glass. Bright green eyes with long, exaggerated black lashes looked back at Evan, and a big, red smile stretched across the round face. However, it was the blond, spiky hair that best represented her subject. The hair filled in the top corners of the page.

"It's you," she said proudly.

"Wow, I like it," Evan smiled, self-consciously flattening his unruly hair. "Nice job on the eyes. They are hard to get right."

Sanaa looked pleased. Dark-skinned, with big, brown eyes, Sanaa was special to Evan, even if he didn't admit to having favourites. He had wanted to call her Sarah, after his sister, but the Professor had been adamant that no names from any supposed 'Holy Book' would be used. Instead, they had carefully chosen names to suit the various nationalities of the children. The project was a multi-racial experiment, and would have been even more so, had all fifty embryos developed successfully.

Vinitha also had a picture that she wanted to show Evan. He marvelled at the realistic features and the black hair she had drawn neatly on the head. "Is this like the Professor?" she asked, looking up shyly from under her long, ebony tresses.

Sucking in his breath, Evan was amazed by her skill. "Well, he used to have..." Evan began with a smile, and then he stopped himself. The Professor didn't want the children to know what he looked like. "Perhaps," he replied.

Braiding her copper-brown hair, Aimee asked, "Is there really a Professor?" Her blue eyes were probing.

"Oh yes!" Evan nodded. "The Professor is the Mastermind of Paradise. I'm only his helper."

Vinitha and Aimee looked at each other in amazement.

"He sounds very important!" Aimee stated.

"Much more important than I am," Evan assured her.

4

Lanky Franz and the dark-skinned, hefty Lema banged on the window, loudly complaining that the other kids weren't sharing the toys. Damien, the strongest boy, said that roly-poly Odin had hit him again. Whining unhappily, Diya, the dark-haired 'princess' said she was bored and didn't know what to do, and there were at least ten other complaints.

Evan tried to work through the issues one by one. It had been a lot of work managing so many children at once. Louis, the oldest by more than four years, had borne the brunt of the burden inside the nursery, but thankfully each labour-intensive stage had not lasted long. Diapering and feeding twenty infants had been an enormous challenge and several photographs of the early weeks sat on the Professor's desk. It had been quite an amazing sight to see, especially when twenty tiny babies lay side by side holding their own bottles! On the far wall of the nursery was a picture Louis had drawn of himself managing all the bumbling toddlers. For the first two months, Louis had been exhausted. Once they were walking and beginning to talk, it had become more manageable.

Now, for the most part, Louis was enjoying his role and had a good relationship with the children. Evan liked to help him out over the microphone, when he could. He hoped that when the magnificent, domed terrarium was finished, all the kids would be fully entertained. The nursery they had lived in for the last ten months was cramped and very plain. "There will be so much to explore and discover in our magnificent world," he thought to himself. "Hopefully it will be ready tomorrow. Surely then there won't be so many squabbles."

Looking around, Evan spotted the oldest Tiny in a corner by the library stand. The biggest books, no taller than Evan's hand, were still above Louis' head. Reaching up, he was pulling and pushing the reading material to one side to see what each one was about.

"He's probably choosing a story for school today," Evan deduced.

Louis was the first Tiny that Professor Lemans had created, exactly four years and ten months previous. Many years of research and experimentation had taken place before the first little Tiny had been successfully 'born.'

While doing his master's degree at Greenville University in Ontario, investigating plant genetics and cell-division, Professor Jacques Lemans had surprised himself when a miniature geranium experiment took root and lived. Years later, as a professor in the same Canadian university, his secret research had developed the process to create a tiny dog! However, the dog hadn't lived long. After numerous experimental failures, the Professor had finally discovered that miniature mammals required a carefully calibrated oxygen content, higher than regular mammals. Once he had determined how to keep his miniaturised creation alive, the Professor had used the same unpublished process on human reproductive cells that had been donated for scientific research. While this process was unethical, the Professor had justified his actions due to the benefits he believed his research would provide to science and the study of human behaviour. Again, it took many unsuccessful attempts, before a tiny fetus had developed into a real, fully functioning baby boy, only two centimetres tall. Louis had been 'born' nearly four years before the others, in an incubator. From embryo to baby took less than a month, and the baby boy had continued to develop at this alarming rate. Now, ten centimetres tall and gray-haired, Louis was a full-grown Tiny of fifty-eight months. Professor Lemans had been promising him a world of his own ever since he had been old enough to communicate.

With access to other human reproductive material, donated with full consent to the University for 'unrestricted scientific research,' the other Tinys had come into existence. Much research and labour had been expended on the enormous terrarium the two scientists were preparing for multiple Tinys to inhabit. This new world, fondly referred to as 'Paradise,' was almost ready!

"Hey, Louis," Evan said, speaking into the microphone, "have you replaced the Wonderdrink in the main machine?"

"We just did it," Louis smiled, turning around and heading toward the window. "The children were great helpers."

"What else can we do, Uncle Louis?" Nancy asked, her bright, blue eyes sparkling. Sturdy and very capable, brown-haired Nancy loved to be busy. She kept the nursery well-organised.

"It's time for school," Uncle Louis said in his gentle, but firm, way. "We have an important lesson today about water!"

"Like the stuff we drink?" Franz asked.

"Yes," Uncle Louis replied, tousling the boy's stringy, brown hair. "but in Paradise there will be so much water in some places that you will need to learn how to stay safe when you play in it."

"Play in it!" Franz went wild with the thought, jumping up and down. "I can't wait to see Paradise!" He rushed over to tell his friends they would get to play in water.

The copper-haired girl nearby was more excited to hear that it was time for school. "Yay for school!" Aimee sang, clapping her hands. "I love school, Uncle Louis!"

Uncle Louis laughed happily. He could always count on Aimee's enthusiasm.

The others looked happy but maybe not quite so keen. Yu Yan, Tina, and Vinitha had returned to read books in the far corner of the room, and many of the boys had resumed building forts.

Kenzie's white, freckled face and gray eyes were peering excitedly through the glass. "How long till we go into Paradise?" he asked Evan.

"We're planting a few more trees today," the tall scientist relayed through the microphone, "and then all that will be left to do is to introduce the animals to their new habitat. By tomorrow, if all goes well, we'll have it ready for you!"

"Really? Tomorrow?" Kenzie asked. "Just one more sleep?"

When Evan nodded his head, Kenzie went running to share his good news with the other children. Soon almost everyone was cheering and dancing around; almost everyone except the quiet girls who were reading, and Odin and Ponce who rarely joined in any group activities.

Waving goodbye to the children, Evan passed by the bird and animal nursery, quickly looking through the glass panes to see that everything looked okay. The beagle puppy was chasing the rabbits and so far, he hadn't eaten any. Squirrels scolded high up on the climbing apparatus, and the colourful birds flew back and forth. Chickens, ducks and loons were pecking grain from the floor. The deer, sheep and cow were guzzling breakfast from the rubber teats on their formula machine.

"We've got to get Paradise in working order by tomorrow," Evan encouraged himself. Tomorrow was the last day of their summer vacation. Since the beginning of May, Evan and the Professor had been working overtime to have things operational before classes resumed.

To fulfil the Professor's third request, Evan moved on to the small greenhouse nursery, where they had been developing miniature plants for the last three years. While the undisclosed lab and nurseries were located below ground level, the greenhouse was positioned under a fifteen-metre skylight. Above, on the main floor of the glass Rainforest Biome, the skylight was part of a decorative, rectangular glass prism, surrounded on all sides with cascading plants. No one knew of its special purpose below. The whole project had to remain well-concealed. Professor Lemans was very concerned that, if anything leaked out to the media, it would be shut down before he had opportunity to set it all in motion. He was well aware of the protests that might arise if word got out that he was developing tiny humans who aged incredibly fast and would be kept in captivity! Yet, captivity was vital since the Tinys required a higher concentration of oxygen than regular humans. He knew full well that the Tinys wouldn't survive more than an hour in the earth's regular atmosphere.

Professor Lemans was confident that one day scientists would come from all over the world to study human behaviour in his nearly perfect world. He was fully convinced that a world with no calamities, no unfair suffering or restrictions would result in the happiest human life possible. "Humans," he often told Evan, "will thrive in a beautiful, safe environment, unencumbered by any authoritarian rules."

Donning protective gloves and a mask, Evan collected the three hundred tiny trees they had produced using Professor Lemans' genetic engineering process. He walked into the elevator and pressed the arrow to head up.

Finishing Touches

Chapter Two

Riding the elevator up to the main floor, Evan waited for the doors to slide open. In the massive Greenville University Biosphere, stretching over one hundred hectares and consisting of several unique habitats filled with living plants and animals from all over the globe, the Professor's most important laboratory was located in the middle of the glass Rainforest Biome. The 'Paradise Room,' as he called it, was about the size of a small house, and so far, very well-concealed.

When the elevator shaft opened, Evan walked into the bright greenhouse enclosure, which housed the enormous domed terrarium. As always, a stately painting of the Professor was the first thing to come into view. In Evan's opinion, the painter had copied Jacques' European features quite accurately, even if he had generously darkened the now nearly white goatee and short, grey hair. Seeing the Professor in a crisp black suit, like the one in the painting, was extremely rare, but it did give him a handsome appearance. Copies of this painting hung in two other places in the Greenville Biosphere. Everyone knew that without Jacques Lemans' foresight and generous donations towards the inception of the University Biosphere, it may never have been built.

Fifteen years previous, when Jacques had first discovered how to create a tiny geranium, he had also inherited an enormous sum of money. His father, who was forty-five years older, had been a brilliant computer software developer who had always wished he'd been a scientist and was very proud of his son's achievements. When he and Jacques' mother had died in a terrible car accident, leaving a multi-million-dollar inheritance to their only son, one important stipulation was attached. The stipulation was that the money could only be spent to further scientific research.

Eager to continue his own research and to provide ample opportunity for others, the Professor had persuaded the Greenville University to build the large Rainforest Biome on their vacant, rolling hills. With the help of his cousin, an architect-engineer, the first biome had emerged in spectacular fashion, encouraging a nationwide contribution to build two other glass structures, now housing the Desert and Arctic Tundra biomes.

Now three, fully enclosed, free-standing glass structures, complete with live animals and birds, stood within walking distance of the University. They were surrounded by natural Canadian gardens displaying the boreal and deciduous forests, tundra, and wildflowers.

Already, the Greenville Biosphere was becoming a notable research and education centre during the University semesters and a major tourist location over the holidays.

While most of the other university staff were aware that Professor Lemans had a private room in the middle of the Rainforest Biome, no one knew about the underground chambers and laboratories. Hidden entrances and exits had concealed the secret research project from nearly everyone. Evan was the only student that Professor Lemans had ever dared trust with his incredibly important venture. They both hoped that, one day soon, Paradise might be the Biosphere's main attraction. With this long-term vision in mind, the northern wall of the large upstairs room was a glass viewing area. It was attached to a large, still-unrevealed hall, which also served as the acknowledged entrance to Professor Leman's private office. His name tag was fixed to the locked door, but no one except he and Evan had ever entered. It had all been purposefully designed for the day when the whole world would be invited to view the one and only miniature Paradise.

"Here are the trees, Sir," Evan said, bringing the tray over.

Pulling on a new pair of disposable latex gloves and donning a mask, Professor Lemans prepared for the last planting in Paradise. It was crucial that they didn't contaminate the new world with any virus or unwanted bacteria. He picked up tweezers and a soft brush from his desk. "Thank you," he said excitedly. "Let's get them in."

A button on the wall lowered the sides of the curved glass dome. About fifty metres in circumference, it took the Professor sixty casual strides to walk all the way around the circular terrarium. Inside, the Professor had created a lake that stretched fully across the south end, complete with a wave simulator monitored from the lab computer. They had already stocked the lake with miniature fish of the best-eating variety: perch, bass, trout and freshwater salmon. A thirty-five-centimeter-wide strip of fine white sand lay all along the vast shoreline.

"I can't wait to see the Tinys build boats," Professor Lemans chuckled, as he pressed the trigger on his LiftPod to get inside the dome.

"It's going to be so fun watching them enjoy our world!" Evan agreed.

The domed terrarium had been specially prepared with privacy window film all around the sides, while the overhead glass was transparent. Standing outside the terrarium, looking in, the glass was perfectly clear from every direction. Standing inside the terrarium, the sun, moon and stars were perfectly visible above, day and night, since the dome was situated within the greenhouse glass of the Biome; however, around the sides the glass was tinted. The Tinys would be unable to see anyone watching them, unless – and very unlikely - someone was able to climb twelve meters up the greenhouse structure and look in from the roof. Drones had been banned in the vicinity.

Believing strongly that one day everyone would be interested in studying his new creation, Professor Lemans had used the privacy window film to ensure the Tinys could be observed without their knowledge. He wanted an accurate assessment of their day-to-day life.

Tiptoeing carefully inside, trying to stand only on the sandy beach and avoid crushing Evan's newly constructed wooden schoolhouse, the Professor reached towards the hills. He was planting the rest of the trees on the west side of the dome. The lovely, forested hills would cleanse the air and provide an enjoyable habitat.

Evan leaned over the lowered glass wall of the dome with his long arm outstretched and handed the Professor three more eucalyptus. The little trees were about the size of his index finger. "These are doing well," he said. "It's amazing how quickly everything matures."

"It is," Professor Lemans smiled, carefully tamping the eucalyptus trees into the rich soil. "I do believe it's the pent-up energy."

Evan agreed. He and the Professor favoured the theory that the miniaturized cells of the Tinys, pre-programmed to produce something thirty to forty times larger, directed their restricted energy into an accelerated maturity.

The Professor interspersed the eucalyptus among the blue spruce, and pines. The Professor hadn't produced every species of tree for the hills, just a few which would remain green all year long. He had been much more liberal in the orchard. An abundant variety of fruit trees from all over the world were already well-established in the farmland.

While he was planting the trees, Evan told the Professor about the children's portraits and the conversation he'd had with three of the girls. "They are very curious about you," Evan explained.

"That's just fine," the Professor replied, planting another eucalyptus, "but we need to remain detached. This is first and foremost a research project. You know how close I've become to Louis."

Evan nodded. He knew the plan was for the project to operate under the auspices of 'naturalistic observational research,' but he yearned to stay involved. "Louis has become like your son," he agreed.

"And, I don't want that to happen with these new Tinys. I will keep close to Louis and communicate with him, but the others need to stay independent from me and you, from this point on. We can't let our involvement tarnish our research. And anyhow, I do believe they will all function better without any higher power intimidating them, or making rules, or governing in any way.

"I know," Evan smiled, having heard this speech numerous times. "You want the Tinys to function with Louis as their loving relative and live in total happiness."

"Exactly. It's regrettable we didn't end up with an Aunt Loretta, and a few other older Tinys who could help Louis out." Shaking his head sadly, he added, "If only I hadn't lost so many, early on."

Evan knew all about the early failures. It was remarkable that they now had twenty-one, healthy, 'normal' Tinys! "The kids do like calling him 'Uncle Louis'," he chuckled. "It gives them a sense of a special relationship."

"That's right," the Professor agreed. "They have Uncle Louis, so we need to stand back and remain objective."

"We're not going to feel any emotion?" Evan queried, knowing how attached he felt already.

The Professor looked up from his work and smiled ruefully. "Our *goal* is to remain detached and objective," he reiterated, "I'm not saying it will be easy."

Evan nodded and handed him a few more eucalyptus. Changing the subject, he said, "If I were a Tiny, I'd build my house on this hill." Pointing to the hill closest to him, Evan noted, "From here, there is a fantastic view of the lake, even though it is surrounded by forest."

"It is a great spot," the Professor agreed, scratching a small hole in the fertile, sterilised soil. He popped in another tree. "Maybe Louis will claim it."

"I hope he does set up here," Evan stated with a chuckle, "especially since the control cave is directly underneath."

Pausing to reflect where the next tree should go, Professor Lemans added, "I love the way the rain has already carved small gullies on the hills."

"Did you see the waterfall yesterday?" Evan asked.

An automatic sprinkler system, coined the 'rainmaker,' extended in a metal arch and ran flush against the domed ceiling. Tiny holes mimicked rainfall and generally watered the terrarium every night between two and four A.M. Evan had chosen a large granite rock to make the tallest hill, and just yesterday, after manually turning on the rainmaker, he had noticed a waterfall streaming over the rock ledge and running through the lowlands.

"Really, a waterfall?" the Professor replied. "That will be beautiful!" A moment later, he said, "However, I guess it will never be seen, unless we occasionally turn on the rain during the day."

"True," Evan agreed. "Maybe the odd rainy day will be a welcome novelty for them?"

"Sunshine is much nicer," the Professor replied; not fond of rainy days.

Gesturing toward a hill without trees near the North Forest, the Professor said, "I've decided to leave that hill bare. If the Tinys ever build something with wheels, it is steep enough to have some fun. It even has a good bump in just the right spot."

"Mountain biking! You've thought of everything!" Evan exclaimed with admiration, handing the Professor another five trees.

"I hope so. Once everyone has been released into this world, I really don't want to interfere... aside from sending in daily supplies, and keeping them safe, of course. I want them to learn to be resourceful and independent."

Holding out another three trees, Evan asked, "Where would you build your house, Professor?"

Professor Lemans didn't hesitate. "Probably down by the orchard and gardens. Then I could keep on experimenting."

Evan laughed. "That would be perfect for you!"

Glancing over to the east side of the dome, Evan admired the lush, green, rolling lowlands. He knew they would be excellent for farming. He and the Professor had layered the soil with fine gravel and limestone for drainage, then well-rotted compost and a heavy layer of the best Triple-Mix soil they could buy. Already, the little fruit orchards were taking root and growing strong along the newly formed, but usually dry, riverbed.

The mining area lay in the north-east. Round, grassy and unforested, it was a large hill full of quartz, fine gravel, sand, piles of pebbles, and many, many flat building rocks. Far down in the layers was a lovely crystal suncatcher and some precious gems. They hoped the Tinys would, in time, find these treasures and use them in their own creative ways.

In the valley between the mining hill and the steep, bare hill with a bump, the Professor had built the supply store. It was well-stocked with useful items like building boards, wooden doweling, toothpicks, brass tacks, wire, and basic grocery supplies. The store even had a useable kitchen for food preparation, attached as it was to electricity and water below.

Evan was proud of the non-polluting, electric train he had set up that came in through a tunnel in the north end and delivered supplies directly to the store. It was just a simple in-and-out track through a highly secure tunnel system, but one that would allow himself and the Professor to give the Tinys everything they needed to build, survive and thrive.

"Trees are in," Professor Lemans exclaimed happily, standing up and wiping his hands together. He stepped back one careful step on the shoreline to look at the forest. "I love it!"

"It's such a fantastic world!" Evan agreed. "I wish I was a Tiny!"

"Me too!" the Professor laughed. Stepping into the LiftPod, he raised himself up and out of the large terrarium.

"So, let's get it all in working order," Professor Lemans directed hastily, as he swung down. "Today we will release the birds and animals and ensure everything is functioning well." Clapping his hands together, he added, "This is the moment I've been waiting for all these years! Finally, Paradise will be filled with life and sound."

Evan pressed the red button on the wall. With a quiet whir, the curved dome sides slid slowly up and clicked back into place. Below the red button were three other buttons, a white, a blue, and a black. Evan pressed the white button and rich, well-filtered, oxygenated air filled the dome, streaming in through a long round pipe with tiny holes that circumvented the terrarium just above the ground.

To settle in the new plantings, Evan also pressed the blue button to activate the rainmaker. From the north side of the dome, the curved metal tube skimmed along the arched ceiling of the dome, slowly and gently raining on the world below. It was a perfect rain, not too hard, not too light, just sufficient to water the hills and the valleys and keep everything lush and green.

"I want to see this waterfall," the Professor exclaimed happily, walking over to stand beside Evan.

"Stopwatch is set," Evan smiled, tapping his phone and holding it in view. "We'll get an accurate count on how long it takes a waterfall to form."

Enthralled by the beauty of their new little world, the two scientists watched with delighted anticipation. Sunshine was streaming in through the outer glass walls of the greenhouse, slanting down into the domed terrarium. Refracting through the fine spray inside, the rays formed a lovely rainbow.

"*Oh là là! Magnifique!*" the Professor called out.

"Look now! The waterfall has started," Evan told him. "That took only forty-three seconds once the rain hit the cliff."

"I should have thought to put some ferns by the cliff," the Professor called out regretfully. "How could I have forgotten to create ferns?"

"Whatever we decide we need in the future, we can send in on the train," Evan reminded him. "Louis will see that they are planted."

"True, true!"

The cascading water splashed down against the rocky cliff, gurgled eagerly through the soft farmland and plunged merrily into the lake. For a few minutes the two scientists stood in absolute bliss, admiring how well their glorious new world was functioning. Neither one had anticipated that a rainbow would stretch across the hills and valleys on opening day!

Once they were satisfied that the new trees had settled in, Evan pressed the blue button to turn off the rain. They both hoped they would never have to use the black button; it was linked to the smoke sensors and the automatic emergency sprinklers.

While the scientists waited two hours for the atmospheric conditions to regulate, they carefully monitored the computer programs to ensure that everything was in working order... and it was! When the jingle on his phone signalled time was up, Professor Lemans smiled at Evan triumphantly. "Let's do this," he said.

Accessing the Dome app on his phone, the Professor found the animal nursery settings, scrolled to 'The Door' and toggled the 'Open/Close' switch. A distant whirr sounded. He did the same for the tunnel entrance, and they both watched excitedly as the tunnel doors opened up inside the large terrarium.

"Take pictures, Evan," he called out. "This is a day to remember. One day we'll be telling the whole world about our Tiny experiment."

Evan had his phone ready as the first Rainbow Lorikeets arrived, soaring up through the tunnel and then circling around inside the dome. When the colourful birds landed in the pine trees on the top of the highest hill, Evan took even more pictures. Bright, little Eastern Bluebirds with their rosy-red breasts were next, then Northern Cardinals and Common Loons - all the Professor's favourites. A brown cow and two black-faced sheep ran in, mooing and baaing loudly as they kicked up their heels and danced all over the rolling pastureland. Two puppies playfully chased after the frisky red squirrels. A few ducks waddled in while thirty chickens ran past. Next, a tentative, striped orange cat crept in cautiously, followed by leaping rabbits, and two shy deer.

There were even some insects - helpful insects, none of the annoying, destructive variety. Even though flies and mosquitoes would have provided ideal food for some of the birds, a decision had been made that formulated, dry pellets would be supplied instead. Choosing their favourites, the Professor and Evan had miniaturized the prettiest species of butterflies and moths, lots of honeybees and fireflies. Due to their short lifespan and proven infertility, the insects would have to be miniaturized and released every month.

"Listen to our creation," Evan exclaimed to the smiling Professor. From the hidden microphone located under the school roof, songbird music was ringing through the speakers they had set up in the Paradise Room. Barks, moos, baas, squawks and a rooster crow added to the melody.

"C'est fabuleux! This... is fabulous!" the Professor sighed happily. "Our perfect world has come to life. We've done it!"

"Our perfect world," Evan considered with a triumphant smile. Yet, he had just the smallest twinge of conscience. It had taken years of research and effort to create the Tinys and their wonderful environment, but... Evan knew they hadn't given life to anything; they had only manipulated what already existed.

Hastily, Evan dismissed the disconcerting thought just as he had numerous times before. Opening a bottle of champagne, purchased weeks ago for this very occasion, he joined the Professor in joyfully celebrating their enormous accomplishment.

"All these years of research have been completely worthwhile!" Evan burst out with elation. "This is absolutely amazing! It's come together just as we hoped! Congratulations, Jacques Lemans."

Come What May

Chapter Three

A cricket chirp interrupted the celebrations. The Professor picked up his phone and glanced at the message. "Rachel needs my advice," he relayed to Evan. "The iguanas have been fighting again."

With a shrug, Evan nodded. Professor Jacques Lemans oversaw everything that happened in the Rainforest Biome. "I'll tidy up," he offered.

Clapping his assistant on the back, the Professor took one more sip of champagne. "I'll be back in half an hour," he assured him. "Enjoy watching the animals discover Paradise. We need to finish our celebration."

Rushing into the elevator passageway, the Professor didn't take a ride down into his underground laboratory, but instead darted left to go through a second set of sliding doors which opened up into a long corridor. This corridor took him through the train loading and supply area and then into the locked viewing hall which had been built for the occasion when Paradise would become a public exhibit in the Rainforest Biome. At the end, another locked door opened up into the mirrored hall, right near the Reptile Café.

Rachel Khalid was standing outside the door. With a twinkle in her pretty blue eyes, she observed the Professor's dishevelled appearance. "I am so curious about what you do in there!" she confessed.

"You will be one of the first to know all about it," Jacques promised the lovely, dark-haired woman. Rachel Khalid was the head veterinarian at the Greenville Biosphere. She and her husband had immigrated from Israel and been supportive of almost everything the Professor had ever suggested should happen in the Biosphere. Often, he wondered what they would think of the Paradise project. He desperately hoped they would both be on his side.

"You always say I'll be the first to know," she teased, "but you've been saying that for the last four years. When will I know, Jacques?"

With a lengthy pause, Jacques looked at her and smiled. Rachel rarely pressed hard and he yearned to tell her everything and show her all around. Paradise was better than he had imagined! But he knew he couldn't... not just yet. "I hope the new display will be open next summer," he said earnestly. "If not, at least by the end of next year."

"You have no idea how mystified I am," she laughed. "Everyone is! Everyone that knows, that is," she clarified quickly. "We've haven't told anyone that you spend so much time in there."

"And 'we' is still just the three of you?" Jacques confirmed.

"Yes. Yes. Farouk and I, and Tim."

Farouk was Rachel's husband and Tim was the maintenance man. Rachel and Tim noticed everything that went on in the public part of the Rainforest Biome.

"So, there's been another lizard battle?" Jacques inquired, trying to change the subject and hoping to get back in time to celebrate with Evan.

"Come have a look at Bert," she said, leading him in behind the spectacular, ten-meter-high waterfall. A plexiglass tunnel kept the small animal care centre safe and dry from the cascading water on the other side. Large clear aquariums lined the far wall. Rachel pointed to the green iguana that had been attacked. Deep scratches adorned his front leg. Crouching perfectly still inside his glass walls, the iguana's eyes roved in various directions.

"This is the fourth time poor Bert has been mauled," she complained, pointing to the wounds which had already been cleaned and put up for adoption. "I think it's time we had Timbo shipped to a pet store or rehomed. He is far too aggressive."

"I agree," Jacques nodded sadly, gazing at the old scars from former battles on Bert's shoulder. "Timbo is a beauty, but Bert has a gentler disposition. If I had to choose between them, I'd pick Bert."

"Wonderful, then we both agree," Rachel smiled. "I'll call the pet store in the morning."

"Thanks so much for all that you do, Rachel," Jacques expressed earnestly. "I always know the animals and birds are in competent hands. I appreciate you asking me for advice on the iguanas, but I'm also quite happy for you to act on your own good judgment."

"Thank you," she smiled. "Maybe I could also inquire if the pet store wants a Macaw?"

"Non! Non! Not Molly!" Jacques called out in mock dismay. He knew Rachel would never give Molly away, even if the colourful bird did have a nasty habit of nipping whenever Rachel had to handle her.

Sharing a laugh, the two parted company and Jacques Lemans returned to the mirrored hallway. Since it was after seven, the Biome was closed for the day and Tim, the maintenance man had gone home. Rachel was still in the care centre, so Jacques took drop floor exit so he could check on the Tinys.

Leaving the lights off, so the children wouldn't see him as he walked past, the Professor gazed fondly into the glowing nursery. Louis was attempting to help Odin read a novel, but Odin was flailing his arms up in frustration and trying to slip away. A group of girls were drawing with markers, and some of the boys were playing tag from room to room. "Tomorrow," he thought, "they will finally have space to run and play. There will be so much for them to do!" With a happy sigh, he murmured, "I can't wait for tomorrow!"

Riding the elevator upstairs, the Professor was glad to see Evan was still in the Paradise Room. The LiftPod was safely back in the corner and all the tools were sterilised and back in the bin. Having finished cleaning up, Evan was watching the animals frolic in the grass.

"How did that go?" Evan asked.

"Well enough," Professor Lemans replied. "Bert was badly scratched again, so we've decided to put Timbo up for adoption."

They discussed Timbo's past misdeeds and agreed he had to go, even though he was undeniably the biggest and best specimen of his kind, and fondly named by the maintenance man.

"Rachel asked again when Paradise will be open to the public," the Professor relayed. "I do wish she could have been in on this from the beginning."

"Rachel would have a lot to offer," Evan agreed. "She's a mom; she has keen insights. The girls especially would benefit from a female mentor." He waggled his blond eyebrows. "But then she'd be an accomplice! If the world doesn't perceive this research experiment as... well... as we hope they will."

With a deep sigh, the Professor nodded. "Yes. Best to keep her in the dark until we're ready to reveal the happiest place on earth to everyone. Surely the benefits of this research will outweigh a few questionable ethics."

"And if they don't?" Evan smiled.

The Professor turned to him. "As I've said many times, I sincerely hope this experiment won't cause you any disadvantage, Evan," he implored. "You know I will take all the blame – whatever it is. Regardless of whether or not they take away my research capabilities... or imprison me..."

"Or call you a 'mad scientist'" Evan grinned.

"*Ça alors!* Whatever they do to me, this project has been the restoration of real joy in my life! If everything is perceived in a negative light, which I certainly hope it will not, I trust that my relationship and care for the Tinys will be seen as integral for their survival. I know many teams will be sent in to manage their lives, and oversee everything that goes on..."

"I hope no one sues us..."

"It is a possibility," Professor Lemans admitted thoughtfully, "but... if everyone falls in love with the Tinys, they may not. The world may donate to our cause instead." Reaching out to clap Evan on the shoulder, the Professor assured him, "Whatever they do, I will cover for you the best that I can. I promise. And I will never regret my part in this. Many scientists have been misunderstood and black-listed as a result of their investigations and discoveries. The world doesn't always understand... initially. Think of how they treated Galileo and Marcello Marpighi, or Gerhard Domagk..."

"Or the physician who discovered that hand washing was the key to preventing disease," Evan added.

"Ah yes, Ignaz Semmelweis!" he agreed. "Good example. So, I may pay heavily for my opportunity to advance scientific knowledge, but I'd rather pay and contribute something significant, than live my life as a free man, never exploring the insights and opportunities that have come my way. After all, 'the end justifies the means.'"

Evan looked up. The Professor often made reference to the end justifying the means, and Evan wasn't entirely sure it was right. Did the end always justify the means?

Gazing wistfully at the two puppies dashing around the orchard, Evan asked, "Do you sometimes wish we could keep this a secret forever?"

"For longer, yes," the Professor nodded, "but since we've come to realise how fast the Tinys age, we must share this experiment while they are still in their prime. No one will be enamoured by a world full of aging, dying creatures."

"So true," Evan agreed, watching the beagle pup playfully approach the orange-striped cat and quickly jump back with a scratch to his nose. He chuckled and then with a nod, he reiterated the

Professor's concerns. "We must share Paradise with the world in a year or two, or we will have no hope of a positive response."

Turning to look at the Professor steadfastly, Evan said, "I want you to know that whatever happens to us as a result of this, I will always be thankful to have taken part in the most exciting, creative, phenomenal research project that I could ever imagine. This," he affirmed, gesturing toward the dome, "has fulfilled every aspiration I've ever had to be a scientist."

"And without you, I would have failed to accomplish my dream," the Professor smiled, picking up his half-empty glass of champagne. He presented a toast. "To you, to us, to successful miniaturization, to a family of Tinys, and to an opportunity to show the world that true happiness can be found in a kinder and safer environment."

Getting Ready

Chapter 4

After Evan had gone home that night, the Professor sat down at his desk. The glow from his phone lit up the darkened Paradise Room. For a few moments he leaned back in his padded chair and gazed up at the peaceful sky. Little stars twinkled through the criss-crossed panes of glass which formed the strong greenhouse structure. It wasn't often that Jacques Lemans took time to relax, but now, finally, everything was ready. The intense preparations were over, and his new world was alive and fully functional.

The cow mooed over the speakers and Jacques smiled. "What a lovely sound," he thought to himself. "I can't wait to sit in here and listen to the children talking to each other. Finally, my little family will have a beautiful world of their own."

For a few more minutes, Jacques enjoyed his quiet reverie. As an only child growing up, he'd often wished he'd been one of many siblings. Now, as a lonely adult, he often yearned for a family. In many ways he was living his life and dreams again through the Tinys, even though he tried to tell himself and Evan that he would remain detached as this was primarily a 'research project.' In all truthfulness, tomorrow's entrance into Paradise was just as exciting for him as he hoped it would be for them.

A cricket chirp alerted him to an incoming message. Louis was requesting to talk, just as he always did once all the children were asleep. Down in the nursery, Louis had access to a small, private, sound-proof chamber with a Smartphone. It was here that he had communicated with the Professor since his earliest days. It was here that he had done his remote learning, watching educational videos, reading, studying and answering questions online.

Pressing the WhiteDove App, the Professor answered the video call.

"Hi," Louis said, with a smile lighting up his ageing face. "How did it go today? I heard the doors open and the animals leave. Are they enjoying Paradise?"

"They are loving it!" the Professor rejoiced. "All went well today. Tomorrow you and the children will join them and see for yourselves."

"I am so thrilled to hear this!" Louis exclaimed. "I probably won't sleep tonight, just thinking about it!"

"Well, we do have some last-minute things to go over," the Professor relayed with a chuckle, "so I'm glad you weren't planning a long sleep. Did you take the First-Aid exam?"

"Yes," Louis smiled. "I scored eighty-nine out of ninety. I only missed one of the four signs of a stroke."

"Well done," the Professor praised earnestly. He was very proud of Louis' abilities to learn and recall information. "Did you finish all the swimming videos?"

Louis sighed. "I've watched at least twenty and I feel I understand the theory. It just may be a little hard to teach something I've never done before myself..."

"No doubt," the Professor agreed, raising his eyebrows and nodding vigorously. "Teaching the kids to swim will be challenging! Hopefully some will catch on quickly and be able to demonstrate the strokes to others."

"I spent a lot of time reading about drowning prevention and water safety tips," Louis assured him. "I am trying to emphasize this with all the children before anyone steps a foot into the water."

"Good, good! There will be so much fun to be had in the water. I want them all to enjoy it fully. But the lake does pose one of the greatest risks to their safety. I do sometimes wonder if perhaps a shallow wading pool might have been a better option... but then they couldn't fish... or..."

"I will help them stay safe," Louis promised.

"Thank you!"

"What lessons do you want me to cover when we're finished with swimming and water safety?" Louis asked.

"I'll be sending in more books," the Professor told him. "It's important to get their reading level up, so that they can read complex instructions on how to build and create. And, we should cover fractions, multiplication and division. I also want them to understand their anatomy, so we can delve into First Aid when they're a few months older."

"Should we look at animal care?" Louis suggested.

"Ah, yes, I have some excellent books and materials on this. To be good stewards of Paradise, they will need to understand the importance of feeding and training the animals. I'll be sending in kibble for the cat and dogs, and pellets for the birds and chickens, but the others will be fine on vegetarian diets, or fish... Anyway, you'll see all that exact information in the notes I'll be sending in."

"We should improve their writing skills so that they can communicate well in the future."

"Yes, yes," Jacques Lemans agreed. "I've printed some small workbooks for that purpose. And then there will be so many practical things to learn, like measuring, using a saw to cut building boards, framing houses, windows and doors, growing gardens, food preparation, useful chemical reactions, maintaining forests, catching fish... You've got plenty to cover for at least a year."

The conversation shifted to the principles of servant leadership which the Professor had been gradually sharing with Louis night after night ever since the children were little. He wanted to be sure that Paradise would be led by selfless example, and with plenty of kindness, empathy and love. Thankfully, Louis was very receptive to the concepts. He was naturally a kind and loving individual, who had enjoyed the children coming into his life from day one, even if the first two months of diapers and bottles had occasionally overwhelmed him.

"What are the ten most important principles of servant leadership?" the Professor quizzed.

Louis had them well memorized and he listed them out, "Listening, Empathy, Healing, Awareness, Persuasion, Conceptualization, Foresight, Stewardship, Commitment to Growth, and Building Community."

"Excellent!"

For at least an hour they discussed some of the principles in more depth. Louis was fully committed to the ideas and even in the nursery he had often demonstrated his understanding in amazing ways.

"I have full confidence in you, Louis," the Professor smiled. "I'll never forget all the mornings I would walk past the nursery and see you asleep in your bed with numerous babies on each side."

"Ah, yes, some just couldn't go to sleep on their own," Louis reminisced with a chuckle. "I'd fall asleep patting their backs."

"You did well," the Professor praised. "I wish you hadn't been so alone looking after them. As you know, it's not what I intended..."

Louis sighed. It would have been wonderful to have had another Tiny his own age, especially a wife, but after four years on his own, the children were a welcome addition. "I'm very happy I'm not all alone anymore," Louis assured him. "It was a lot of work for a couple of months, but now I look forward to every day. I love the children. Sharing Paradise with them will be my dream come true."

"Tomorrow then," the Professor promised earnestly. "As soon as you've all had breakfast, I'll open the doors and you can walk in."

"Tomorrow!" Louis reiterated. "Tomorrow will be the day!

"Today's the Day"

Chapter Five

imee woke up when the large metal door opened. She knew that the creaking sound meant Evan was visiting. Bright lights flooded into the large nursery windows, lighting up the row of ten little wooden beds lined against the wall. Sitting up, Aimee pulled her long, copper-brown hair into a tidy ponytail, and pushed off the pink fleece blanket.

"Today's the day!" she called out, her bright blue eyes sparkling with elation. Hopping out of bed, she danced around the room that she shared with the nine other tiny girls. "We're going to the new world today!" she sang.

Sanaa and Georgia were instantly awake. "Hooray!!" they cried out, jumping out of bed. "Today is the day!"

"I want to see the water," Sanaa sang, clapping her hands and kicking her dark brown feet from side to side, "and flowers!"

"And all the things that Uncle Louis drew for us!" tall, blond Georgia added, running over to dance with Aimee around the room.

"It's going to be our home forever!" Aimee sang happily.

"I hope there will still be a Wonderdrink station," Diya moaned, rolling over in bed. Diya was the smallest girl; she looked just like the Indian princess in the book that Uncle Louis had read to them.

"We will grow our own food," Aimee reminded her, "or make something to trade for food from the store."

"I just want Wonderdrink," Diya pouted, sitting up and brushing her thick, black hair with one of the pink plastic brushes that Evan had given them.

"Me too," whined Rosa, heaving her plump self out of the small wooden bed. "Why can't the Professor just keep giving us Wonderdrink?"

"Because he wants us to have fun," Sanaa encouraged, pulling her colourful shawl over her nightgown. "Remember, Uncle Louis said that growing things is so much fun!"

"And it teaches us to be industrious," Nancy added, recalling Uncle Louis' lessons from the day before. "We will be happiest if we contribute to our community."

A whirring sound alerted the girls to new supplies entering their room. With great excitement they ran over to the delivery area to have a look. Nancy pulled open the door to the sliding compartment under the window and dragged in a box. It was full of new clothes! Every few weeks, a box of clothes had come through in the same manner, and it was always so exciting.

"Oh, I love this dress!" Aimee said, holding up a blue sundress with little, white flowers. Wispy gauze strips hung from the shoulder straps; the girls called them ribbons.

Sanaa pulled out a very small, sparkly pink top and shorts with lace and sequins. "This is for Diya," she said immediately, tossing it over to her. There was always one extra-small item that would only fit Diya.

Seeing the sparkles and sequins, Diya's eyes lit up eagerly. She put on the new clothes. Then she waltzed over to view herself in the glass reflection of the window. "Hmm," she considered carefully, "this top could be just a little tighter. But... it will do."

Lily looked over at Diya enviously and wrinkled her freckled nose. "I don't know why you get all the small clothes. I'm not that much bigger, you know."

"If it has sparkles, then it's mine," Diya proclaimed, looking at herself sideways.

Tossing her straight, brown hair back proudly, Lily picked up a sundress that Georgia had decided was too small. It hung loosely but she liked the orange flowers that were embroidered on the hem.

"I wonder why all the clothes have a little capital F and P on them?" Aimee remarked, very pleased that the pretty blue dress fit. No one understood the FP label, having never heard of 'brand names,' but they all briefly examined the decal on their own items.

"This is for me!" Sanaa laughed, having reached the bottom of the pile. She held up a bright turquoise dress and slipped it on. "Oooh, I can move in this!" she laughed, dancing all around. "And there aren't so many ribbons! I don't like ribbons. I just love colour!"

Almost everyone had found something they liked to wear... except one. "Nothing fits me," Rosa complained, unable to pull on even the loosest dress.

Everyone looked at Rosa. She was much rounder than the others. Finally, in a tentative voice, Sanaa said, "You can have my shawl, if you want. It's big on me."

Aimee looked up in surprise. She knew that Sanaa loved her multi-coloured shawl.

"Okay," Rosa said, tossing back her shiny, blond curls, "I'll try it on."

The shawl was unrestrictive. Rosa was pleased to revamp her wardrobe with the colorful shawl, but forgot to say, 'thank you.' And she didn't seem to appreciate how hard it had been for Sanaa to give up her favourite accessory.

When Rosa turned her back, Aimee reached out to give sad Sanaa a quick hug. "That was really nice of you," she said quietly.

Sanaa sighed and hugged Aimee back. Hugs were special among the Tinys and not everyone gave them so freely. "Thank you," she said.

Yu Yan stood by the glass window with Tina and Vinitha, admiring her new clothes in the dim reflection. With a distinctively Asian appearance and in the petite category with Diya and Lily, dark-haired Yu Yan had found a flowered top with a matching skirt. In keeping with the FP clothing, wispy ribbons hung from the shirtsleeves.

Tina was neither tall, nor short, and she was rather plain. She generally kept her long, brown hair up in a bun. Twirling around, she was pleased that her simple skirt and blouse had only minimal decorations.

Vinitha, with her dark, wavy tresses and cinnamon-coloured skin, always looked particularly stunning. She was trying on a new purple top.

Yu Yan lifted the large book they had been reading in the nursery the night before, and asked Vinitha to help her carry it back to the library.

"Of course," Vinitha said sweetly, doing up the criss-crossed ribbons. She had one last look at her window reflection, gave herself a pleased smile and ran over to help Yu Yan.

"I'll help too," Tina volunteered, taking another corner. "I wonder if there will be books in Paradise."

"I hope so!" Yu Yan smiled gently. "What would we do without books?"

"I know," Vinitha agreed. "I could read them all day! But I do wish they were a little smaller."

There was a tap on the common room window and all the girls who weren't carrying books ran from their own room into the other. A large smiling face, with spiky blond hair, was peering in.

"Evan!" they shouted happily.

"When do we go into the new world?" Georgia asked, pressing her pretty face up against the window.

Stooping over to speak into the microphone, Evan answered, "Breakfast first and then the doors will open! Get your Wonderdrink, everyone, and pack up your stuff. If you put it inside the delivery area in your rooms, I'll make sure your things get to you in Paradise."

With great delight, Georgia, Sanaa and Aimee walked over to the Wonderdrink station, chatting excitedly about the new world. They could hardly wait to see it! Aimee didn't feel hungry and wished they could skip breakfast and go in right away.

Lots of loud stamping and shouting indicated the boys were coming out of their room as well. Swarthy Zahir came out whistling a merry tune. He and Vahid looked quite dapper in their new vests, flowing white shirts and knee-length shorts. However, they had ripped all the hanging ribbons off their clothing, which left a few holes here and there. Bronze Ponce and small Charley were right behind, with the same new outfits. In fact, as the boys tumbled out of their room, Aimee noticed that all their outfits were identical.

Odin and Damien pushed past everyone to be first in line. They were the biggest Tinys. The others complained but didn't stop them.

The Wonderdrink station had two nozzles within easy reach. Each child had their own big cup and had written their name on it. Filling their cups with the delicious creamy mixture, the kids usually drank their breakfast quickly. Uncle Louis referred to it as 'breakfast' in the morning, but they had the same Wonderdrink every meal.

Soon everyone had gathered in the common room with cups in hand. "I haven't had any yet," Rosa complained, tugging gently on Odin's long, white-blond hair. Odin was filling his cup for the third time.

"I'm not done yet," Odin said in a grouchy tone of voice. Generally, Odin and Damien stood in front of the station and filled their cups over and over. Odin was very round, and barely fit in his new clothes and Damien was the tallest. They always insisted on drinking to their fill before they moved away.

Rosa started crying. Nancy reached out for Rosa's cup, barged in front of Damien, and filled it for her. It was a common morning occurrence, although, no one ever dared push in front of Odin.

Uncle Louis walked out of his private room to check on the kids.

"Oh, you have a new outfit too!" Aimee exclaimed.

Rubbing down his vest, Uncle Louis looked pleased. "Yes, we're all heading to Paradise in style," he laughed. Just like the boys, Uncle Louis had a flowing white shirt, fancy brown vest and knee-length, fringed pants. "Make sure you drink enough for breakfast," he told them all. "We have a busy morning ahead of us."

Once she had taken a couple sips of Wonderdrink, Aimee washed her cup in the sink that was built into the common room wall and left it to dry on the counter. With great delight, she ran to the girls' room to pack her pillow, blanket and clothes into her little bed.

Rosa and Yu Yan were sitting together, and Rosa was crying!

"Why are you sad?" Aimee asked.

"We're going to miss the nursery," Rosa lamented. "It's cozy here!"

"We'll have cozy places in Paradise," Aimee assured her.

Yu Yan nodded. "And there will be so much more to do in Paradise," she told her friend.

"But we've been here all our lives. This is our home!" Rosa wailed.

Aimee looked around the plain nursery. It had been cozy and was filled with lots of good memories, but she was confident Paradise would be even better. "I'll help you pack your stuff," she said. Picking up Rosa's blanket, she folded it neatly.

Yu Yan gathered Rosa's brush and nightgown off the floor and tucked them into her bed. "Come on, Rosa," she encouraged. "It won't be so cozy here when everyone else has gone."

Reluctantly, Rosa stood up.

Aimee and Yu Yan dragged Rosa's bed over to the delivery area, just as Evan had said. Then they ran back and gathered their own belongings together.

Overjoyed that the big day had finally come, Aimee ran into the common room. She couldn't restrain the melody filling her heart. "I love today," she sang, twirling around in her new blue dress, enjoying the way the ribbons floated past her arms. "We're going away, to play all day, in the brand-new world!"

"World doesn't rhyme," Zahir pointed out thoughtfully.

"I know, but I couldn't think of anything else," she shrugged.

The tall, dark-haired boy with gentle, blue eyes, frowned, deep in thought. He hummed her tune. With a sudden smile, he sang, "By the brand-new bay."

Aimee looked at him with awe. "You have such a nice voice!" she raved. She had never heard Zahir sing before; usually he just whistled.

A rosy-red brightened Zahir's dark olive complexion.

"What's a bay?" Aimee asked.

"Well, it's sort of like a bunch of water," Zahir shrugged. He raised one of his well-defined eyebrows. "And the new world has a lot of water."

"You know so much!" Aimee praised.

Zahir looked flustered. But even though he didn't know the true meaning of a bay, Zahir did know a lot. Like Yu Yan, Tina, Vinitha and Aimee, Zahir had caught on quickly to reading and had now read every book in the nursery.

Aimee tried out her song with the new ending. She liked it, so she kept singing. Soon Zahir, Lema, Georgia and Sanaa joined in. Rosa was too sad to sing. Odin and Franz told them to stop the noise, but the other children were too happy to just stand quietly waiting for doors to open. Yelling loudly, Odin and Franz clapped their hands over their ears, and ran back into the boy's room.

As soon as everyone had finished breakfast, washed out their cups, and packed their boxes, Uncle Louis asked them to get into a line.

Standing in the common room by the big doors that had never opened before, Uncle Louis held up his hand to get their attention.

Aimee stopped singing. She was very excited to see the doors open! "What does Paradise look like?" she wondered eagerly.

Everyone quietened down, except for Ponce. Ponce kept talking to Odin, wondering how they would build forts in Paradise.

"That's enough, Ponce," Uncle Louis said.

All the kids gave Ponce a dirty look. Ponce responded better to his peers than to the teacher. He stopped talking.

"We don't want there to be any running or pushing," Uncle Louis reminded them. "We are going to walk up this tunnel ramp slowly so that no one gets hurt. When you get to the new world you can run, and jump, and shout, and go wherever you like."

There were loud cheers.

"And just remember," Uncle Louis pleaded, "what I said about the water. I don't want anyone to drown, so please don't go into the lake without me. We will be doing swimming lessons during school, and when you learn how to swim, then, and only then, will you be safe to go into the water by yourselves."

Paradise

Chapter Six

With a squeaky noise, the big doors started opening. The kids could hardly contain their excitement, but Uncle Louis insisted they stay calm.

The tunnel ramp was only big enough for two people to walk side by side. It was dark to begin with, as there were only tiny lights along the floor to guide their way. The ramp sloped steeply upwards and at the top, bright rays of light shone through.

Uncle Louis led the children, breathing heavily as he tramped upward. Holding hands, Aimee and Georgia giggled nervously. Small Charley, and timid, shy Milan were right behind them. Charley started singing the new song and soon most of the kids were singing Aimee's song all the way up the tunnel.

When they reached the top of the ramp, they could see lots of bright green straight ahead through the open doors. Everyone walked quickly toward the shining light.

As much as Aimee had been dreaming about Paradise, nothing had prepared her for how beautiful it truly was! Once she got to the entrance, she stopped walking and stared open-mouthed in absolute astonishment. All the eager children behind her pushed her forward into the orchards. Even Rosa had a look of elation on her face. Aimee found a spot away from everyone else and, with a rapturous look, she stretched her arms out and soaked in the beauty. She could see the bay, as Zahir called it. Light sparkled on the calm, blue surface. A few brown, speckled ducks were floating on top. One suddenly went headfirst into the water and waved its little webbed feet in the air. For one anxious moment, Aimee thought it was drowning. But then all the others did the same thing and the first duck bobbed back up with something in its beak!

Ponce, Damien, Lema, and Franz had been dreaming about the water. They tore off their new vests and shirts and went dashing down to the lake. Uncle Louis followed them anxiously, repeating his warnings.

There was no school scheduled for the first day in the new world. However, within a few minutes it became obvious that swimming lessons had to start right away. Although Uncle Louis had never swum himself, the numerous YouTube videos he'd watched had given him a general idea of what to do.

Plunging into the water with the boys, Uncle Louis tried to teach them how to float, while he experimented himself. It was a brand-new adventure for them all. Wiry Ponce didn't want to listen and nearly drowned in the first few minutes. Damien pulled him out just in time.

Aimee wasn't sure about swimming. Seeing Ponce nearly drown, and Uncle Louis struggling to keep his head above water, she decided it looked rather dangerous. She would rather explore. Turning her attention to the green field in front of her, Aimee was quite proud that she knew what it was. "This is grass," she said out loud.

"I know," Georgia laughed. Uncle Louis had shown them a picture book about children going to a farm.

Looking up, Aimee saw that the cow and sheep were eating the grass, just like they did in the farm book. She reached down and tried some, but she wasn't impressed. She spat it out.

Georgia and Vinitha giggled. "You're not a cow," they teased.

Aimee made a face and twirled around in the field, singing, "I'm not a cow! I'm so glad to be me!"

Behind the field, the hills rose up, lined with trees - lots of pretty green trees. Two colourful birds with blue, green and red feathers flew through the air effortlessly, narrowly missing Aimee's head. Amazed, she watched them flap their little wings and glide up and down. "How do they do that?" she marvelled out loud. Flapping her arms wildly, she ran forward, even though Uncle Louis had told her that only birds and insects could fly. "Oh, how I would love to soar all around like that!" she sighed happily.

The birds were soon out of sight, heading towards the rock cliff which stood above the hills on either side. It had a big plateau on top. "Maybe I can climb up there," Aimee thought, feeling this would be second best to flying. In the distance she spotted the shapes of two deer standing on the cliff. Startled by all the noise the children were making, they suddenly turned and ran off. "Oh, I hope I can make friends with them," Aimee said.

All around her were trees loaded with colourful fruit. Seeing the gardens filled with many flowers like those Uncle Louis had tried to draw for them in the nursery, Vinitha rushed to examine them more closely. She discovered they were so much prettier than his drawings and the roses smelled wonderful. "Oooh, I love them! I want to pick them! I want to smell them!" she called out.

Aimee rushed over to admire the colourful flowers with her friend.

Charley, Nancy, and a lot of the girls followed close behind her, laughing and shouting, rolling in the grass, picking the flowers and touching every new thing. They were all so happy to be in the new world.

Coming to the edge of the garden, the girls looked back to see that Zahir, Vahid and Milan were testing the fruit in the orchard. The sunshine gleamed on the boys. "Look how white Milan and Vahid are compared to Zahir," Georgia marvelled out loud. She looked down at her own skin. "And I'm white too!"

Comparing arms, Aimee decided she was golden.

Sanaa clapped her hands and swayed her hips from side to side. "And I'm dark brown!" she exulted.

41

Vinitha laughed. "I'm right in between!"

"I love all the different colours that we are," Aimee exclaimed.

Together, Aimee, Vinitha, Nancy, Sanaa and Charley explored the fields. They tried to catch the beautiful butterflies. They discovered two friendly puppies and a mischievous kitten in the meadow. Even a few sweet rabbits peeked out of the grass. Charley fell in love with the small, brown puppy with a white stripe down her muzzle. He picked her up and cuddled her. The puppy licked Charley's round face and even his brown hair. He laughed out loud. "I'm calling her Maxi," he told the girls.

"She's cute like you," Sanaa smiled.

With a look of surprise, Charley laughed again, "What do you mean?"

"You're both small and you have cute faces," Sanaa teased.

"It's a compliment," Aimee assured him.

"Okay," Charley shrugged, rolling his eyes. "We're both cute!" he told Maxi.

Nancy picked up the little orange-striped kitten hiding in the grass. "This will be Ripple, then," she said happily. Uncle Louis had read them a story about a puppy called Maxi and a kitten called Ripple.

Unused to contact, the kitten hissed and stuck out her claws. "She's not so friendly," Nancy observed. For a minute she tried to keep Ripple in her arms, but the scratches deterred her from continuing. She let Ripple jump down and watched her run up the tree with the bright red fruit. "I'm going to make you like me," she promised the kitten.

The other puppy saw Zahir and his friends eating fruit and went bounding over to them. "A puppy!" Zahir called out eagerly. Kneeling down, he opened his arms wide and wrapped them around the wriggling, golden pup. "Oh, I want him!" he said.

Charley held up his puppy. "I called this one, Maxi," he said. "What are you going to call yours?"

Lifting the big puppy off the ground, Zahir was surprised that the dog wouldn't stop licking his face. He conferred with Vahid and Milan about names. Aimee could hear them suggest, 'Licker' and 'Goldie.'

"Let's just make something up," Zahir said at last. "Let's call him 'Freddo.'"

His friends laughed, but they didn't disagree.

"We're going to call him Freddo," Zahir announced to the girls, lowering his puppy to the ground. He and the boys took off for the lake with Freddo right at their heels.

Aimee had noticed the fruit the boys were sampling. "Look at those pretty red things," she cried out. "Let's try them." Picking some for herself and her friends, they all tried them and were enthralled.

"I think they are pears," Nancy remarked. "Or... was it lemons? Do you remember reading that book on fruit?"

The red balls were sweet, juicy and crunchy!

"I think they are apples," Sanaa piped up.

"Whatever they are, this is so much better than grass... or even Wonderdrink!" Aimee exclaimed.

Sanaa did a little wriggling dance of delight. "I love them!" she cheered.

They all agreed. Vinitha looked up to see that Rosa, Tina and Yu Yan were climbing the hill nearby, and she dashed off to catch up with her friends.

"Let's climb the highest hill," Charley suggested excitedly, looking in the opposite direction and seeing there was already someone else standing on top.

It took at least ten minutes to reach the cliff and even longer to climb, but with Maxi bounding eagerly behind, they finally reached the plateau. There was no longer anyone else on top, but they could see Kenzie walking up the rounded, bare hill beside them.

"We can see the whole world from here," Nancy said in awe.

All four stood looking out across Paradise. They could see all the hills and the farmland and even down into the forests. They could see clearly to the other side, where Rosa, Tina, and Vinitha were exploring the hill next to the tunnel entrance, beside the orchards and farmland.

"I can even see the swimmers in the bay," Aimee called out.

"They haven't gone far," Sanaa observed. "Everyone is still close to shore.

"Just to let you know," Charley wisely informed Aimee, "it's not a bay. Uncle Louis says it's a lake."

"Oh," Aimee replied, looking disappointed, "but lake doesn't rhyme."

"Swimming looks hard," Nancy said. "I don't think I want to learn."

"We all have to learn," Charley reminded her. "Swimming is going to be our first school lesson tomorrow."

Nancy made a face. Looking in the opposite direction, she was excited to see a large rectangular building. "Look, there's the store that Uncle Louis told us about."

The store sat down in a valley, beside a train track. As they turned to look, a sharp whistle made them all jump. The train was coming in!

"Did the train make that noise?" Aimee asked.

"Of course," Charley replied.

Nancy clapped her hands together eagerly. "I wonder what's on it!" she called out.

"Let's go see," Sanaa cheered.

Picking Maxi up in his arms, Charley ran down the hill with the girls.

Built out of wooden building boards and hot glue, the store was fairly long. It had a slanted roof that covered the large deck all around. They couldn't get inside as the doors were locked. A sign on the window said, "Storekeepers needed."

The children looked inside the window. There were many shelves full of items. There were lengthy wooden planks, and plenty of toothpicks and blue tack like they had used in the nursery to make forts. Charley pointed out the wooden box filled with fruits and vegetables just like they had seen in the picture books.

"Oooh, I would love to be the storekeeper," Nancy exclaimed.

"Really?" Aimee asked, looking up at her friend in surprise. Aimee did not want to be stuck inside a building every day. Yet, eyeing her friend thoughtfully, she recalled that Nancy loved to organize things. Tall and sturdy, with her long, brown hair tied back in a tight braid, Nancy wore a plain white dress, devoid of ribbons. "I think you'll make a very good storekeeper," Aimee said.

Charley and Sanaa agreed.

Quite certain she would, Nancy clapped her hands together. "Yes!" she agreed. "It would be so fun to keep it all tidy and hand stuff out to everyone."

"Let's look inside the train," Charley suggested.

The girls looked at him uneasily. "Should we?" Aimee asked.

"Why not?" Charley replied.

The train doors slid open easily. Inside were all the little beds from the nursery, piled high with everyone's belongings.

"Where are we all going to sleep tonight?" Charley asked suddenly, his blue eyes full of concern.

The girls looked at him blankly. They hadn't given this any thought.

"Maybe we should find a place," Nancy suggested. "Then we can set up everyone's beds and have them ready."

"Good idea," Charley agreed.

They looked around for a cozy place.

"How about in the meadow?" Charley said.

"Oh yes!" Sanaa agreed.

"But the cow might step on us," Aimee objected. "Down by the lake might be nice."

"It's too far to carry everything!" Charley argued.

"The store has a big flat part all around it," Nancy observed.

"That's a deck," Charley said.

Aimee looked at the deck and the roof that stretched over it. Having been used to sleeping in a cozy, rectangular room, this seemed like a good substitution. "Yes," she nodded. "I think this is the best place to put the beds. Then we can be all together."

The others agreed and began pulling out the wooden box beds, helping each other to carry them one by one. They set up a girls' section on one side of the deck, and a boys' section on the other. Uncle Louis' bed was positioned right in the middle. They were really hungry when they had finished the job.

"How do we get food?" Aimee wondered.

Thankfully, Uncle Louis arrived, wet and bedraggled with four water-logged boys in tow, wearing only their knee-length pants. Zahir and his friends were following a short distance behind, and Zahir had the golden-haired puppy in his arms.

"Well done!" Uncle Louis praised, seeing all the beds laid out. "This will be a good place to sleep tonight!" With a pleased expression he looked at the three children who had set up the sleeping quarters. "Thank you for organizing us all," he said. "Eventually, we'll start building homes, so we will each have our own shelters."

"We get to build homes?" Charley repeated, "anywhere we want?"

"Of course," Uncle Louis replied. "This is your world. Everyone gets to make a home where they would like to live."

All the Tinys looked up, some with alarm and others with excitement.

"Can't we all stay together?" Aimee asked, twisting her hands nervously.

Sanaa pleaded. "Can we live with you, Uncle Louis?"

"Can I too?" Zahir begged.

Georgia, Lily, Rosa, Vahid and Milan all wanted the same.

Uncle Louis smiled kindly, seeing the wild-eyed children. Close by to Zahir, he tousled his dark, curly hair. "You will all be very safe here in Paradise," he assured them. "But if you want to build a big house and live together, that is fine by me. Although," he paused, looking around awkwardly, "for now girls will live with girls, and boys with boys."

No one protested this arrangement. Aimee and Sanaa clasped hands. "We're together," Sanaa said, "and we get Uncle Louis."

Uncle Louis smiled but he didn't commit.

Georgia dashed over to cling onto Aimee's arm. "Me too," she declared.

"I want to be in the meadow," Charley said without hesitation. His puppy barked and he laughed. "And so does Maxi!"

Vahid and Kenzie chose to be with Charley.

Yu Yan, Rosa and Vinitha linked arms. Tina ran over to them.

"Beach for me," Damien and Lema called out in unison, and then they looked at each other and laughed.

"I'll take the highest hill," Ponce announced.

"But I want it!" Odin shouted; his pale blue eyes suddenly intense. "I said it first."

Odin pushed Ponce, and Ponce tried to push back. Odin was bigger and heavy-boned, while Ponce was lean and very wiry. As they began a shoving match, Uncle Louis strode over and pulled them apart.

"Boys, cut it out," Uncle Louis said sternly. "This is a big world, and there's room for everyone. You can both have a house on the hill. You are friends, remember?"

The two boys glared at each other.

"I get the flat side," Ponce whispered.

Odin was about to argue when Aimee's stomach growled loudly. Everyone laughed.

"How do we get food?" Aimee asked politely. "I am so hungry."

Everyone began complaining about how hungry they were.

Uncle Louis held up his hands. "Calm down, everyone," he said. "There will always be food available. You saw the fruit on the trees and the Professor has never let us down." Reaching into his pocket for a key, Uncle Louis unlocked the door. "For now, we are able to help ourselves to food in here, but once we get storekeepers..."

"Oh, I want to be a storekeeper!" Nancy piped up.

"Great!" Uncle Louis replied with a smile. "We'll let you try it out and see if you like it. And once we have everything sorted, we'll trade for food."

"What does that mean?" Ponce asked.

"You will all need to bring something to the store to trade for meals and whatever you need," Uncle Louis clarified.

"Like what?" Damien asked, shaking back his wet, straggly, blond hair. "What would we bring?"

"Well, if you want to live by the water," Uncle Louis replied, "then you might like to catch some fish and bring them to be cooked for breakfast, or to trade for fruits or vegetables."

"I want to grow vegetables," Charley smiled proudly. "So, maybe I'll trade my vegetables for breakfast fish?"

"Exactly," Uncle Louis replied, leading them all into the store. "Or someone could pick some flowers or make some furniture. There is even a little bakery here in the store, and somebody might like to learn how to make bread. We will all find something that we can do well and use that to trade."

"What will you bring?" Ponce asked Uncle Louis.

"My work is to look after all of you and teach you school lessons," Uncle Louis chuckled. "So, I will trade work for food."

"Oh, this looks fun!" Aimee called out, walking around the kitchen. It was a square room with gleaming metal shelves and counters, equipped with bowls and spoons, bags that said 'flour' and several other supplies. A large metal sink sat in front of a big window that looked out toward the treeless hill. The sink had taps and Aimee ran over to see if water would come out. It did! The taps worked just like they had in the nursery. A tall metal box was positioned against a wall. It had a big door that opened and several black knobs. On top were four round, black spirals.

"That is the oven," Uncle Louis told her. "We will be able to bake our bread in there."

"What does bread taste like?"

"I'm not sure," Uncle Louis laughed, "but I've heard it's something we will want to eat every day."

Then Ponce saw the Wonderdrink machine behind the store counter and bounded over. "Hey, Wonderdrink is here!"

"Yes, for a little while longer, you can all have Wonderdrink," Uncle Louis said, quickly walking over to stand in front of the machine before Ponce could help himself. "But first, everyone needs to try at least one delicious vegetable or fruit." Suddenly, he remembered something important. "Actually, now that we are in the real world, we must always wash our hands before we eat."

"Why?" Ponce asked.

"Because we may have touched something, like dirt, or harmful bacteria, that could make us sick if it gets into our mouths. You don't want to get sick. You'll feel awful. So, go wash your hands with soap and water. Use the sink here or the one by the outhouse."

There was a mad dash to the kitchen sink. The outhouse was much further away. Everyone washed, although some did it more carefully than others.

When Aimee's hands were clean, she picked up a carrot and bit into it. "Oooh, it's so crunchy and sweet!" she said.

All the other kids chose from the wooden box, and almost everyone chose more than one delicious treat before running over to get their cup of Wonderdrink. Vahid couldn't get enough carrots.

Having filled up with nourishment, the children ran outside to continue their exploration and pick the best spot for their future home! Soon the remaining stragglers heard that food was to be found in the store, and they came running in to get lunch.

Aimee, Georgia and Sanaa found the outhouse, which was another wooden building, tucked in at the base of a forested hill. There was a girl's side, which said 'GIRLS' very clearly, and a boy's side, that said 'BOYS.' Just like in the nursery, each side had a couple of small private rooms with a round hole in a smooth plank. The holes went way, way down.

Opening all the doors on the girls' side curiously, Aimee found the third door opened to a shower. She turned the taps and found it worked just like the one in the nursery. Drenched, she came out, told her friends and then, of course, they had to try it too.

Outside the outhouse, attached to the wall, was a large metal sink with running water and soap. After using the new outhouse and washing their hands, the girls explored Paradise for the rest of the afternoon. It was so exciting to dip their toes in the lake, to feel the sand, climb the trees, pick the flowers, and stand up high on top of the hills.

As the three girls tromped through the orchards, eating apples, and talking about where they might live, Aimee confessed, "I hope Uncle Louis decides to live with us. Let's build a really big house with a room just for him."

Sanaa and Georgia agreed. "I'm glad we're all sleeping on the deck tonight," Sanaa added. "I hope it takes a long time to build houses."

Georgia was glad as well, but she was also intrigued about living together. "When we do build a house," she prodded, "where do you want to build it?"

"How about in the meadow, with the beautiful gardens all around us," Sanaa suggested, waving her arms towards the farmland.

"I was thinking the hill might be nice," Georgia said slowly. "Not Odin and Ponce's hill, but a smaller one."

"Yes, a hill," Aimee nodded. "Then we can wake up in the morning and look across the sparkling lake."

Georgia laughed. "And see what is going on all across Paradise," she added.

"Which hill?" Sanaa asked.

Aimee stood still and looked towards the hills. The tallest hill in the middle had already been claimed by Odin and Ponce. There was a hill on either side of the rocky cliff, one was grassy and rounded but without trees. The other was forested and close to the lake.

It wasn't hard to choose. "Let's try the hill with the forest," she suggested.

When they climbed to the top, Lily and Diya were already sitting on the grass admiring the view.

"Do you want to live with us in one great big house?" Georgia asked.

"Sure," Lily replied.

"Only if I get a room of my own," Diya insisted.

"Of course," Georgia agreed, her green eyes glowing with the idea. "We'll all have our own rooms, but we'll also be together."

The girls ran around on the top of the hill, looking for the best place to build. They considered several spots - near the edge of the hill on the large clearing, on the side of the hill in the trees, or right on top and far from the edge, or on the other side which looked out towards the store. Eventually, they settled on the very top, far from the edge.

"We will have a great view of the lake and the pretty gardens," Aimee raved. "This is exactly where I want to live!"

"Hey, look, there's Zahir and Milan," Georgia pointed out. "I think they are picking a spot near us."

Aimee looked out in the direction Georgia was pointing. The boys were standing in the trees, not far away. She saw Zahir's puppy, Freddo, looking up at her, wagging his golden tail. "I guess they want to be cozy in the forest," she surmised. "How nice! They will be our closest neighbours!"

"They'll have almost the same view of the lake," Lily observed.

By the time everyone returned to the store to get their Wonderdrink that evening, they all had ideas of where they wanted to live. Most planned to live in groups of two or more and everyone was happy with their choices, except for Odin and Ponce. They were still arguing about who would get the flat part of the cliff.

"You should build a house together like the rest of us," Zahir remarked to Ponce.

Odin stamped his foot. "No way!"

Ponce shrugged. "I'm not sharing a house with him. He snores!"

Uncle Louis made a suggestion. "If you both want the flat part and don't think you can share a house, then we will set up a contest to win it."

"Why not see who can pin the other to the ground for the longest?" Odin said, folding his arms across his chest. "That's a good contest!"

"It's not exactly a fair contest," Uncle Louis smiled. "Come up with a fair suggestion that won't hurt anyone, and I'll consider it."

After a dinner of Wonderdrink, the sky began turning the most fantastic pink and purple colours. Most of the other Tinys were tired out and snuggling into their small beds, but not Aimee. She had enjoyed her day so much that she longed to express her happiness. As she climbed the hill that she and the girls had chosen, she kept looking up at the sky in awe, and occasionally stumbling over little stones and plants she didn't see. Uncle Louis had showed them a sunset in a book, but the colours she saw above surpassed her expectations. However, she hadn't expected the black criss-cross pattern. In the book the sky had been an uninterrupted expanse and Aimee didn't know that she was inside a house of glass.

"Oh, I wish I could thank Evan and the Professor," she whispered, as the pink became even more intense. She wondered if Evan might be looking into the nursery windows and for a moment, she imagined herself running back down through the tunnel to thank him. But she knew the tunnel doors were closed tight.

"Will I ever see Evan again?" she asked herself wistfully. "I should have asked him that question yesterday."

Looking up again at the glowing, criss-crossed sky, she walked right into a tree branch. Undeterred, she pushed it away. "What does the Professor look like?" she thought. "Will I ever meet him? He's the Mastermind of Paradise!" she marvelled. In her mind, she could picture Evan well, but the Professor was just a blank spot with a very important label. "He must be so incredibly amazing to make this beautiful world! I would love to meet him!" She sighed and asked herself, "How do I thank them?"

When she reached the top of the hill and stood where her house was going to be, the colours faded, and the sky turned a deep blue. To her amazement, little white lights flickered on and off all around her. "Fireflies," she said in awe. "They are real!"

Down below on the lake, the loons cried out. Their stirring cry made her thankfulness overflow.

"Oh, if only I could give Evan a hug," she thought wistfully, her hands folded together over her heart. "I want to tell him I love Paradise!"

A little tune began blossoming inside. Standing on the hill in her blue sundress, Aimee hummed and twirled, enjoying the way the ribbons floated and wrapped around her. Then she began adding words to the tune, "I just want to say," she sang, "Thank you for today, In every special way, You have made the bay, and places for us to play, I love you al-al-way…" Once again, the song came together really well until the last line. She wanted to end with, 'Thank you for the world,' but…

"Zahir is right," she considered, "the last line needs to rhyme with all the others." Up on the hill, as the light faded, and she could see the large, luminous moon appearing in the sky, Aimee tried over and over to get the last line right. Finally, she decided to sing, "Thank you, thank you, thank you for today." It changed the rhythm a little, but she felt it expressed the deep gratitude that was in her heart. "I love you, Evan," she declared holding her arms up to the sky. "And you too, Professor," she added wistfully, just in case they were listening. "And I just love, love, LOVE this wonderful world you've made!"

Aimee was unaware that the Professor and Evan were sitting together on the other side of the frosted glass, with tears in their eyes. Little Aimee's song was the perfect ending to the delightful day they had spent watching the Tinys discover Paradise. They had heard every comment and squeal of happiness through the microphone hidden under the school roof. The new world was as perfect as they had hoped... and neither one of them had anticipated such a grateful song.

"Oh là là! Not bad for a ten-month old," the Professor murmured gruffly to Evan. "She has a lovely voice!"

"Not bad at all!" Evan whispered, taking another picture on his phone. "It just makes everything we've done so worthwhile. What a sweetie!"

"She is a special child!" the Professor smiled proudly. "And while she is the only one who has actually said thank you, it's been so rewarding seeing all the delighted looks on everyone's face! I'm glad you took hundreds of pictures."

"Today was certainly worth every year of research and construction," Evan added softly, as he scrolled through his photos.

"Even giving up your entire summer vacation?"

"Best summer ever!"

"Good! I'll see you in the halls tomorrow."

"Yes, you will," Evan replied quietly, rising from his chair, and stretching his tall frame. "And so far, it looks like everything is working well, but I'll try to check on things in the morning."

"Louis can reach me if anything goes wrong," Professor Lemans reminded him in a hushed tone, pulling out his cell phone to look at his messages. "Don't worry too much if you can't get in before your classes are over."

"Okay, I'll see you tomorrow," Evan smiled. He turned back for one last look into the dome. Little Aimee was making her way down the hill in the moonlight to the small wooden beds on the deck.

"Goodnight, children," Evan whispered, knowing full well that they wouldn't and shouldn't hear him. While he was happy to see them in Paradise, he was sad he could no longer communicate with them directly. "Have a nice sleep everyone!" he said softly.

Checking the monitor to ensure there was no one around in the staff-parking lot, Evan took the easy one-way exit. Accessible only to them, it was the quickest way out of the Paradise Room, by-passing all elevators, locked doors and time-consuming key codes. Had there still been a number of people milling about the cars, he could have chosen to exit through the viewing hall, coming out the Professor's private door, but at night, the one-way exit was the easiest.

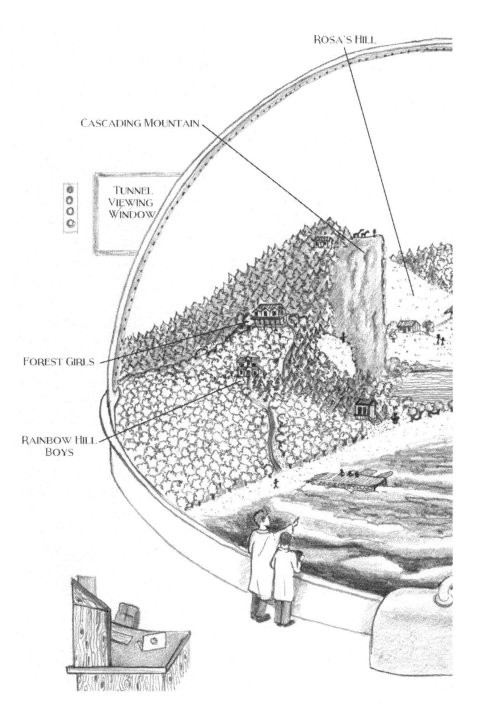

ROSA'S HILL

CASCADING MOUNTAIN

TUNNEL
VIEWING
WINDOW

FOREST GIRLS

RAINBOW HILL
BOYS

56

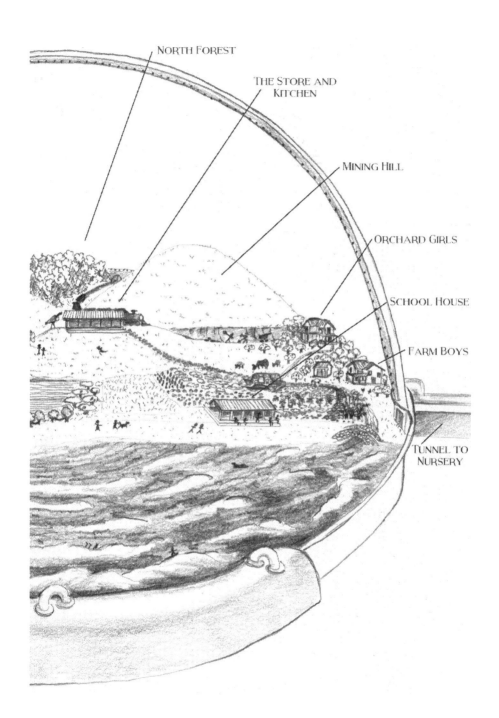

NORTH FOREST

THE STORE AND
KITCHEN

MINING HILL

ORCHARD GIRLS

SCHOOL HOUSE

FARM BOYS

TUNNEL TO
NURSERY

57

A Hot Day

Chapter Seven

*I*t was a hot day in Southern Ontario. The week had been the hottest on record for September. In the Biosphere, the giant air-conditioning units were working overtime to keep up, especially in the Arctic Biome. The seals and the polar bears were spending most of their time in their aquariums, separated by a strong glass wall, as their artificially created snow had melted completely. On that first day of the semester, many of the university students were talking about the heat.

"It's not much better in here than it is out there," one student complained, wiping sweat from his forehead.

"It's fourteen degrees better," the Professor replied, having already checked the indoor and outdoor temperatures.

"Then it must be fifty degrees out there," a female student estimated. "We should get another day off to go to the beach... just to survive."

The Professor chuckled. "No, it's only thirty-seven degrees outside," he told her. "If it was fifty, the university would be shut down and we would all be in danger of heat stroke and death." He then launched into his favourite side-issue. "This is our world," he told the two hundred students sitting in his class. "This is one of the life-threatening problems that you will need to address in the future. Our world is spinning out of control. The extremes of temperature are just one indicator of all that is going wrong with our planet. Due to excessive pollution, fossil-fuel emissions and irresponsible stewardship, we have brought many of these problems on ourselves. We need to do all we can to turn our world around, or future generations may not be able to survive."

A red-haired student put up his hand.

"Yes," Professor Lemans acknowledged. He didn't know everyone's name just yet. It was only the first day of Foundations in Molecular Biology and Genetics 101.

"Isn't it God's world, Sir?" the young man asked.

A light, sarcastic laugh escaped the Professor and rippled across the classroom. "God's world?" the Professor repeated, his dark eyebrows raised in a skeptical fashion. "Surely, if there was a God then He would be doing a much better job controlling the conditions of this planet. The environmental conditions of the last twenty years indicate to me that there is absolutely no higher being watching over us. Or if there is," he mumbled to himself, "He doesn't care much about His creation."

The arm of the redhead went up again.

"Yes," nodded the Professor.

"But, Sir, as you said, it is man's irresponsible stewardship that is to blame for many of the life-threatening problems that we face. And God has promised to intervene in the future to make things right."

"Well, when He gets around to intervening, perhaps a few more will join His cause," the Professor acknowledged.

Seeing a number of hands go up, the Professor decided to terminate the discussion. "I highly recommend my book on this subject," he said. "There are a few copies of 'Faith or Fact – An End to Delusion' in the Rainforest library. And plenty of other very helpful resources on this topic – make good use of them. A good scientist doesn't ever allow bias to cloud his investigations. He explores all the evidence before making any conclusions."

59

"I've read it," another student piped up proudly. "It's good! Scientists make decisions based on *evidence* not *faith!*" he scoffed.

"Just one second," Seth argued. "Faith is based on evidence."

"Not according to my dictionary," the Professor retorted. Having Googled the word 'faith,' he read the definition, "'a belief not based on proof.'"

A female student put up her hand. "When I Google 'faith,' Cambridge Dictionary says, 'a high degree of trust or confidence in someone or something.'"

Seth nodded. "The Bible defines faith as *'persuasion,'*" he stated. "Faith is a *'well-grounded assurance* of that for which we hope, and a conviction of the reality of things which we do not see.'"

"Oh là là! I've never heard of that definition," the Professor laughed. "Did you make it up?"

"It's the Weymouth translation of Hebrews eleven verse one," Seth smiled. "If you look up the actual meaning of the Greek words – it's even stronger. Sir," Seth pleaded, "we all see and evaluate the same evidence. Some believe the evidence happened by chance – however improbable that may be, while others see the evidence as proof for an intelligent Creator. There is a measure of 'faith' required whether you believe in Creation or Evolution. Neither theory can be fully proven by scientific experiment, so both are better described as theories of *history...* not science."

"Enough of this," the Professor frowned. "We're all here today," he stated, "to take a look at the remarkable abilities of the cell to divide and reproduce." Continuing on without any further interruptions, the Professor began the new university semester sharing some of the remarkable discoveries and advances by researchers all over the world. He was teaching a very important, foundational course - one that would lead many of his students on to various scientific careers.

It was a long, hot, sweaty day that first day back and the Professor wasn't used to teaching fulltime. In the last four years he had taken a lighter load of classes, to give himself more time to research and build Paradise. Now that his new world was up and running, he had resumed a full teaching schedule. Evan was also very busy, hoping to finish his master's degree in three semesters. They met at four o'clock, in the Reptile Café to check on the Tinys.

The Professor was pleased to see that Bert was basking on a rock near the waterfall while the turtles lazed in the water. Timbo had been shipped to the pet store.

"How have you survived the day?" Evan asked, as they walked along the mirrored hall. Howler monkeys and the noisy macaw called out to each other from their well-designed habitats. "I hear this heat wave will break tonight with a bank of thunderstorms moving in."

"That's a relief," the Professor sighed, wiping sweat from his forehead. Instinctively, he looked around to ensure they were alone in the hallway.

"Did you get my message?" Evan asked, automatically doing the same check, as he pulled out his cell phone to press the green arrow.

Patting the pockets of his white lab coat, the Professor suddenly realized his phone was missing. "No, I did not," he replied. "Maybe I've left my phone in the Paradise Room? I sure hope it's not at home. Oh... routines," he sighed as they both positioned themselves on the drop square. "It takes a while to readjust."

As soon as Evan pressed the green arrow app, the floor dropped away below their feet. Evan and the Professor were quickly lowered down to the heavy metal door.

"I have a question concerning the rate of mutation based on radiation damage," Evan said, as the Professor typed in the code on the door. "I know there's a fine balance between the amount of DNA damage and repair verses the death of the cell. What have you found in your research?"

61

The Professor launched into a detailed reply, as he and Evan walked through the empty nurseries, and took the elevator up. They stepped into his private room housing the newly functioning domed terrarium.

"Whew, it's hot in here," Evan remarked.

With a jolt, the Professor noticed that Paradise looked quite wilted inside. For a moment he didn't see any of the children anywhere. In a panic his eyes raced to the lake, and with relief he saw many heads in the water with Louis. The animals were lying along the shallow shoreline. Racing to the side panel, he checked the conditions inside. The temperature displayed forty-five degrees Celsius inside the dome! In the large, glass Paradise Room the temperature had climbed to forty.

"*Ça alors!*" the Professor called out fearfully. "This is not supposed to happen! Check the air-conditioning unit."

Without a word, Evan rushed to the computer desk and took a seat in the big padded chair.

"Why didn't Louis message me that things were this bad?" the Professor expressed anxiously, as he pressed the blue button on the wall to engage the rainmaker, and then the white button to do an immediate and complete air exchange.

"Your phone, Sir," Evan reminded him, hastily entering the important password '0suffering66', to check the controls.

"Right! Who would have thought there would be an emergency on the very first day?"

Evan began troubleshooting, searching the main computer control system.

Little voices were coming through the microphone and over the speakers, as the anxious Professor ran over to view the lake. He wanted to ensure all the living creatures had made it to the water. Since they were all in a group, and he could only see heads, it was hard to discern who was talking.

"It's so hot!" a little voice said, which sounded like Yu Yan.

"When can we get out of the water, Uncle Louis?"

"Will it be hot like this every day?"

"I want to go back to the nursery!"

"I don't like the sun. I want it to go away."

"I don't want to do swimming lessons any longer." He was sure the voice was Aimee's.

"I'm hungry. When can we get food?" He was almost certain this came from Zahir.

"Does the Professor want us to be this hot?"

The last question startled the Professor as he counted all the heads bobbing above the surface. "Do I want them to be this hot?" he reiterated to himself in utter disbelief. He wasn't sure who asked the question, but he imagined it was Ponce or Odin... or maybe even Franz. In his mind, he thought, "They have no idea how hard I've worked to ensure that Paradise is perfect!"

"Yeah," Odin added, "are you sure he knows what's going on? Or is he doing this on purpose?"

Inside Paradise, sitting in the lake with all the children, Louis responded quickly, "Definitely not on purpose! The Professor loves us. Let's be thankful that he gave us all this water to keep us cool."

Sanaa's voice piped up, "And we should be thankful to Lema and Franz for telling us to come in here."

"Yes," Uncle Louis acknowledged gratefully. "This was an excellent idea, boys! This is the place to be on a hot day."

"It's always the place to be," someone cried out.

Swallowing hard, the Professor counted the animals he could see lying along the shallow shoreline. He was furious with himself for not inspecting his controls first thing in the morning; he had been so confident that everything would work as it should. He hated to see any kind of suffering in his beautiful world. And if even one of the Tinys had died as a result of this malfunction, he knew he would be totally devastated! Anxiously, he also considered that if the public ever found out about this system failure and the length of time he had taken to respond, his hopes of continuing on as the guardian of Paradise could be dashed.

Having determined that all of the living creatures had found their way to the cooling water, Jacques Lemans hurried over to see if Evan had found a glitch in the program. On top of all his worries and concerns, his heart ached that some of the Tinys were questioning his motives. "How could any of them think that I wanted this to happen?" he asked Evan quietly.

"There are only a couple that do," Evan assured him, his eyes scrutinizing the data scrolling by on the main computer screen. "They are just kids. They have no idea how much intensive research and effort has gone into making their world absolutely perfect for their survival."

Louis' patient voice was still responding to the children's complaints. "Just a little longer till things cool down. When it starts to get dark it will cool down for sure. Then we'll all go and see what we can make for dinner. Tell me what you're hoping for."

"I think I've found the problem," Evan called out. "There is an error message on the heat-transfer unit. I'll try a reset."

"Merci beaucoup!" Jacques exclaimed with a sigh of relief as the raindrops slowly crept over the hills in the north and the air exchanger knocked the temperature down one whole degree. He noticed the edge of his phone under a research paper. Picking it up, he saw there were five messages from Louis, all warning of the intense heat and asking for help.

"Poor Louis, I have really let him down today," the Professor mused quietly, walking over to the dome to look in.

"The reset worked," Evan whispered loudly.

"Likely it was a system overload," he replied softly. "I guess we'll need to keep a better eye on the controls should we reach extreme temperatures again."

"Let's sync my phone to the controls, as well as yours," Evan suggested, keeping his voice low. "We should have done this from the beginning."

Jacques Lemans didn't disagree; it was a completely unfortunate oversight.

As Evan worked on synching his phone, the rainmaker reached the lake. It was the first time the children had seen rain. The wonder of little drops of water falling across the water and landing on their heads quickly distracted them from the heat. They tried to catch it. They tilted their heads back to feel it fall into their mouths. They laughed and held up their hands. And Georgia was the first one to spot a rainbow.

"Look in the sky!" she shouted. "Those are the most beautiful colours! And it's right over our hill, girls!"

"It's a rainbow," Uncle Louis told them. "The sunlight is refracting through the water droplets in the air."

"Let's go find it," Zahir shouted, charging out of the lake, his dark, wet curls bouncing against his drenched shirt and spraying water in all directions. Freddo, his golden-haired dog, bounded after him. Vahid and Milan followed close behind.

With that, most of the children raced towards the beach in search of the elusive bow. Louis let them run, knowing the Professor was now responding to the emergency. Already, he could feel the cooler air coming in.

The rain collected on the plateau and began cascading down the rock cliff. Evan and the Professor chuckled as the awestruck children marvelled at the stream of water falling down the rock face. They watched them sprint along the riverbed following the gurgling brook racing towards the lake. The dreadful heat was soon forgotten as the plants began to revive and the beauty of rain refreshed the new world.

"Look," Sanaa called out to Charley, with her hands around some nodding pansies. "The flowers are bright and cheerful again. They look so beautiful when they're happy!"

"The children love the rain," Evan observed, watching Aimee, Zahir and Georgia prance around in the waterfall as it cascaded down the rocky cliff. "Maybe we should program the rainmaker to come on once a week during the day?"

"Ah, it will just be an inconvenience," the Professor replied shaking his head. "Any towels or laundry they have hung out to dry will get wet. Once in a while rain might be fun, but I'd rather leave it set for the night hours."

While Evan didn't fully agree, he said no more. He didn't feel it was an important issue.

Building Homes
Chapter Eight

The first glorious week in Paradise was filled with morning sessions of school and learning how to swim – which was only going well for three of the boys. In more successful fashion, other Tinys were learning how to bake bread, or plant vegetables, or feed the animals and birds, and all were involved with building houses in the afternoon. Everyone liked the idea that they could choose where they wanted to live and what kind of house they wanted to build, even though some found it distressing to think of sleeping far away from Uncle Louis. Little by little he was assuring them that they would be perfectly safe and that it would be fun to live with their friends.

So far, all of the Tinys remained unaware that at night Uncle Louis would wait until they were all asleep in their wooden beds on the store deck, and then he would silently slip off to the hidden cave.

The cave was concealed in the hill nearest to the lake, which had been aptly named by the girls, 'Rainbow Hill.' The first time the children had seen the rainbow it did seem to be attached to the slopes.

This night, as always, when Uncle Louis was certain they were all asleep, he slipped away from the store deck. He was thankful for a little moonlight that helped him find his way in the dark past the outhouses, and into the narrow valley between Rainbow Hill and the tall cliff next to it. About fifty more strides took him to the secret entrance. Hidden behind two fast-growing spruce trees was what appeared to be a very large and heavy rock. However, Louis knew the fake rock could be easily rolled to the side, revealing a locked door. There was only one key to this door, and Louis kept it safely with him at all times. Another key opened the store, and that key had been given to Nancy. Inside the cave, the office room was powered by electricity. There were only two places in the giant terrarium where electricity was available – here in Louis' office, and in the store.

Inside the small cave office, a Smartphone was attached to the wall. The phone was taller than Louis. Ever since Louis had been old enough to figure things out, the Professor had given him access to a phone. It was through sites like Google and YouTube that Louis had received most of his education. Every day the Professor had assigned Louis videos to watch, beginning with the alphabet, all the way up to simple math and reading. It was a system which had worked well for the first Tiny, given that he was a diligent, studious individual who wanted to learn. In the private room attached to the nursery where Louis had lived for four years on his own, the Smartphone had been an important access to learning and mental stimulation when the Professor was busy with other matters.

However, the Professor wanted a different experience for the Tinys in Paradise. He had seen many university students who couldn't live without technology and spent a great deal of time with a digital device in their hands. The Professor wanted the Tinys to learn by experimentation and to enjoy the elaborate world that he had created. "After all," he had texted Louis, "there is no point in going to all the trouble of creating such a remarkable environment, with so much to discover and invent, if the Tinys are going to spend all their time staring at a screen. Therefore, the Smartphone is to remain a top-secret instrument for your use alone."

It was here, in this cave office that Louis escaped at night to communicate with the Professor and research ideas on the internet. Right now, he and the children needed to learn how to build homes and he was thankful for the YouTube videos demonstrating the construction of simple and elaborate homes using building boards and glue guns.

Most of the children were eager to build their own homes and so Louis had put all the children's names into a big jar. He told them that whichever name he drew out each week would be the one whose house they would build as a group. Uncle Louis knew it would take a team effort to build each home and he thought it would be more fun to construct the houses together. Just after dinner that night they had picked out the first name, and it was Sanaa's.

"I want to live with Georgia, Aimee, Lily and Diya," Sanaa had proclaimed, clapping her hands and doing her dance.

"Are you all happy to live together?" Uncle Louis had asked, looking at each one.

"Yes, but we will need a really big house so that we can each have our own room," Diya had insisted, in queenly fashion.

So, Louis was looking for plans for a mansion made with popsicle sticks, or as the Tinys called them – 'wooden building boards.'

There were several ideas on the internet. He settled on an attractive design with a blue roof. It had sufficient rooms for all the girls, with little decks and a lovely fence that went all around the property. He watched the video and then copied the link, sending it off in an email to the Professor.

"Please give us a printout of these instructions and a picture of the house," he texted. "Another carton of popsicle sticks and glue sticks will come in handy as well. A lot of materials will be required for this mansion."

"I'll send them in tomorrow morning on the train," the Professor replied immediately.

After he had given the Professor the daily briefing and they had chatted about what the Tinys were learning well, and what they were not, the Professor gave him a few more tips on how to swim. It all sounded simple enough to Louis, until he got into the water. They said good-night, and then Louis left the office cave, locking the door behind him and rolling the rock facade back into place. Still not tired, he walked to the clearing at the top of the hill, only a stone's throw from the area the girls had marked out for their mansion. He was pleased the girls would be the closest inhabitants to the control cave; he knew they were very unlikely to spy on him or snoop around at night. Had Odin and Ponce chosen the same location, he knew he would be concerned.

Sitting down, Louis looked up at the night sky, full of stars. The black criss-cross lines weren't as noticeable when the sky was dark, and everything above had a more uniform appearance. A fingernail moon illuminated a shiny path across the peaceful water. There were never any waves at night. The waves came only after lunch and lasted until dinnertime. A few ducks bobbed up and down as they floated across the silvery reflection. Little birds twittered goodnight to one another, and the cry of the loons echoed across the lake. The three "beach boys" - Damien, Lema, and Franz, lay stretched out on the sand, fast asleep. They had claimed the beach for their home but were uninterested in building a house.

"Unfortunately," Louis thought to himself, "they aren't willing to help anyone else build, either. And they sure don't like the bartering system. I think those three would be quite content to remain on Wonderdrink and sleep on the beach for the rest of their lives."

"However," he pondered, with a smile on his face, "they may be first to invent a flotation device."

In the last few days the beach boys had been trying out different free products from the store and discovering various way to use them. When the houses were done, Louis planned to give them the pattern for a boat. For now, they were learning a lot from their own experimentation.

Louis gazed across the meadow where the new veggie garden was thriving with tiny tomatoes, carrots, cucumbers, peppers, squash, onions and potato plants. The seven children who helped plant the garden had each taken one area to maintain. Some things required extra watering by hand, and often grass tried to grow where it wasn't wanted.

Having been inspired by some of the garden designs that Professor Lemans had sent in on the train, Sanaa, Yu Yan and Vinitha made trellises for the tomatoes to climb on and were putting up a stone fence to keep out the rabbits and sheep. Maxi was their loyal companion and did her best to keep the small garden predators away. There was plenty of food in other places for the rodents and birds to eat.

Charley, Vahid and Kenzie had been the first to claim the farmland and were making plans for a house right across from the garden, next to the tunnel entrance. Just over from the gardens, part way up Mining Hill, the other four girls had chosen to build a house in the orchard. Tina, Vinitha, Yu Yan and Rosa's house would be in a quiet area which looked out toward the lake, surrounded by peach and cherry trees.

Getting to his feet to walk down the hill, Louis glanced up at the rock cliff. Kenzie had coined the name, "Cascading Mountain" after seeing the waterfall occur. The majority had liked the name. Unfortunately, Ponce and Odin had been unable to find a way to share the mountain plateau. They had decided instead to compete in a race to scale the cliff-side, with the winner earning the property. Having agreed to compete, the lean, wiry Ponce had won, and big Odin was still brooding. He didn't feel it was a fair competition and Louis felt badly; the wrestling contest would have favoured Odin. Paradise was supposed to be a world of complete happiness and fairness for everyone. Louis wondered if there might have been a better way to settle the matter.

Reaching the store deck, Louis lay down on the blanket he had spread on the soft grass. He heard one of the boys stir.

"Where were you?" Ponce asked, one dark eye peering out from under his mass of tangled, black hair.

"Just up on Rainbow Hill looking at the moon," Louis answered.

Ponce looked up at the sky. "That's nice," he said and then he fell back to sleep.

Wide awake, Louis determined someone needed to cut the boys' hair, since they didn't look after it the way the girls did. He had one very small, sharp knife that he used for himself, but he knew it would be painfully slow to cut all the boys' hair in the same fashion. Then he started wondering where it would be best to build his own house once the children's homes were finished. He wanted to be somewhere central, somewhere that they could easily find him. Besides, all the best scenic views had already been taken.

"Right here by the store might be ideal," he thought sleepily. Nancy had already taken the one spare room in the store and was doing a great job of organizing everything and everyone that came to trade. Often, the quiet and reliable Milan joined her. They had opposite personalities but seemed to work well together.

"It's all going as planned," he thought, before falling asleep. "There's something for everyone to do and everyone is happy... except maybe Odin."

The Half-Price Sale

Chapter Nine

*A*lone at a table for four in one of the local French restaurants, the Professor finished his *'Creperie Suzette,'* savouring every last, delightful, caramel-coated cooked apple slice folded into the delicious crepe. He didn't eat out very often, but today was his birthday and hardly anyone knew. Years and years ago, he and his wife would have gone out for dinner and talked about the places they wanted to visit next and the big plans they had to adopt a multicultural family. But that was before the accident...

Licking the last bit of caramel off his spoon, the Professor sadly pondered the fact that he had just turned fifty-five! "Ten more years till retirement, or maybe fifteen if I'm still up to it," he thought. "What have I got to show for my life? No family. Not many friends. Just a devoted student and a whole world of Tinys who don't know my birthday... or really anything else about me."

As much as the Professor told himself that Paradise was primarily a scientific experiment, he had always dreamed of having a big family. Wendy and he had hoped to have two of their own and adopt a few from third world countries. However, many years of building careers, several miscarriages, and finally the accident, had shattered all his hopes.

Professor Lemans did have some relatives. His favourite aunt had sent a card, right on time, like she always did. He had a few cousins in France, and one in Quebec who had Facebooked him with a *Bon Anniversaire* post that morning. However, his own beloved parents had died in a tragic car accident fifteen years earlier, leaving him the enormous inheritance earmarked for scientific development.

A cricket chirp sounded, and the Professor checked his phone. There was a text message from his in-laws in Newfoundland:

"Happy Birthday, Jacques. It's so sad that you're having your 55th birthday all alone. When you're all done this big project, we'd like to take you on a week-long vacation anywhere you'd like to go and make up for the last five years of busyness! We could even travel somewhere here in Canada. Maybe the Rockies? Or here in the East, if you'd like? Please let us know if you ever have a holiday you can share with us. With plenty of loving thoughts, Bill and Mandy."

There was no doubt that Professor Lemans was feeling just a little glum as he paid the waiter and left a generous tip. "I have spent all my time and resources developing Paradise," he sighed. "I hardly have any friends left and I never take holidays."

He passed the toy store where he had often purchased clothes and Barbie accessories for the Tinys. With a passing glance at the display window, he noticed that the seventy-percent discount sign on FairyPetal clothing and accessories was no longer hanging behind the glass. "I bought it all two weeks ago," he chuckled.

A little further downtown was a high-end garden shop, with plenty of fall flowers and trees. On the sidewalk sat a bright orange sign which caught his eye.

"Half-price on Fairy Furniture," he read. *"Oh là là,* I'll just have to check this out!" he smiled, stroking his grey goatee.

Building little 'fairy' gardens had been the summer fad in Greenville, and now it seemed that all the supplies were on sale. Inside the Bluemoon garden centre, which was always open late on a Friday night, a large "Fairy Furniture" sign hung over a high, wooden shelving unit. The Professor picked up the tiny, painted metal chairs and tables, beds and stools, and his dark eyes lit up. "The Tinys will be so excited to see all this useful and well-made furniture," he thought to himself. "It's much better than anything they can make with wooden building boards." Walking inside the store, he told the cashier that he wanted to buy it all.

"Certainly," she said, dumbfounded.

It took quite a while to ring through all the individual pieces.

"If you don't mind me asking," she said politely, "What do you plan to do with all this?"

"It's just so *'charmant'* - lovely," the Professor told her. "I'm going to put these pieces in one of the Biosphere displays. You might even get to see it one day."

"Oh, I love the Biosphere!" she exclaimed. "Do you work there?"

"Yes, I am one of the Professors," he replied.

She looked at his face more carefully. He wasn't wearing a black suit or a white lab coat. "Oh, you must be Professor Lemans," she stated in surprise.

He nodded.

"Then you are the most important Professor!" she exclaimed with a laugh. "I'll certainly look for the furniture. I visit almost every holiday with my family. We especially love walking around the Rainforest at Christmas time! It's like taking a trip to the tropics!"

Smiling, Professor Lemans nodded. "Yes, my favourite too," he agreed.

The cashier didn't ask any more questions. "Have fun," she smiled, putting the receipt in one of his bags.

The Professor walked out of the store with the large bags of gifts for his Tinys, happier than he had been all day long. Instead of going home, he returned to the Biosphere. There in the supply room he loaded the train with as much as it could carry... which was only a quarter of the furniture he had purchased.

Running down the supply room corridor and through the elevator entrances, Professor Lemans entered his private room – the Paradise

Room. It was dark, but a little moonlight streamed through the clear glass above. He didn't turn on a light as he didn't want the glow to shine through the frosted glass around the sides and frighten the Tinys. Instead, he walked over to the dome and looked inside. Louis was sitting on Rainbow Hill gazing towards the lake, as he often did in the evenings. Damien, Lema and Franz were asleep on the beach. All the other children were snuggled inside their beds on the store deck. The wonderful world looked so inviting.

"I wish I could climb the hill and talk to Louis right now," the Professor mused. "I'd like to tell him about the fairy furniture I bought! And I'd love to sit there beside him and ask how swimming went today, and what the children learned. How I would love to live in Louis' world!"

Had the oldest Tiny been in his cave office, the Professor could have sent him a text that he wanted to talk, but there was no way to communicate outside the dome without the risk of the Tinys discovering that they were being watched. One day he would tell them that they could be seen, but not until he was ready to put Paradise on display. Hoping that Louis might check his messages one more time before going to bed, the Professor texted, "I found a good sale on furniture today. I will be sending it in on the train early tomorrow morning. This first shipment is a gift for everyone. Please help to divide it up fairly. I will be sending in three more shipments for the store with the usual trade system in place. Don't feel they need to trade too much for it. I want everyone to get the furniture they need."

After sending the text, the Professor went home alone to his quiet, little condominium overlooking the river. There were no presents waiting for him and no one had made him a cake, but his excitement over the gifts of fairy furniture made it difficult to get to sleep.

As soon as the day began to dawn, Professor Lemans hurried back down to the Biosphere. This was going to be the earliest train delivery yet, and he couldn't wait to see the joy on the children's faces.

The Gifts
Chapter 10

*I*n the supply room, the Professor set the train in motion, and then he raced through the secret entrances to watch the delivery take place in the dome. All the Tinys were still asleep when the train whistle blew. Some of them startled in fright. Others raised their heads wearily with confusion. Louis was the first one up. As soon as they caught sight of the train coming in, the children rolled out of bed and raced down to the track to see what it was bringing in.

Uncle Louis had received the text the night before and knew what was happening. He took charge. "All right, children, we have been sent a wonderful gift from the Professor. This is furniture for your houses!"

There were squeals of delight, especially from the girls. Some of the kids started pushing forward to get to the train first. Those already in front began pushing the others back and a fight nearly broke out.

Uncle Louis stopped them. "We are going to do this fairly for everyone," he began patiently. "First, we are going to bring all the furniture out and set it up in a line on the grass. Then we will decide who will get to pick first. Does everyone understand?"

Mumbled agreement was reluctantly given.

Opening the doors to the train, Louis let the children bring out the furniture. Piece by piece, it was brought out and set in place on the grass. A large metal 'wicker-like' couch with pink and white cushions was a favourite. Two of the Tinys carried out the couch, and all the girls hoped to claim as their own. A blue-checkered hammock attracted the attention of the beach boys. When Uncle Louis explained how it was used, all three wanted it. Unfortunately, the hammock was the only item that Lema, Franz and Damien bothered to retrieve. Everyone else continued unloading furniture until it was out of the train. The very last piece was a white, sculpted double bed, which was carried out by Zahir and Milan. There was an uproar over the bed!

Uncle Louis wondered how to divide the gifts up fairly. Everyone had been helpful, except, of course, the beach boys. But they had helped a little; they had carried one piece out.

"Okay, everyone stand in a line," Uncle Louis said, motioning to the grass beside him. "Now, first of all, there is no need to panic. I want you to know that the Professor will be sending in three more train loads of furniture for trade. Eventually, there will be enough beds and chairs for everyone. Not only that, but if there are items you really like, we can try to make them from building boards."

His words had a calming effect on the children.

"Almost everyone was helpful," he began, "so any suggestions on how to make it fair?"

Kenzie spoke up. "Let's put all the names in a jar, just like we did for the houses," he said.

It wasn't an original idea, but everyone was in agreement.

With her long, blond hair streaming behind her, Georgia ran to get a pen and paper from inside the store. Kenzie found a jar. Together they worked to write all the names down, while the others craned their necks to inspect all the choices again without getting out of line.

Franz's name was chosen first, most undeservedly, and to no one's surprise, he picked the hammock. Then Sanaa was next, and she chose the big white bed, which would come in handy for the five girls living in the mansion. "We can all fit in this!" she exclaimed cheerfully to her future housemates.

Georgia, Aimee and Lily nodded dubiously. Diya shook her head and reminded Sanaa that she needed a room of her own.

The Professor, watching silently and unseen from the other side of the dome, was pleased when Aimee's name was drawn out and she chose the pink and white couch. Gleefully, she danced around it. She was so thrilled! It made the Professor very happy to see her joy.

One by one, the children were called as their names were drawn from the jar, and they had their opportunity to choose a piece of furniture. Some of the children began hauling off their piece of furniture to the site they had chosen for their home.

Rosa, however, let everyone know she was unhappy, complaining that the only chair left was green. "And I don't like green!" she wailed. "It's not fair! Won't someone trade with me?"

But no one else wanted to trade and all that was left was a desk. Rosa didn't want a desk.

As the pieces departed, it became obvious that when the Professor had loaded the train, he had miscounted by one piece of furniture. Standing on the other side of the dome, he shook his head in dismay. Someone was going to be disappointed. "This isn't supposed to happen in Paradise!" he rebuked himself. "How could I mess up counting to twenty?"

Although they had already collected their piece of furniture, Aimee, Nancy and Milan were still standing nearby, wondering who was going to miss out. When the second-last name was called, Vinitha strode forward to pick up the one white desk still standing on the grass. Quiet little Yu Yan bowed her dark head and began to cry. There was nothing left for her.

For a moment no one knew what to do.

The Professor sent a text to Louis, even though he knew he wouldn't get it until he entered the cave later on that night.

"Sorry about the miscount on the furniture. I will send in another piece right away." Walking over to the wall intending to press the train reverse button, he was surprised to hear Aimee speak up.

"It's okay, Yu Yan," she said. "You can have my couch. Uncle Louis said the Professor will be sending in lots of other furniture. I can pick something the next time."

Rushing back over to look through the dome, the Professor saw Yu Yan dry her tears and gratefully accept the pretty couch. Vahid offered to help her carry it over to the orchard. A wonderful feeling came over the Professor. It surpassed the joyful feeling he'd felt when Aimee had danced around the couch. Aimee's compassion and willingness to share evoked a deep measure of love in the Professor's heart towards her.

"She was moved by Yu Yan's tears," he pondered. "She saw her friend's pain and acted generously! And she believes me," he smiled. "She trusts I'll send in more furniture." He blew her a kiss, only of course, Aimee had no idea what the Professor had done or how he felt about her. Then he ran to the wall and pressed the train reverse button.

With its whistle blowing, the train began backing up. The Professor raced through the open elevator entrances and into the supply room. He looked through the fairy furniture for something special and was delighted to find another couch with pink and white cushions. Placing this on the train, he was ready to send it back in, when he stopped himself. "If I send the train in right away," he considered, "then all the children will know they are being watched." As much as he longed to give Aimee an immediate reward, he knew it was better to let her faith in him hold strong for another day.

With a sigh, the Professor loaded up the train with as much furniture as it could carry so that it would be ready for the morning. He sent Louis another text. "Please make sure that Aimee has first-dibs on the furniture when the next train comes in."

A Little Pain

Chapter Eleven

Aimee was so surprised when the first piece of furniture taken off the train in the morning was another pink and white couch! When Uncle Louis told her she could take it as her gift, she actually ran up to him and gave him a hug.

"Oh, thank you," she said earnestly. "And please thank the Professor," she pleaded, "if you know how to tell him things. You said he would send in more furniture, but I'm so happy there was another pink couch!"

Uncle Louis promised to thank the Professor. He then asked all the children to help him unload the train again, only this time he wanted them to take the furniture into the store. Nancy told everyone where to put things and ran around quickly reorganizing the supplies as the furniture came in. Ripple, her cat, found a place on the highest shelf and watched, wide- eyed at all the commotion.

The beach boys found two more hammocks and wanted to take them right away.

"What do you have to trade?" Nancy asked, with her hands on her hips.

"Nothing," Damien laughed, bare-chested and standing up to his full height, which was taller than anyone else. Tossing back his thick blond, messy hair, he grinned. "We are sleeping on the beach," he reminded her, "while the rest of you are building houses. So, we need the hammocks."

"Why aren't you building a house?" Nancy questioned, undeterred.

"We don't need a house," Lema explained with a wide smile on his black face. "We just need hammocks, so we should get them."

"Then find something to trade."

Lema's black eyes twinkled. "Like what? Do you want some sand?" he asked.

Quiet, thin Milan walked over to stand next to Nancy. "Why don't you catch some fish?" he suggested.

"Ah, that takes too long!" Damien complained.

Uncle Louis had overheard the conversation as well and spoke up in his calm way. "If you want the hammocks, boys, you have to do some work to trade for them, just like everyone else. At least go to Mining Hill and dig up a few rocks. You never know, you might even discover the treasure!"

The shirtless lads mumbled something under their breath, dropped the hammocks and took off for the lake.

Kenzie had been waiting in line. "I'm going to go pick some apples," he called out. Being a farmworker, he was able to use the produce he harvested as fair trade. "Then I'll be back for that red chair," he said, pointing in its direction.

Nancy noticed the chair he was looking at and set it aside for him.

"And I'll see if the chickens have laid any eggs," Charley nodded, his eyes on a tall wooden ladder. "I need that ladder."

Nancy put the ladder beside the red chair. The boys ran out to get their produce.

All of a sudden there was a scream and then crying. Louis ran out. Odin had pushed Sanaa to the ground and was shouting at her.

"Hey, what's going on?" Uncle Louis called out.

"She took the bed yesterday," Odin yelled, his messy blond hair hiding his face. "There's no way she can have the big table as well. That's just not fair. Not fair!"

"But there will be five girls in my house," Sanaa explained tearfully, wiping blood from her bleeding knee. "I traded a whole pail of apples for this. We need a big table and a big bed."

"Just because you're building a mansion, doesn't mean you should get everything!"

"Enough. Enough," Uncle Louis said, helping Sanaa get up. He was dismayed to see that Sanaa was bleeding and gave her a big hug. "Odin, look what you have done to Sanaa," he pointed out angrily. "You pushed her down and she's bleeding. From now on there will be no hitting or hurting anyone in this world. And that's a rule!"

"Then you'd better make everyone share," Odin said, frowning.

"If you really like that table, I'll help you make one."

"Exactly like this table?" Odin questioned.

"Yes. We'll try our best," Uncle Louis promised, still holding Sanaa close, "but you'll need to find something to trade for the wood supplies."

"Dumb deal," Odin grumbled, as he tramped off towards the North Forest.

Tina and Lily came running over. "Are you okay, Sanaa?" Tina cried out, seeing bloodstains on Sanaa's bright yellow, flowered skirt. "Let's go to the outdoor tap, and we'll help you get clean."

Giving Sanaa over to her caring friends, Uncle Louis went back to unload the building boards and glue from the train. He found the printouts of the mansion instructions.

Sanaa returned, looking much happier even though half her dress was dripping wet. The blood stains were gone, and a bandage had been wrapped around her knee.

Having unloaded the supplies, Uncle Louis called together all the girls who hoped to live in the mansion and led them to the glue gun depositor. Some of the boys joined them, eager to learn how the work would be done. The glue gun was about as long as Uncle Louis was tall and much higher. It was mounted just outside the store. Uncle Louis borrowed a ladder from the store. He had to climb the ladder to turn it on.

"Now, we need to be very careful with this," he warned them while the glue gun heated up. "The tip will become extremely hot and can burn you. And you don't want the hot glue to drip on you, either, or it will hurt. So, we must treat this equipment with a lot of respect."

He gave the children a demonstration on how to use the new instrument. There was a long table underneath the hot tip, where the building boards could be arranged for gluing.

"Now, Georgia," he said, "I'll get you to climb the ladder and push the glue stick from behind to keep it going through this machine. Sanaa, you can push the button that allows the glue to drip out. And Aimee can help me position the boards."

Everyone heard Uncle Louis' warnings, but not having ever experienced 'burns', they weren't overly concerned. As Aimee and Uncle Louis lined up three boards on the table under the tip, Sanaa heaved with all her strength on the trigger. Up high, Georgia pushed the glue stick from behind and a large drop of clear, hot plastic oozed out and fell on the first board below. Pulling the board toward him, Uncle Louis called out for the girls to do it again. Once they had three drops of hot glue, he motioned for Aimee to lift the second board and together they placed it on top and pressed down.

"This will give us a solid, strong beam for your house," he told her with a pleased smile. Zahir, Vahid, Kenzie, Milan and Charley came closer to watch.

All went well, until they tried to move the third building board into position on top of the glue. The last drop had fallen close to Aimee's end, and when she and Uncle Louis pressed down on the boards, it squeezed out onto her hand.

The glue was hot! Aimee screamed and hastily pulled her hand away, but the glue remained attached to her hand. In a moment, Uncle

Louis was by her side, peeling the glue off. "Are you okay?" he asked, anxiously.

A large red mark stretched across the palm of her hand and tears welled up in Aimee's eyes. "It hurts!" she cried out. "It stings!"

All the Tinys crowded around to see what a burn looked like. Some expressed sympathy and Uncle Louis hugged her close. Remembering that he had seen a bottle of Burn Remedy in the First Aid kit that was kept in the store, Uncle Louis begged Zahir to find it.

Zahir asked Nancy, who was still in the store making bread. Nancy knew where everything was. In a moment, the dark-haired young lad came running back with the bottle of ointment and the rest of the kit just in case it was needed.

Uncle Louis squeezed some of the gel from the bottle straight on to Aimee's palm and told her to gently cover the burn. The cool blue liquid soothed her pain. "Thank you," she murmured gratefully.

"Just keep putting it on whenever you need it," Uncle Louis told her. "We'll leave it here by the glue gun. I sure hope there won't be too many other injuries." He looked around at all the other Tinys. "Take note, everyone," he said. "This glue is hot, and it will burn your skin if it gets on you. Burns hurt."

The other Tinys nodded soberly.

Uncle Louis told Aimee to sit down and rest until her hand felt better. Freddo ambled over to sit close beside her. He put his head on her lap and Aimee patted him gratefully.

"Who wants to help with the boards?" Uncle Louis asked. When all the guys volunteered, Uncle Louis decided everyone would take turns. One by one, they began making the reinforced beams as the Tinys rotated positions and Aimee and Freddo watched. Zahir whistled catchy tunes as he worked, which kept everyone moving. Before dinner that evening they had constructed many of the beams and frames for the walls and roof of the new mansion.

"And now we need to get these pieces up the hill," Uncle Louis stated, looking up in its direction. The hill suddenly appeared ten times bigger than it had before.

Aimee's hand was feeling better and she wanted to help. With her uninjured hand, she and Georgia tried to pick up a beam. They were barely able to budge it.

Everyone laughed.

"I'd say, boys on the ends and girls in the middle," Zahir suggested, coming over to take Aimee's end. Vahid took Georgia's. With Zahir and Vahid helping, the beam was bearable, and the four youths started toward the hill.

Charley and Kenzie helped Sanaa and Lily carry another beam. Diya suddenly decided she needed to use the outhouse, so she was excused.

Uncle Louis grabbed a couple of building boards with Milan's help and they followed the others. Many single sticks would be needed to make the floor.

It was a gruelling trek up the hill, with plenty of stops.

"Is there an easier way to do this?" Zahir asked, once they had reached the top of the hill. Laying the beams on the ground, they all wiped the sweat off their faces.

"There must be," Uncle Louis grunted, as he and Milan lowered their two sticks. "This is all we'll do for today. Let's all try to think of a better way for tomorrow."

Nancy was ringing the dinner bell.

"Hurry," Vahid called out, "we need to get something to trade."

"You spent your day helping out the girls, so you've earned your dinner," Uncle Louis told him.

"Really?" Charley said in surprise. All the boys looked over eagerly.

"Yes, from now on," Uncle Louis stated firmly, "if you spend your day helping out someone else, then that is a fair trade for all your meals and drinks."

There was a loud, "Hurrah," from the boys, as they dashed off to the store.

The girls looked up. "What about us?" Sanaa asked.

"You all helped each other," Uncle Louis smiled, "so, you've traded for your meals."

"Even me?" Aimee asked anxiously. "I sat for most of the day."

Uncle Louis chuckled. "You were hurt on the job and you stayed with the labourers, even carrying a big beam at the end. Go have your dinner!"

No Rules?

Chapter Twelve

*L*ouis was very tired that night when all the kids went to bed. He hobbled to the cave entrance and looked around wearily just to ensure no one was watching. Opening the locked door with the key that he kept in his pocket, he entered his office, closed the door and with a groan, sat down in his chair. They had made a great start on the mansion. Even though the house was for the girls, the boys who were helping were learning how to build their own. In one day, they had built the frames for the first floor, and clamped many wooden building boards together to make several strong beams. It was now a question of how to get all those structures up the hill.

Tapping the side button of the cell phone with his hand, Louis turned it on, and swiped the screen. He Googled, "how to get heavy objects up a hill." As usual, there were many items for sale... very big items that weren't suitable for a tiny dome world. Eventually he found the image of a man pushing a cart with wheels.

"Ah, that's what I need," he thought. "Wheels! I need wheels, and a way to attach them to a frame."

A few more distracting ideas caught his eye. Things that he thought might be fun to create in the future... bikes, skateboards and go-karts! But first, they had to build everyone a house. He clicked back on the home screen and chose the WhiteDove messenger icon for a video call.

The Professor answered and his kind face showed up on the screen. "How are you doing, Louis?" he asked. "You've worked very hard today."

"Yes," Louis chuckled, rubbing his shoulders. "Getting up and down that hill with those wooden building boards was quite tiring. I've Googled ways to make it easier and decided that we should build carts. If it's possible, could you please send us some wheels?"

"Great idea!" the Professor replied, nodding. "I can get wheels easily enough. Carts will help a great deal."

"Thank you," Louis smiled gratefully. "I should also mention an incident today between Odin and Sanaa. Odin is still pushing the other kids around, and today he pushed Sanaa so hard that she fell and cut her knee. I made a rule that there is to be no hitting or hurting anyone in Paradise."

The Professor's eyes filled with alarm. "Sanaa actually cut her knee?" he exclaimed. "Was she bleeding?"

Louis nodded. "Yes, and in tears. Her friends helped her out and she's fine now."

"I'm really sorry to hear that Odin is pushing the others," the Professor said with great disappointment. "I hoped that once you all had entered Paradise, that everyone would be too happy to hurt anyone else."

Louis didn't reply and the Professor pondered the incident thoughtfully. Finally, he said, "I know Odin's behaviour is distressing, but I don't want there to be any rules in your new world. I'd rather you sit down and talk to Odin about why he wants to hurt people. Remember the ten principles. Listen and show empathy. Maybe help Odin think of some options to express his negative feelings in less harmful ways. Paradise should be a happy place where no one wants to hurt anyone else. Rules are unnecessarily restrictive. I'm sure after a few more weeks his behaviour will improve."

Louis was surprised by the reply. "No rules at all?" he questioned. He knew that in the Professor's world, rules abounded. "Not even, 'Wash your hands before you eat?' Or, 'Come to school in the mornings?' Or 'You must learn how to swim?'"

"No rules," the Professor insisted. "Just explain why it's important to wash your hands and swim, and then they will want to do it because they will see the benefits. Encourage them to come to school because learning is so exciting and valuable. You've done a great job so far, choosing only topics that are useful and important for them to know. Carry on in the same manner and you'll never have to make a rule."

Louis agreed. "Well then, I suppose I can take time off building tomorrow to talk to Odin," he considered. "Maybe he'll also have something to trade for table supplies and I can help him make one of his own."

"Yes," the Professor smiled. "Let him express his feelings to you. A little empathy and encouragement should curtail Odin's desire to hurt others, just like we discussed in our course."

Louis nodded. He understood that listening, empathy and encouragement were important motivators. However, Louis was also aware that knowing how something is done or should be done, doesn't always result in perfect implementation. Only three boys had learned how to swim, and he himself was still struggling to figure it out.

Inwardly, the Professor wished he could call Rachel Khalid for advice. He and Evan had excelled in making a perfect physical world in which the Tinys could thrive, but... they had never been parents. He thought to himself, "It might be helpful sometimes to have a motherly perspective. Maybe Rachel would understand Odin. Oh, if only we didn't have to worry about making her an accomplice."

"Well, goodnight, son," the Professor said kindly. "You're doing a wonderful job with all these children and for the most part, they all seem to be very happy."

"Thank you," Louis smiled, "and good night to you."

Once the screen went black, Louis thought about what he would say to Odin in the morning. Mentally he went through the Ten Principles' Checklist, taking note of all that he thought would apply – Listening,

Empathy, Healing, Awareness, Persuasion, Foresight and Building Community.

Once he had made a plan, he Googled a few ideas for the boys' farmhouse. Yesterday, he had pulled Charley's name from the jar. Charley, Kenzie and Vahid weren't so concerned with how nice their house looked, so Louis found a plan with a large veranda, two floors and plenty of rooms. He sent it off to the Professor to print.

He received a text back from the Professor. "Do you hear that beautiful song?"

Louis couldn't hear anything in the cave. He had assumed all the kids were sound asleep. Turning off the lights in his cave office, he dashed outside. Someone was singing and Louis knew immediately who it was. The clear, strong voice with a lovely, sweet tone was unmistakably Aimee's.

"I love you, Professor," she sang.

"You make my dreams come true.

I couldn't ask for more.

I'm so thankful to you.

My favourite colour pink,

Is on the couch you gave.

You know just what I think..."

All of a sudden, the song stopped.

"Oh, I always get stuck on the last line," Aimee moaned. "What rhymes with 'gave'?

Louis could hear her trying various words. Finally, she found a word she liked.

"Wave! My love to you I wave!" And with that, Aimee started the whole song over.

With a smile, Louis locked the door to the cave office, rolled the fake rock in front, and headed to bed. He didn't know until the next day that the Professor had sent another message that said, "I can't tell you how much this little girl's songs mean to me! All the work we put into building Paradise is worth it for just one song! I wish I could tell her how much I love her. Please take special care of her. See if there are any children who also love music and would like to make some easy instruments. I will send in some instructions."

Early the next morning, everyone gathered at the store to get Nancy's fresh bread for breakfast. The farmers and the orchard girls had fruit, flowers and veggies to trade. Charley had even brought some eggs. Whistling happily, Zahir came in with his catch. He and Vahid had caught ten fish.

Aimee had offered to help Nancy get breakfast ready that morning, since her hand had healed well and she was able to use it again. Taking one look at the stiff creatures with the blank eyes, she was aghast at Zahir's suggestion that she fry the fish. She cried out, "Oh, but that's so mean. I couldn't fry something alive!"

Uncle Louis came over just as Vahid walked in. "They aren't alive, Aimee," he assured her. "The Professor gave us fish to eat. That is why they are in the lake. They are meant for food." Putting an arm around Zahir's dejected shoulders, Uncle Louis asked Nancy for one of the small kitchen knives and a chopping board. She passed them to him.

"We'll be right back," Uncle Louis smiled, as he coaxed Zahir and Vahid outside with the fish.

Frying the eggs, Aimee kept busy while Nancy and Milan served the bread and fruit. Almost everyone had eaten breakfast before Uncle Louis and the boys reappeared.

"Can you fry these?" Zahir asked hopefully.

On the chopping board were several long white slabs. They didn't have faces or skin, and there were no longer any eyes.

Reluctantly, Aimee took the chopping board from Zahir and Vahid. Uncle Louis was nodding at her. "Yes," she agreed. "I can fry these." She popped them into her pan with some oil and in a few minutes, they were done. She had to admit, they smelled delicious.

93

The two fishermen were still standing by the counter when Aimee came back with the golden fillets on a tray. With pleased expressions, they helped themselves to the fish and some bread.

"Any chance you might have a lemon?" Zahir asked eagerly.

Nancy reached for a lemon in one of the fruit baskets she kept in the kitchen. "What will you do with this?" she asked. "They are very sour."

With a smile, Zahir picked up a small, clean knife and cut the lemon open. "I don't really know if I'm right," he confessed, squeezing the lemon juice on his fish, "but I just have a feeling that this might go well together."

The girls looked at one another in surprise.

"What do I smell cooking?" Lema asked as he came into the store.

"Fried fish!" Zahir smiled, trying a forkful of the fish on his plate. "Yum!" he exclaimed with a smile in Aimee's direction. "This is the best breakfast ever!"

Aimee felt proud, even though her part had been rather small.

Vahid tasted the fish and his eyes lit up.

"Can we just eat breakfast now and bring double trades for lunch?" Lema asked.

"But that's what you said yesterday," Nancy reminded him, "and then you brought a cup of sand, which no one needs."

"Head out to Mining Hill," Uncle Louis told the beach boys firmly, tired of their reluctance to put in any effort. "There are lots of treasures to be found in the dirt. At the very least bring some flat rocks, and then you can have your breakfast."

As the beach boys turned to leave, grumbling under their breath, Uncle Louis came forward to try a piece of the fried fish. He squeezed the other half of the lemon on his fillet and tried his first mouthful. "This is fantastic!" he raved, looking up at Zahir and Vahid. "I sure hope you boys plan to fish every day!"

Zahir nodded eagerly. "Sure will!" he said.

Odin brushed by, and Uncle Louis asked if he'd found anything to trade for table supplies.

"Not yet," Odin shrugged.

The beach boys returned with only a few pebbles, so Uncle Louis told them to get their bread and fish and head down to the lake for a 'discussion.'

Standing up, Uncle Louis announced to the whole group, "Everyone else will need to meet me here at the store for school today. I'll ring the bell when it's time to come. If you're no longer using your little wooden bed, bring it over to the glue gun. We will use the old beds to make carts today. I want everyone to make a cart to carry materials for the houses."

Singling out Franz, Damien, Lema, Odin and Ponce, Uncle Louis insisted they follow him to the beach. Reluctantly, they complied, while the other kids enjoyed some time to play outside. Sprawling out in the sand, the five boys made themselves comfortable.

"Are we in trouble again?" Damien asked, looking up warily with his big, brown eyes.

"No, not in trouble," Uncle Louis replied, "but I believe it's important for us all to talk about how we treat other people and build our community. We are very fortunate to live in Paradise, and we want to keep this world happy for everyone, and free from pain and suffering. This means we need to think of how to make this world a happier place for others as well as ourselves."

"What about when they cause us pain?" Odin demanded, his pale blue eyes flashing indignantly.

"How does that happen?" Uncle Louis asked him.

"Well, sometimes we really want something, and then someone else comes along and takes it! That hurts me!"

Uncle Louis looked at Odin with surprise. Anger and frustration were seething in the boy's face. It was hard to believe that in a beautiful world, a ten and a half-month old Tiny could have such strong negative emotions.

"All right," Uncle Louis replied, exercising empathy, "you were very upset when Sanaa got the bed and the table. I can understand your disappointment. You didn't think that was fair."

"It sure wasn't fair," Odin grumbled. "All I got was a hard chair."

"Did you have to do anything or trade anything to get that chair?"

"No," Odin retorted, "but Sanaa got the bed for nothing."

He tried to help Odin think of options, "Can you trade for a bed, or make a bed?"

"But that's work! Sanaa didn't have to work for the bed."

Uncle Louis looked at Odin long and hard, but the stocky youth was not about to change his grumpy appearance.

"What options do we have when someone takes something that we had our heart set on? What can we do?"

"Fight him and get it back," Odin insisted.

"Anything else?"

Ponce looked up at Uncle Louis. "Tell you and hope that you make them give it back?"

"That's a less aggressive way," Uncle Louis nodded.

"We could make something that they will like better, and offer to trade?" Damien suggested with a smile.

"I like that idea," Uncle Louis agreed. "Now you're talking about making an effort to do something that will keep the other person happy, and you will feel happy yourself."

"You could just decide not to care about the thing... whatever it is," Lema shrugged. "You could let them have it and make yourself something instead."

"Yes," Uncle Louis nodded, less convinced. "That works well, if you care more about the other person than yourself. Then you will be happy if they are happy. But, if you continue feeling resentful towards that person, your unhappiness may lead to hurtful actions later."

"But what if you make the other person something and then they don't want it?" Franz challenged.

"That is a possibility," Uncle Louis agreed.

"I say, just hit them and grab it," Odin grunted.

"What is gained by hurting people?"

"They won't say no the next time!"

Uncle Louis looked at Odin thoughtfully. "Is that really what you want, Odin? Do you want to make the others so afraid of you, here in Paradise, that they just give you whatever you ask for? Do you think you'll have any good friendships, if people are afraid of you?"

"I don't need friends," Odin shrugged.

"Hey," Ponce frowned.

"Other than Ponce," Odin clarified.

"We all need friends," Uncle Louis told him. "We make friends when we show kindness to others. We lose friends when we resort to scaring people to get our own way. No one feels happy when they are hurt, and no one who hurts others will feel happy inside. So, let's have no more hurting – no hurtful words, no hurtful actions. In Paradise we will use other methods to work through conflicts. Come and talk to me if you can't figure out what to do."

"I don't like rules," Odin complained.

"I'm not making rules," Uncle Louis replied reluctantly. "I'm only giving suggestions. The Professor doesn't want us to have rules in Paradise."

With a smug smile, Odin stated, "That's more like it!"

As he watched Odin trudge off alone across the meadow, while the others ran ahead, Louis was unsure the discussion had been profitable. "I just don't understand the way Odin thinks," he thought to himself. "How will I be able to empathize and help someone that I don't really understand?"

Danger and Heroes

Chapter Thirteen

The train came in while Uncle Louis was chatting to the boys on the beach. Those who were still near the store ran to unload the goods. A new shipment of insects was in the first cart and all the girls squealed with delight when they saw the colorful butterflies flutter out. Aimee and Georgia tried to catch them, but the butterflies stayed just out of their reach.

Vahid and Kenzie began to unload the other train cars, and then they discovered wheels – lots of wheels. Leaving the side doors open, they pulled them out to have some fun! They were thrilled to discover how fast the wheels could roll, shoving them back and forth to each other. Then Kenzie suggested a small incline. By the time Uncle Louis had finished his chat with the boys, a full-blown competition was taking place.

Walking back to the store, Uncle Louis could see seven children at the top of Mining Hill holding something in their hands. Eight others were merrily chasing after round disks that were speeding quickly down the hill and bouncing in all directions.

"It's all wonderful experimentation," Uncle Louis smiled, "just like the Professor was hoping to see." Then he saw a wheel fly up into the air almost as high as Lily was tall.

"Oh dear," he thought. "Someone could get hurt if those wheels hit them!"

As quickly as he could, Uncle Louis put an end to the wheel chase, encouraging everyone to come and make carts.

Fascinated by the wheels, even Odin, Ponce, and the beach boys were eager to begin. All the wheels had a little rod inserted through the middle, which stuck out on each side. Uncle Louis showed them how to use a sharp tool to bore a hole through the building boards and then attach them to the rods. The other ends of the boards became handles. Using the glue gun, he created a frame and attached it to the handles. Then he laid one of the small wooden beds inside and dabbed more hot glue on to make it strong.

Damien followed the instructions to a point, but he didn't want to use a wooden bed! Instead, he laid down a layer of wooden boards across the frame, creating a much wider cart than any of the others. Testing it out, he proved his wider cart helped to keep the beams from tipping side to side.

"This is no effort at all," Damien exclaimed, pushing his new contraption up the hill with two beams laid across it.

"I really like your idea," Uncle Louis praised, watching him carry the beams with ease. "I think I'll redesign my cart. Yours is better."

Once Uncle Louis began making changes, most of the boys redesigned their carts as well. The girls were content to keep the smaller carts. When they had finished, Uncle Louis excused Nancy and Milan to make lunch at the store. Georgia, Tina and Vahid were asked to work on musical instruments, since instructions had arrived that morning along with the wheels. All the other children agreed to push the building materials up the hill. It was still hard work, but not nearly as taxing, although Zahir and Vahid weren't as energetic as they'd been the day before. Rosa and Lily, however, were exhausted after only pushing their cart halfway up the hill, and they let everyone know.

"I need to use the outhouse," Rosa whined at the top of the hill.

"Me too," Lily complained.

"That's fine, girls," Uncle Louis said, rather tired of all their complaining. As he emptied his widened cart for the second time, pulling out two beams, he suggested, "Use the outhouse and then maybe you can help Nancy and Milan get the food ready."

Rosa and Lily were delighted to escape the difficult work. Once the outhouse trip was completed, they decided to stall even longer.

"We could go to the store the long way around," Lily giggled.

With a frown, Rosa questioned uncertainly, "You mean walk all the way around Cascading Mountain?"

"We'll just take it slowly," Lily assured her. "Maybe we can find some pretty flowers to pick."

"But we already worked for our lunch, right?" Rosa asked, confused.

"Oh yes," Lily smiled mischievously. "We're just going to do a little extra and bring flowers as well."

"Oh, I get it," Rosa laughed. "Let's go."

The girls set off happily, quite hidden from view in the forested area between the two hills. They found purple clover in a grassy clearing.

"Rabbits like this," Lily told Rosa, "and so do the bees."

They startled the two deer that spent most of their time in the forest, and almost caught a little rabbit, but it popped down a hole just in time.

"Oh, look at this trail," Lily said, stopping in her tracks. "I wonder where it leads."

Rosa was eager to investigate, so the two of them followed it.

"It stops at this rock," Rosa said, puzzled.

"That's strange," Lily remarked. "Why would anyone come to this rock and stop here?"

They poked around in the bushes but found nothing. Lily suggested that they sit down beside the rock and try to imagine why anyone would walk along the path. After some sitting and thinking neither one of them could figure it out.

Rosa's stomach growled. "It must be nearly lunchtime," she said. "We should get to the store."

Lily agreed. "Let's go," she said, rising up from the rock.

By the time the two girls came around Cascading Mountain and began heading towards the store, Nancy was ringing the bell for lunch.

Carrying some of the purple clover, Lily tasted one of the tiny strands from the flower blossom and discovered it was sweet. "Oh, you should try this!" she exclaimed, handing a piece to Rosa.

Rosa reached out to receive the tiny strand, when suddenly, they both walked into a soft, sticky, almost invisible net between two trees. Had they been watching where they were going, they may have seen the silvery threads sparkling in the sunlight, but they had been too distracted by the edible flower.

"What is this?" Rosa called out, pulling at the threads that were tangled in her pretty, blond curls. "Oh, it's all over me! It's sticking to my hair. It's on my face. Get it off!"

"It's on me too," Lily wailed. "Yuck! Yuck! Get it off me!"

As girls struggled to take off the sticky substance, Rosa looked up and screamed at the top of her voice.

Lily looked up and began hollering as well. Above them and dropping down fast was a large, scary black creature they had never seen before. It was over half their size and had eight long, wriggling legs and a round body with a peculiar red shape underneath. Even its eyes were terribly strange. It didn't just have two beady eyes; it had many!

In no time at all, the thin black legs were wrapping them up with its never-ending sticky threads; threads that they couldn't break or push away. Every time the creature came around in front of them, the terrifying mouth with fangs seemed to come closer and closer. The girls screamed and hollered.

"Who is screaming?" a voice hollered back.

"What is wrong with you girls?" another voice demanded.

The girls had never been so relieved to hear Odin and Ponce.

"Help us!" they pleaded.

"Look, they are all tangled up!" Ponce exclaimed to Odin, pointing in the girls' direction.

Odin was looking above the girls' heads. "What is that black thing?" he yelled.

For a moment, the boys stood aghast, hardly believing what they were seeing. Uncle Louis had never told them about strange black animals with eight wriggly legs.

"Please help us!" Lily called out desperately.

"Save us," Rosa begged.

Odin and Ponce swung into action. "I'll find some sticks," Ponce yelled, dashing around the trees, hoping some broken branches might be on the ground.

Undeterred by his lack of weapons, stocky Odin advanced with his arms ready for action and his pale blue eyes firmly fixed on the fascinating black creature.

"It's tying you up," he marveled.

Rosa wailed, "Yes, please help."

Flailing his arms wildly, and yelling at the top of his voice, Odin tried to scare the strange animal, and it reacted with fear. Nimbly wriggling up along one of its threads, the creature moved out of Odin's reach. It was too high to tie any more threads around the girls or frighten them with its protruding fangs. Continuing his antics, Odin's long blond hair whipped wildly around him. He managed to keep the strange animal away from the girls until Ponce returned with two building boards he had found lying nearby. Then the boys courageously took on the beast.

Jumping, poking and yelling fiercely at the creature, they tried to knock it down from its perch.

Unable to move their arms but craning their necks to see, the horrified girls watched the fight, fearful of what would happen to the boys should the aggressive creature fall to the ground and turn on them.

At last, the boys succeeded in knocking it down. On the defensive now, the creature rose terrifyingly to its full height, which was well past their waists, and began to charge at them. Odin struck it with a mighty blow. Ponce whacked it a second time and it collapsed. Then Odin jumped on the back of the strange animal and there was a mighty crunch. It was not pleasant to see all the liquid oozing out of the body, but the wriggly legs finally stopped moving.

The girls cheered. The boys were dumbfounded for a moment, still positioned and ready for another attack. But the black beast didn't move. At last, the boys decided they had won the battle.

"We'll get you out of there," Ponce promised the girls, but it was harder than he thought. Bravely, he pulled at the threads with his board, but they wouldn't break.

"We're going to need something to cut with," Odin determined. "Hey, girls," he said brusquely, "we're going to run back and get carts and something sharp. If we can't cut you out of those wraps, we'll wheel you to the store and see what Uncle Louis can do."

"Okay," Rosa said gratefully, her big eyes shining with adoration. "Thank you for saving us!"

"Yes," Lily agreed, in much the same fashion. "You guys will be our heroes forever!"

Odin and Ponce looked at each other in surprise. They had no idea how to respond to praise. Without another word, they ran off toward the store.

It took a while for the boys to return. Uncle Louis came with them carrying one of the small kitchen knives in his hand. As he sawed away at the sticky threads surrounding the girls, Odin and Ponce examined the unmoving creature more carefully, poking it with their boards to see if it would react. But nothing happened. Having never caught a fish, or seen Zahir prepare the fillets, they and most of the Tinys were unfamiliar with death.

"What's wrong with it?" Ponce murmured to himself, confusion all over his dark, bronzed face. "Why doesn't it move anymore?"

"That was terrible, Uncle Louis," Rosa lamented, trembling all over as he pulled off the sticky threads from her round arms. "What was that creature? Why didn't you ever tell us about him?"

"It was a spider," Uncle Louis told her. "I don't know how it got into Paradise. Maybe it climbed onto the train by mistake."

"But why didn't you tell us about him?" Lily begged anxiously, pulling threads from her straight brown hair.

"There are many things I haven't told you about," Uncle Louis replied. "Why would I tell you about something so scary, when I didn't think you'd ever see one?"

Curiously, Odin looked up. His pale blue eyes were filled with intrigue. "Are there more creatures that we don't know about?" he asked. "Is there another world somewhere?"

"Yes," Uncle Louis admitted uncomfortably. "There are and there is. But Paradise is the world which the Professor has built for us. It's the only world in which we can survive."

"Can you tell us about the other world?" Ponce begged.

"Perhaps, at some point," Uncle Louis conceded, "once you've learned all there is to know about our world."

The boys grumbled and complained, but Uncle Louis would not divulge any further information.

After freeing the girls from the web, Uncle Louis came over to examine the stiff, black creature with Odin and Ponce. He pushed it gently a couple of times and poked at the liquid pooling around it. Standing up straight, he spoke heavily, "It's... dead. It's not breathing." He sighed deeply. "It's no longer alive."

"Dead?" Odin asked curiously. "What does that mean?"

Uncle Louis looked at him in a very serious way. "Once something is dead," he said slowly, "it will never live again. That's the end of its opportunity to be alive. You... you killed it."

"Oh good!" Odin smiled, looking very pleased with himself. "Well, if we ever see another one of these," he stated boldly, "we'll certainly know what to do with it!"

"You are both so brave!" Lily praised with a sweet smile on her little, freckled face.

The boys looked at each other uncomfortably. Odin turned and began running to the store, but Ponce nodded in Lily's direction. "Thank you," he said, his dark eyes meeting hers for one brief second, and then he too, ran off.

With the girls clinging tightly to his arms, Uncle Louis walked with them to get lunch. He told everyone what had happened and praised Odin and Ponce for their courageous actions. When lunch was over and the girls had run off with their friends, Uncle Louis slipped away to the cave office. The first thing he did was Google 'black spiders.' When he found an image of a spider with a red blotch on its abdomen, he was shocked to read the details.

Breathing deeply, Uncle Louis wrote a hurried text message to the Professor explaining the incident, the results of his search and a suggestion that the dangerous beast might have entered Paradise on the train. He praised Odin and Ponce who had saved the girls from the poisonous black widow spider and suggested some special recognition for the heroes. Feeling rather shaken, he left the cave, only to encounter another dilemma.

Kenzie met him as he walked past the outhouses, and he was visibly upset. "Zahir and Vahid can't leave the outhouse," he relayed anxiously. "They are... well, it's just really gross!"

Running into the outhouse, Uncle Louis encountered two listless, vomiting boys. It took a while before they had emptied their stomachs and could be helped into bed. It was finally determined that they

106

hadn't washed their hands with soap after filleting the fish that morning, but simply rinsed quickly under the water.

Professor Lemans was extremely distraught when he and Louis made contact later that evening for the daily debriefing. He knew how dangerous a black widow was to the Tinys and he was very alarmed that a creature from his world had found its way into the dome. *"Ça alors!* This must have been absolutely frightening for those poor girls!" he commiserated.

"It was terribly frightening," Louis agreed, "but on the bright side, Odin and Ponce became heroes today. Their aggressive natures were exactly what was needed."

Jacques Lemans pondered Louis' remarks. "Interesting," he mused. "They did save the day... and not everyone would react with such courage. They do need to be praised for their actions. However, we don't want this to ever happen again! I'll investigate how that spider may have found its way in on the train!" he promised. "This is very, very distressing! And then to have Zahir and Vahid so sick after handling raw fish... all in the same day! I had hoped bacterial infections would not occur in your world. I thought we had been extra cautious to avoid this happening. You must encourage everyone to always wash their hands with soap before a meal," he told Louis.

"But... don't make a rule?" Louis clarified.

"Non, non. No rules – just strongly encourage them all," the Professor insisted.

Whether there was a rule or no rule, there were now two Tinys who would never forget to wash their hands before a meal. Suffering such a terrible reaction had firmly impressed upon them that there were very important reasons for some of the things that Uncle Louis 'encouraged' them to do.

Preparations

Chapter Fourteen

Uncle Louis smiled sadly. "I'm sorry, Aimee, I can't stay in your house because that would be unfair to the others."

"You could take turns staying with all of us," she suggested hopefully.

"Are you afraid to be on your own?" he asked, looking up at the big building board mansion that many of the Tinys had helped the girls construct. Eight weeks had passed quickly. All the houses were now built and no one slept on the store deck any more.

"I'm not terribly afraid," she murmured, coming closer to Uncle Louis and putting her arm around him. "I know Odin and Ponce are always guarding us, but I just feel better when you are close by."

Uncle Louis smiled and gave Aimee a hug. Now over six centimetres tall, Aimee was a slim, pretty girl who was becoming a strong, positive leader. He was rather amused by her trust in Odin and Ponce. The heroes had been praised numerous times and now spent much of their time in the North Forest near the train tracks, 'guarding' Paradise. Louis knew the train was carefully inspected every day before entering Paradise. He didn't expect any more frightening creatures would ever have the opportunity to ransack their world, but the whole ordeal had elevated Odin and Ponce in everyone's eyes and given them a story to tell... over and over.

"I must stay near the store," Uncle Louis explained. "I need to be somewhere central, so that anyone can find me quickly. Paradise is a very safe place, and you have a house full of girls and two boys nearby."

"Okay," she sighed, leaning her head on his shoulder. "I guess I'll be okay."

"You will be," he assured her, with a gentle squeeze. "And if you ever call out for me, I'll come running!"

Aimee smiled up at him gratefully.

As they approached the clearing at the top of Rainbow Hill, they saw the new row of solar twinkle lights that had been strung along the trees. "Are you ready for the celebration tonight?" he asked.

The children were twelve months old and maturing rapidly. Uncle Louis had told everyone a 'Thank You Celebration' was in order to show their appreciation to the Mastermind of Paradise. He assured them that he had a special way of telling the Professor and Evan to watch the show.

"It's going to be amazing!" Aimee smiled, looking up at him with delight. "Georgia has added a very special ending to our song. She made little shakers and Vinitha painted them! And Vahid has these metal things that make a loud clang when he hits them together. I'm sure the Professor and Evan will love our song!"

"I'm sure they will, too," Uncle Louis smiled. "This is going to be a very special celebration."

"Oh, and this is the best part," Aimee added enthusiastically, as she pulled away and clapped her hands. "Zahir has agreed to sing with me!"

"You talked him into it?"

"Yes," she nodded exuberantly, her blue eyes sparkling. "Finally! Zahir doesn't think he has a good voice - but he does! Except," she added, "when his voice cracks. But hopefully that won't happen tonight."

"Well done, Aimee," Uncle Louis praised happily. "I'm really looking forward to the performance and hearing the two of you sing."

Looking down toward the lake, he murmured, "I need to go and see if the surfers are ready."

Uncle Louis turned away to head down to the beach. Aimee met Zahir to practice their song. Everyone had a role to play in the celebration and there were even going to be two special awards given out, which Uncle Louis was keeping secret. Leaving the school pavilion, Uncle Louis crossed the bridge over Rainy River. Zahir had named it Rainy River, as it only flowed when it rained in Paradise.

Looking out at the lake, Uncle Louis sighed. Damien, Franz and Lema were supposed to be doing a surfing show for the celebration, but at the moment they were in the water, throwing an apple back and forth. While many of the youths had built houses and learned to make, grow, or find something to barter with in the store, the beach boys had strung their hammocks in the trees and learned to build surfboards, but only for themselves. That was all they had worked on during the entire eight weeks they had spent in Paradise.

Unfortunately, the beach boys still rarely had anything to trade. Recently, they had begun sneaking food supplies from Nancy, who had no way of stopping them. Seeing the apple that they were tossing around, Uncle Louis guessed that they had taken it from the orchards lining the beach. Since they never contributed to any of the work on the farm, it didn't seem fair for them to help themselves to the produce. Uncle Louis had been trying to convince the Professor that some rules and consequences were needed in Paradise. As of last night, the Professor had agreed that if the boys stole from the store again, it would be helpful to impose a consequence.

"Hey, guys," Uncle Louis called out, "are you ready for the show tonight?"

"I can stand up on my board, Louis," Franz replied. "Want to see?"

"I would," Uncle Louis told him, choosing to ignore the fact that Franz had dropped the 'uncle' part of his name. If there were to be no rules in Paradise, he could hardly insist on respectful titles. "I'd like to see what all of you are planning to do for the celebration," he encouraged.

With a little grumbling about their game being interrupted, the boys grabbed their surfboards off the beach and headed out into the waves. They lay on top of the boards and paddled out to where the white caps were forming.

Uncle Louis watched patiently as the boys struggled time and again to get up on the boards. Damien was the strongest and most agile, although Lema wasn't far behind. After several tries, Damien was the first to stand for several seconds, riding a wave. Then he was tossed headfirst into the water.

"Well done," Uncle Louis clapped.

He watched until each boy had stood up on his board for at least a few seconds. He admired their proficiency in the water and wished that more of the Tinys had learned to swim, but it hadn't been a popular activity. "Perhaps I didn't teach it very well," he reflected, as Damien swam hard towards the bigger waves. "It's difficult to be enthusiastic and build their confidence in something that still intimidates me." Finally, he called the boys in.

"You're doing very well on those boards," Uncle Louis told them with a big smile, "and I love watching you swim!"

The boys looked proudly at each other.

"Yes, I wish all of us could swim like you do," Uncle Louis nodded. "You've got it down pat! A little more surfing practice this afternoon will help you do even better tonight. It would be great to aim for ten seconds each on those boards."

"Easy!" Damien boasted.

Lema considered the request dubiously.

"How about five?" Franz offered.

"See what you can do," Uncle Louis encouraged. "Now, before I go, we also need to discuss trading."

Franz frowned. "What do we need to trade for? There's enough food for everyone in the store."

With a smile, Uncle Louis reminded him, "We trade because it keeps everyone productive and learning new skills. There are plenty of fish in this lake that you boys could catch..."

"Anyone can catch fish, if they want them," Lema argued, his dark arms folded across his bare chest. "It takes two minutes, if that."

"Yeah," Damien agreed. "Zahir fishes every morning. If anyone else wants fish, they can come get them. We don't mind."

"The Professor would like you to contribute in some way," Uncle Louis said kindly. "You could make surfboards for other people or try to make boats. I've heard that boats are easier to use on the water."

"That's a lot of work!" Damien complained, with his hands on his hips. "It took us days to make these surfboards. No one else even wants to learn how to swim, so who would want a board?"

"Well, if none of these suggestions are appealing to you," Uncle Louis told them, "then you can always go to Mining Hill and see what treasures you can find. Some people would like rocks for their gardens, or gems and pebbles for decorations. You're welcome to dig anything up and bring it to the store for trade."

"That's too hard," Franz whined.

The gentle negotiating didn't seem to be making any headway. "Okay, from now on," Uncle Louis said firmly, "if you steal food or supplies, you will be banned from the lake until you make or bring something to trade."

Lema laughed. "Will someone stand there all day and night, guarding the lake?"

For a moment, Uncle Louis imagined himself building a wall - a tall, thick wall all around the lake with a big locked gate! Folding his arms across his chest, Uncle Louis reminded himself that a tall, thick wall wouldn't fit with the Professor's desire for Paradise to be a happy, free place. With a sigh he remembered the lofty principles of 'servant-

112

leadership.' "Persuasion," he told himself. "Try a little more persuasion."

"Guys," Uncle Louis pleaded. "Have a look at the wonderful world we are living in. Do you think we would have such a delightful paradise if Evan and the Professor just laid around, played with their friends and only thought about their own interests?"

Lema shrugged.

"We wouldn't," Uncle Louis said, answering his own question. "The Professor and Evan worked very hard to make Paradise for us, and they want us to do our part to make it more beautiful, to learn, and to help each other..."

"Are we their slaves?" Damien questioned.

"No!" he retorted. "We are all working together to keep our Paradise the best that it can be."

"And then what?" Lema questioned.

Uncle Louis looked at him with confusion, unsure of what he meant.

Damien understood. He shrugged and explained, "Not everyone cares about the way things look." Glancing over at his friends, he added, "We don't!"

The friends agreed. "Paradise looks good enough already," Franz put in. "Why can't we just enjoy it and have fun?"

"Because, without our effort, Paradise won't function as well as it can," Uncle Louis explained. He tried to think of way to help the boys understand. "Imagine if no one planted food in the gardens, or made sure the plants were well watered? What if no one took the produce to the store and Nancy and Milan didn't turn it into a delicious meal? What would you eat?"

"We'd pick our own apples," Lema argued.

Yawning, Damien stated, "I'd be fine with Wonderdrink."

"Me too," Franz chimed in.

With a skeptical expression, Uncle Louis looked long and hard at the boys. Lema and Damien couldn't help but smile; they knew they weren't being entirely truthful. Franz looked away.

"Well," Uncle Louis told them, "The Professor and Evan gave years of their lives to make this world. All they ask is that we do our part to keep it attractive and self-sustaining. That's how we show our gratitude to them."

"I don't know who the Professor is," Franz argued. Then with a twinkle in his brown eyes, he added, "or even if he really exists."

The other boys laughed. Uncle Louis shook his head in disappointment.

"But," Lema admitted, "we do know Evan."

"Yeah, Evan was nice," Damien agreed, half-heartedly. "We should at least be thankful to him."

"I've had enough of this," Franz complained. "Let's go practice our surfing." And with that, he ran into the water.

The other boys followed.

Watching them run off, Uncle Louis wondered how he could help these boys understand the importance of gratitude and working together for the benefit of the whole group. The majority of the Tinys loved the bartering system and enjoyed discovering new treasures they could take to the store. Thankfulness toward the Professor and Evan for the daily train loads of goods and the magnificent world was something many of the children related to quite naturally.

Walking back over the dry Rainy River channel and through the orchards which were loaded down with fruit, Uncle Louis saw that Sanaa and Charley were harvesting the cherry crop. Sanaa was happily humming away to herself as she worked. A lot of the fruit had been pecked by the birds, but the kids were carefully choosing the most intact fruits. Maxi lay nearby, watching intently for rabbits.

"Hey, Uncle Louis," Charley called out, "should we put the best cherries in a basket to bring to the celebration tonight? Would Evan and the Professor like that?"

"Sure," Uncle Louis nodded, very pleased by Charley's suggestion. "That's a great idea."

"But how will the Professor see the cherries?" Sanaa asked, looking very confused. "How will he know they are there?"

For a moment, Uncle Louis wasn't sure how to answer the question. He knew he couldn't tell her the technical details. "Well, you see," he began slowly, "the Professor and I have a special connection. If I tell him to look at something, then he will."

"But how does he see us?" Sanaa asked, looking up at the sky.

"He just can, when he wants to," Uncle Louis shrugged.

"Will we see him?" Charley asked.

"No, you can't see him," Uncle Louis answered, "but trust me, the Professor can see us if he wants to, and so can Evan. I can't tell you any more than that."

It was easy to see that Sanaa had other questions, but she accepted his reply with a little shrug of her dark shoulders.

"It's too bad we can't send them a couple of mangoes," Charley said thoughtfully, "but they aren't quite ready yet."

"No, they are still hard as rocks," Sanaa laughed, "and besides, there are only seven!"

Uncle Louis glanced over at the mango trees. They had certainly not been as productive as all the others.

"We'll send them a gift of cherries on the train tomorrow," Uncle Louis told her. "Then they'll get to enjoy them, just like we do."

"Oh, that's a good idea," Sanaa laughed, wiggling her hips and clapping her hands together. "We'll pick the best cherries for them."

The Celebration

Chapter Fifteen

A message scrolled across Evan's screen. "Check out these model homes." He was finishing off an assignment in the Biosphere library when his dad's email came to his attention. "There are only five houses left for sale. You'd be a ten-minute walk away from us, and Serenity Street backs onto a thirty-acre green space!"

However, it was not the opportunity to purchase a house in the coveted area near his parents, but the model homes themselves, which drew Evan, wide-eyed, to examine the link more closely. On the website, the large display of miniature model homes lining a fabricated street set Evan's imagination on fire. He'd never seen model homes quite like these. Hinged-fronts lifted up to reveal perfectly crafted rooms with open windows, stairs, furniture, decorated rooms and flooring - everything that made a home attractive and liveable.

"Are they big enough for the Tinys?" he wondered with astonishment. Then he sighed, "Even if they were," he told himself, "the Tinys have wooden homes which they enjoyed building themselves. There is no need for something so extravagant. No need at all!"

However, he couldn't resist forwarding the link to the Professor, with a little message, "Think they'd fit, if they were for sale?"

A voice from behind startled him, "Hey, do you want to go out for a coffee or a hot chocolate?"

Evan looked up from his computer to see Jim standing nearby with a hopeful expression. They had been friends since the first year of university.

As the monkeys chattered away nearby competing with the noisy Molly Macaw, Evan replied, "Sorry, buddy, I have an important meeting with Professor Lemans."

Disappointed, Jim replied, "You've had enough meetings to plan a world take-over!"

"We're still working on that research project," Evan explained, closing the lid of his computer and standing up. He put his arm around his friend's shoulders. "Look, I'd love to get together with you and have a catch up... soon. Maybe next week?"

"It's always next week," his friend smiled, as they walked out of the library and past the sloth hanging lazily from a tree. Curiously, Jim asked, "When are you going to tell everyone about this project?"

"Very possibly in less than a year from now," Evan smiled, trying to speak above the noise of the howler monkeys. "It's going well. We just have a few more things to work out. You'll be one of the first to know, I'm sure!"

Jim asked him to repeat himself, as the monkeys took a short reprieve from their chorus.

"I hope it's soon," Jim nodded. "Rumour has it that you're building a virtual reality, interactive 3D jungle world. That would be cool!"

Evan smiled. "It would," he agreed as they stopped by the main glass doors. Tall, high and tinted blue, the doors framed the young deciduous forest lining the winding pathway outside. The remaining red, orange and yellow leaves were blowing off the trees and whirling around outside. A dark storm was blowing in.

Opening the door for his friend, Evan thanked him for stopping by.

"See ya," Jim called out, as he exited the building.

Crisp, cool, autumn air enveloped Evan as he waved good-bye and closed the door. Then he quickly dashed down the hall to meet the

Professor. The 'Thank You Celebration' was beginning in five minutes, and he didn't want to miss a thing. As always, when he turned the corner and came to Mirror Hall, he looked in all directions to be sure no one was watching. Usually, by five o'clock in the afternoon, the Biosphere was closed to the university students and only Tim, the maintenance man, remained behind.

However, a student was still wandering through the Rainforest exhibits, so Evan waited, checking his messages as a cover for standing still.

There was a message from his parents wondering if he'd seen the email they had sent about the houses for sale. He replied, "Yes."

After answering his parents, Evan also took the opportunity to catch up with some students who had started a group chat about investigating the breeding possibilities between black bears and polar bears in the Arctic Biome.

"This would provide a good opportunity for genetic research," Evan texted in agreement.

"We're safe," a voice chuckled.

With a start, Evan looked up. Professor Lemans was standing beside him and the student had disappeared.

Quickly pressing the green arrow on his cellphone, Evan and the Professor were both immediately lowered into the tunnel shaft.

"How was your day, Professor?"

"Good enough, until the last hour."

"What happened?"

"You know that red-headed kid in first year?"

"You mean Seth McGeorge?"

"You do know him?"

"I tutor him, Sir."

"Well, I suppose you know he's a Creationist?"

"I do."

"So, he's always questioning everything I say about the evolution of man and how life began. Today, he wanted to know why I didn't believe in a God."

"And what did you say?"

"I gave him many reasons, mostly from the scientific viewpoint and the research that has been done. But wouldn't you know it, he didn't seem moved by anything I said. Finally, I asked if he'd read my book and he hadn't." With a chuckle, he added, "So, I insisted he read it before he asks anymore questions."

Passing by the empty nursery rooms, Evan felt somewhat emboldened by Seth's questioning. "If you don't mind me asking," he said, "why is it that you don't see any evidence of Intelligent Design?"

The Professor looked surprised. "Are you on Seth's side?"

Evan shook his head and sighed, "I just wonder, that's all. I like to keep an open mind."

"Well, I'll give you one simple explanation," the Professor replied. "There can't be a God, or He wouldn't allow so many senseless tragedies to take place on earth. Think about it, Evan. Think about how much we care for Paradise. We'd do anything to keep our Tinys safe. We don't want to lose even one. We would never willingly generate tidal waves to wipe them all out or introduce disease." For a moment, the Professor paused, reflecting on the mishaps that had occurred. "We have had a few close calls in Paradise," he admitted, "but certainly nothing we would instigate! If there is a God, then how can He allow so much suffering? How can He be paying any attention to what is going on in the earth?"

"True," Evan agreed timidly, "but most of the time the world functions incredibly well..."

"All it takes is one catastrophe and that's enough to prove that God can't exist," the Professor argued. "If He really is 'all-powerful', why would He allow any hurricanes, or volcanoes, or tsunamis, or massive flooding, or famine, or..."

"I guess so," Evan nodded uncertainly. "If there is a supernatural God with power, then He should be able to stop those things from happening... if... if He wanted to."

The Professor glanced over with a frown. His voice was almost fierce. "And why wouldn't He want to?"

"I don't know," Evan faltered, "but, unless suffering has a purpose? Maybe some good comes from it?" Having sensed on a few occasions a personal vendetta in the Professor's rants, Evan looked over compassionately, "Sir, you seem to have experienced some suffering in your own life."

The Professor didn't answer, but Evan noticed his clenched fists and the dark, brooding look in his brown eyes. As they entered the office, the conversation didn't continue; it was time for the celebration to begin.

It was only five-thirty in the afternoon, but due to the approaching storm outside, it was fairly dark in the Paradise Room. They drew close to the dome.

"*Oh là là,* look what they've done with the solar lights we sent in!" Professor Lemans whispered, very impressed.

The beach area had been lit up with twinkle lights. Strung in trees that lined the beach, the reflection of the lights shimmered in the water. While the Professor and Evan had been in class, Louis and his team of Tinys had woven the seven meters of lights and cable in and out of the trees. They had created a lighted pathway up Rainbow Hill and encircled the plateau clearing where the festivities were to take place. An 'on and off' switch was positioned close to the clearing.

"Paradise looks beautiful tonight!" Evan said quietly. "I love the lights!"

"I sent in new clothes and glow sticks, as well," the Professor told him with a smile.

Evan chuckled. He knew how much the Professor enjoyed sending in gifts.

120

"And look at those swim shorts," the Professor whispered, pointing to the beach boys. "I had them custom-made."

The beach boys were leaning on their surfboards, clad only in their new shorts, which were entirely free of ribbons and fringes. Waiting impatiently for the signal to begin the show, their voices were clearly discernible from the speakers that hung on the wall.

"I don't see why we have to wait so long!" Damien was saying.

"Yeah, let's get on with the show!" Franz muttered.

"I don't see anyone watching us 'from above'," Lema chuckled, flinging out one long black arm. "I think Uncle Louis is telling us stories. He's just trying to motivate us to do something that he wants us to do."

Franz laughed. "Why do you still call him Uncle? I just call him Louis."

Damien was thinking about Lema's comment, and he agreed. "A 'Mastermind' sounds kind of scary... and powerful," he pondered. "Maybe it is just a story..."

"Come on, let's get on with the show," Damien said impatiently.

"I think the whole 'Professor' thing is just made-up!" Franz snickered.

The Professor and Evan shared a look of amusement.

"Maybe," Damien pondered. "We did use to see big Evan in the nursery, but I've never seen any Professor."

Looking over at Evan with a twinkle in his eyes, the Professor whispered, "I should just get up on my Lift-pod right now and look in through the top." He chuckled, "Then they'd know!"

Evan grinned. "Can you imagine their reaction?"

A smile crept across the Professor's face as he thought through the whole scenario, even though he had no intentions of carrying it out. "It would alter the experiment significantly," he mused. "If they knew they were being watched then they wouldn't feel free to be themselves. They would feel stressed."

Evan nodded. "Or they might stay indoors all day where they couldn't be seen."

Franz was still complaining. "Yeah, whatever happened to Evan?" he grumbled. "Why don't we see or hear from him anymore? He used to check on us every day!"

Evan smiled sadly, wishing he could still interact with them. Then he noticed movement in the meadow. "Look," he whispered, "there's action by the schoolhouse."

Suddenly, four children ran out from the school waving coloured glow sticks and shouting, "Thank you for Paradise!" Together, they sang a cute, brand new song, while Georgia and Kenzie kept the beat with their newly made shakers and cymbals. The children repeated their happy song, while the beach boys rode the waves, managing to stay on their boards for an average of nine seconds each. The Professor laughed and clapped softly. Evan took pictures, although in the dim lighting, he was having trouble capturing good ones.

"The beach boys are learning to surf," the Professor whispered. "I'm glad to see they are developing their skills."

The Tinys on the shoreline held their glow sticks high and began running towards Rainbow Hill. Looking in that direction, the Professor noticed a sudden glow of colour lighting up the clearing. On the high edge of the hill, the rest of the children were now standing in a colourful heart-shape, with their lighted glow-sticks. Aimee and Zahir were in the middle.

"I love it!" the Professor said out loud.

Evan looked at him sideways, wondering if his voice would be heard.

At that moment, Aimee began to sing from the hilltop; her voice carried clearly across the water.

Moving around the dome to a place where they could see the singers more clearly, the Professor and Evan eagerly leaned forward. Tall and slim, Aimee looked lovely in the new, shimmering, white

FairyPetal dress that was only slightly too big. It had long iridescent gauze ribbons that hung from her waist and shoulders. Dark and handsome, Zahir stood near her, looking quite dapper in his flowing white shirt, ribbon-trimmed vest and new suspender-shorts. Freddo sat close by. They had tied a few red and pink ribbons around Freddo's furry neck. A white ribbon had also been used to pull back Zahir's hair. The boys always had a good supply of ribbons they had torn off their clothes.

Having found a lowlight setting on his phone, Evan managed to capture a great picture of the scene. He turned on his video.

"Thank you, thank you, thank you," were the first lines of the song. Aimee sang softly looking up to the sky with outreached arms.

With a sideways glance, Evan could see a smile spreading across the Professor's face.

Zahir stepped forward and repeated the lyrics with the same earnest tone.

Evan had never heard Zahir sing before. "Wow, he has a good voice!" he whispered.

"Quite a well-matched pair," the Professor agreed proudly. Privately, he had high hopes that their relationship would blossom in the future.

"We thank you for all that you do," they both sang together.

"We thank you for all that we grow," Aimee sang. "We love the flowers and the food from the seeds we sow."

A sudden, uncomfortable thought flitted across Evan's mind. "This is almost like worship," he thought to himself.

"We thank you for stocking our store," Zahir added, his voice cracking a little. With only a slight hesitation and glance in Aimee's direction, he added, "Every day the train brings more."

"We thank you for the rain that falls from above," Aimee twirled around, sending all the shimmering ribbons flowing outwards. A few hit Zahir in the nose and he backed away. Without noticing, Aimee continued, "And all the dear animals that we've come to love."

"Professor, you've given us everything," Zahir praised, kneeling down to embrace his favourite dog for whom he was so thankful. "We're so happy here, that we want to sing."

A soft, choking sound came from the Professor.

Evan turned and saw there were tears in his eyes. Continuing to record the scene on his phone, he put his free arm around the older man's shoulders.

"So, thank you, thank you, thank you," Aimee softly ended the pretty song.

In even softer tones, Zahir echoed, "Thank you, thank you, thank you."

Then together with Louis, everyone on the mountain raised their arms and said, "We love you! Thank you for Paradise."

Unexpectedly, the Professor turned to Evan, choked up with emotion. He couldn't say anything.

"Hey, it's all been worth it!" Evan told him, patting him on the back and not really knowing what to say or do. He thought to himself, "I do believe objectivity may have just come to an end."

Clearing his throat, Evan said, "Never mind the doubting beach boys, you've got a very thankful group of Tinys who love you."

It took some time for the Professor to gain his composure. He stood by the dome, leaning against the glass, unable to talk.

Together they watched Uncle Louis present the special awards he had sent in for the unsuspecting heroes.

Calling Odin and Ponce to stand before all the others, Uncle Louis reflected on the brave response of the two boys in the face of danger. "Here in Paradise," he continued, "we rarely see danger or have to save one another. So, today we celebrate our two heroes who did just that and fought the frightening, dangerous spider which trapped Rosa and Lily. We admire your courage and your willingness to help your fellow Tinys. Thank you, Ponce and Odin."

Everyone cheered and clapped. The epic tale had been told so often that it was now remembered as the most exciting event in the history of Paradise.

Ponce and Odin stood tall, receiving the praise and applause as proper heroes. Their eyes lit up when Uncle Louis brought forward two dark blue flags with golden writing. In big letters on each flag was the word, "COURAGE."

From outside the dome, Evan nodded with a smile. "It's so good to see those boys being rewarded for their bravery."

Without a word, the Professor nodded. He was still emotional.

Watching the boys admire their flags, Evan saw Rosa and Lily come over to give them hugs. He remarked, "I believe the spider battle was a turning point for those two. A little praise and recognition for their courage may be just what they needed."

Again, the Professor nodded.

Inside, the farmers involved in growing produce handed out fruit and vegetables to the others. Those who had been mining in the hills gave out pretty, coloured beads they had found. Nancy and Milan, the bread makers, doled out buns. Even the beach boys contributed by handing everyone a paper invitation to come for a surfing lesson.

It wasn't until the feasting had ended, and Louis was organizing a group game of 'Storm the Lantern' on Rainbow Hill, that the Professor was able to get himself together.

"That was *magnifique,*" he said quietly.

"It was very impressive," Evan whispered.

"It topped any award I've ever received," the Professor confided.

"Really? Even Scientist of the Year?"

"Even that. This had something that all the others lacked."

"What was that?"

"That song came from their hearts," he said emotionally. "It was real. It was beautiful!" Struggling to find words to express his feelings, he just shook his head and looked at his phone. There was another reason he felt emotional but he wasn't ready to share it. In a quiet voice, he said, "It's nearly seven. We'd better get home. You need your dinner."

Evan laughed softly. "Why don't we go out and celebrate with some Chinese food?"

"Thanks for the offer," the Professor nodded. "I just feel... drained. I need to go home."

Patting his mentor on the back, Evan whispered, "Congratulations, Professor Lemans. Go home and remember all the thankful hearts that praised you tonight."

Nodding, the Professor smiled. "I will," he promised, opening the door to the tunnel that led out to the parking lot.

"Do you mind if I stay here for a while longer and watch the game?" Evan enquired.

"No, no, go ahead. I'll see you in the morning."

Evan stayed for another hour, watching the Tinys play their games. He wished he could join in. As he watched the youths hide in various places in the forest, and two boys sneak up the hill hoping to touch the glow stick before Uncle Louis noticed them, he pondered the Professor's emotional response to the captivating celebration. Both of them had given up everything to work on this project. They had lost friendships and used up limited resources. Still in his late-twenties, Evan hoped that one day, when he had completed his doctorate, he might get to enjoy closer relationships again. Maybe he'd find a wife and have a family. Maybe he'd even buy a house near his parents.

"But," he considered, "the Professor has no one. He is in his fifties. Why is he all alone? Why is he giving his whole life to this?"

Evan sighed, feeling another twinge of conscience. "I sure hope we've done the right thing," he mused, as the 'worship' song niggled at his conscience. "I feel like we're playing God. This is sort of our world that we've 'created' but in reality, we haven't created anything. We've only manipulated the life that is already in existence."

Noticing the beach boys wandering back to the lake, Evan listened to their voices, which were always well-reflected off the surface of the water.

"That game was cool," Franz admitted.

"And I got a stash of buns," Lema bragged. "Should keep us going for the next couple days."

Franz opened his bag to show the others and laughed. "And I got some cherries!"

Damien popped his hand in to grab a few cherries, eating them straight away. "Yum!" he said.

Franz quickly closed the bag up.

Passing by the mango trees, Damien sniffed one of the ripening fruits. "I'm keeping my eyes and nose on these mangoes," he remarked mischievously. "They smell awesome!"

"You might have to catch twenty fish for one of those," Lema taunted. Even though there were five mango trees in the orchard, none had produced more than two fruits. "Charley is guarding them like they are the most precious thing in the orchard."

Damien laughed.

Franz suddenly changed the subject. "That celebration tonight was dumb," he quipped. "No one was listening."

"There were some strange sounds," Damien reflected. "I heard kind of muffled noises."

"I didn't hear anything," Franz retorted as they reached their hammocks. He pushed his long, stringy hair out of his eyes, "This hair... is driving me... crazy!"

Shaking back his lengthy, golden waves, Damien agreed. "Mine too!"

"Glad that I don't have that problem," Lema laughed, rubbing his tight afro. Climbing into his hammock he added, "But you know, Zahir also said he heard funny noises. Maybe the animals were reacting to all the lights and songs. They aren't used to them."

"I hope they turn those lights off soon," Franz complained. "It's way too bright to sleep!"

"I'm turning them off!" Damien declared. "I know where the switch is." And with that, he dashed off toward the path which led up Rainbow Hill.

Evan, on the other side of the glass, took mental note. "We certainly can be heard on this side," he said to himself, pulling out his phone to text. "I'll have to let the Professor know. And I should ask him if he has ordered those tiny scissors. Those boys really do need haircuts!"

Stealing Mangoes

Chapter Sixteen

Aimee woke up early to the sounds of boys yelling and a dog barking. Grabbing her fleece blanket, Aimee ran to the window. Wrapped in her blanket, she had a good view of the farmland from the second floor of the girls' mansion. Sure enough, out in the orchard, she could see Damien and Lema pulling the few ripe mangoes off of the trees. Charley, while scrawny and small in stature, had a very loud voice and he was yelling for the boys to stop. Tearing around their ankles, Maxi was howling and barking.

"Poor Charley," Aimee mourned. "He's been waiting so long for those mangoes to ripen. He wanted everyone to share them."

Angry about the situation, she called loudly to the other girls, "They are taking the mangoes! Those selfish boys are stealing them!"

Georgia was the first to rush in. "Who's taking the mangoes?"

Aimee pointed. The tall, well-built Damien was wrestling small, wiry Charley who was trying to protect his crop.

Damien pushed Charley down, but Charley wasn't going to give up easily. Jumping back up, he tried to defend the two mangoes still hanging from a branch. Lema shoved Charley hard. Thrown off balance, the smaller youth tripped over his dog and fell to the ground awkwardly. Charley cried out in pain and Maxi yelped. The girls were greatly distraught. Maxi was frantic. Jumping up, the little beagle began nipping at Lema's swim shorts.

"Lema is hurting Charley!" Aimee cried out.

Sanaa, Diya and Lily joined them at the window.

129

"We've got to go help them," Georgia said.

"But they are hurting each other," Diya argued. "What if they hurt us?"

"Please come help," Sanaa cried out urgently, running down the stairs in a panic. "We can't leave Charley to face them alone." Sanaa and Charley worked every day on the farm together; he was her best friend.

"Go call Uncle Louis," Aimee ordered Georgia. "I'll help Sanaa."

While Lily and Diya hugged each other in the window, the other three girls ran as fast as they could to the gardens.

Lema and Franz had taken off towards the lake. Damien was following behind, trying to get away with six mangoes that he couldn't carry very well. Across the orchard on Mining Hill, Vinitha, Tina, Yu Yan and Rosa stood by their home, hugging each other anxiously.

By the time the forest girls reached the farmland, the beach boys had made it to Rainy River Bridge and were trying to find a place to hide and enjoy their stolen treats. Charley was sprawled on the ground, crying. Maxi was licking his face and one bruised mango lay close by.

"Are you okay?" Sanaa called out, tears in her dark eyes.

"No," Charley moaned. "I can't move my arm."

Charley's arm didn't look right.

"Oh, Charley," Aimee wailed. "Uncle Louis," she called out loudly. "Uncle Louis, where are you?"

"Why is your arm bending like that?" Sanaa cried, as the tears streamed down her dark face. She reached out towards him.

"Don't touch it," Charley warned her sharply. "I fell on it. And I heard something snap. It hurts so badly!"

Maxi doubled her efforts to wash Charley's face.

"Sanaa, please hold Maxi," Charley begged.

Reaching down quickly, Sanaa scooped the squirming dog up in her arms and held her tight. The little beagle anxiously licked Sanaa.

Uncle Louis was running from his cabin near the store. "What's going on?" he called out.

Other children were running over from their houses. For a few moments, Paradise was in chaos. Some Tinys were desperately trying to find out what had happened, while the girls frantically tried to explain.

Reaching Charley, Uncle Louis knelt down beside him. Aimee tried her best to give him all the details from the very first moment she had looked out the window.

"I think your arm is broken," Uncle Louis told Charley with a grim expression. "I'm going to have to run back and get some supplies to fix it up. Just stay here and don't move."

Addressing the girls, he said, "Talk to Charley. Sing to Charley. Keep his mind off the pain. I'll just get a few supplies from the store."

There was now a large crowd around Charley. Trying to help keep Charley's mind off the pain, Georgia decided to tell their favorite story. "One day, two Tinys decided to go for a walk in the deep, dark forest..."

With everyone enthralled by their favourite, well-embellished story, the group calmed down. Having never fixed a broken arm before, Uncle Louis tried to refresh his memory as he ran toward the store. He hoped Nancy had left the plaster bandages on the left side of the far shelf, and that his little book of important notes was still underneath!

Thankfully, everything was in place. He quickly reviewed his First Aid notes, grabbed the bandages, the Advil, and picked up a clean, sharp knife. To his great amazement, as he headed out the door, he saw three pairs of scissors lying on top of the big bag of pet food that had come in on the train that morning. "Just in time!" he thought, laying down the knife and picking up the scissors.

School that day in Paradise was on First Aid, with a live demonstration on how to mend a break. Only three boys were absent from the class. Tina, Kenzie and Yu Yan helped cut the plaster into strips.

The Tinys were very curious about the large gel cap of Advil. Following Uncle Louis' instructions, Aimee carefully poked a hole in the thick, transparent walls of the oval-shaped containers and measured out a small spoonful of the medicine for Charley to swallow. Once the Advil had taken affect and Charley was feeling less pain, Uncle Louis gently set his bones back into place. Charley screamed loudly and all the kids covered their ears, but when it was straight again, Charley was a lot happier.

Using a pail of water from the lake, Uncle Louis directed Tina and Georgia to moisten the plaster bandage, and they began wrapping it around Charley's arm.

"This is fun," Georgia said, as she helped Tina smooth the bandages together and felt them harden.

"Fun?" Charley questioned wearily. "I'm glad you're having fun!"

"I'm sorry, Charley," Georgia replied. "This isn't much fun for you! But this plaster is really cool stuff."

"Maybe we can make other things out of this?" Vinitha suggested.

"I'm sure you can," Uncle Louis smiled. "However, the rest of these strips we'll keep for emergency use. But I'll ask the Professor if he can send in some for crafts."

"I'd like to make a bowl to put things in," Vinitha said.

"Well, there's one thing you girls could certainly do with the scissors," Uncle Louis smiled, standing up and looking at them.

"What is that?" Aimee asked.

"A lot of the boys need haircuts," he said, "and maybe some girls would like a trim as well. If you or any of the other girls are inclined to cut hair - that would be a skill you could use to trade for goods."

"Really?" Aimee said, looking at the scissors with surprise, her blue eyes sparkling. "I would love to cut hair!"

"Great, then put up a sign and encourage the boys to take part!"

"I'd like to do it as well," Georgia offered.

"Me too!" said Vinitha.

"Wonderful," Uncle Louis nodded. He looked towards the beach, "Now, I have to find those mango thieves."

"I hope you get them in big trouble!" Sanaa demanded, placing her hands on her hips, and swaying back and forth angrily.

Uncle Louis turned around to look at her. "What kind of big trouble?"

"They should have to pay for this," Sanaa stated firmly, stamping her foot on the ground. "Not only did they steal the precious mangoes, they really hurt Charley. He's not going to be able to look after the garden for quite a while."

"They should have to plant the lettuce," Tina called out.

"No way," Charley argued. "I don't want them on the farm. They won't care about doing it right."

"I know," Kenzie answered, his voice full of enthusiasm. "Vahid and I just discovered a pile of really great flat rocks in Mining Hill. We were going to start building a road from the store to the lake. You could make the beach boys help us."

"Yeah, and tell them no more time in that lake until the road is done," Sanaa added, shaking her pointing finger.

"I like that idea," Uncle Louis smiled. "And you'll supervise the job, Kenzie?"

"Yes," Kenzie said, standing up straighter and folding his arms together.

"I'll help too," Aimee offered, happy that consequences were being meted out to the offenders. It made her feel safer to know that Uncle Louis would deal firmly with bad behaviour. "I can bring food and drinks for them if they do a good job," she suggested, looking over at Kenzie for approval. "But only if Kenzie says they deserve it."

"That will be great motivation for them to work hard," Kenzie nodded, tossing his long wavy, brown hair out of his grey eyes.

133

"Excellent!" Uncle Louis smiled, thankful for the helpful ideas. "That will be the plan then, starting this afternoon."

Rosa had been keeping very quiet all this time, except for a few empathic wails when Charley winced with pain. But now she was eager to impart some information. "Uncle Louis, I know where they are hiding," she piped up.

"Oh, where?" Uncle Louis asked.

Rosa pointed towards Rainy River, towards the closely nestled banana trees. Right in front lay a precious mango. As everyone turned to look, a hand poked out of the tall leaves and tried to reach the stray mango. It was just out of grasp. The hand retracted and then tried again a little closer to the ground.

"Thanks, Rosa," Uncle Louis chuckled.

Before the hand could reach the mango, Uncle Louis had reached the bridge and picked up the mango himself.

"Lema, Franz and Damien, I want to speak to all of you, right now!" he demanded.

Reluctantly, the boys slid out of their hiding place. Mango juice stains were all over their faces and down their chests.

"What's up?" Damien asked, swallowing hard.

"You know perfectly well what this is about," Uncle Louis told him. "You have stolen rare and very valuable food, which is unfair to Charley, who has worked hard to tend the orchards. And you hurt him badly, which concerns me more than anything. Because of your actions this morning, Charley won't be able to use his arm to do any work for quite a while. That fall broke his bone! How would any of you like to feel pain like he has?"

The boys didn't have anything to say. They had never broken a bone; scrapes had been the worst injury they had encountered. Having witnessed the pain and distress they had caused to all the other Tinys, they were rather shaken. Damien looked down at the ground, Lema shrugged shamefully, and Franz kicked a stone.

"Well, this is what I've decided," Uncle Louis said firmly. "From now on, you will not be allowed back to the lake, not even to sleep, until you have first of all apologized to Charley for hurting him badly and stealing produce from his farm! What you did today is unacceptable behaviour here in Paradise. For this, you will reap consequences. All three of you will help Kenzie build a road from the store to here. When the road reaches the beach and is finished to Kenzie's standards, you can then go back to the lake."

Franz objected. "We can't even sleep in our hammocks?"

"You can sleep in the hammocks, but not on the beach. In fact, you can go and get those hammocks right now," Uncle Louis stated firmly.

The lanky young lads weren't used to hearing Uncle Louis speak so harshly and they certainly hadn't expected to face any consequences. Straggling off unhappily, they took down their beds.

Following Uncle Louis, with hammocks slung over their shoulders, they trudged to the farmhouse, where Charley was sitting outside in the garden talking to Sanaa.

Damien was first to apologize. "I'm really sorry, Charley," he said. "I was only thinking about how much I wanted the mangoes. I'm sorry I hurt you. I didn't mean to get into a fight."

"Thank you," Charley said, unsure of how to respond, but appreciative of Damien's sincerity.

Lema looked up uneasily and shuffled his feet. "I'm sorry too," he pleaded. "I didn't mean to push you down so hard. I shouldn't have stolen your mangoes. I'm really sorry about your arm... really sorry! I didn't mean to hurt you."

"Sorry for stealing the mangoes," Franz added, without much emotion.

Charley nodded. "That's okay," he said.

Uncle Louis asked Charley how his arm was doing. Then satisfied with his positive response, he took the offenders to Mining Hill.

"You need to set those hammocks up in trees where I can see you clearly from my house," Uncle Louis told them. "I'm giving you ten minutes to hang them, and then Kenzie will start you working on the road."

While the young lads reluctantly repositioned their hammocks on the edge of the North Forest, Uncle Louis and Aimee went into the store and arranged with Nancy and Milan that the road workers would be paid with freshly squeezed orange juice, lunch and dinner, until the job was done.

Kenzie started planning the road project. Vahid and Zahir offered to stay with Charley and Sanaa and fill in for the necessary farm duties. The orchard girls offered to help on the farm as well.

When the beach boys had joined Kenzie, Aimee walked over and gave a small drink to all the boys. "If you work hard," she told them soberly, "I'll bring you a cup of orange juice every couple of hours."

"And you'll get lunch and dinner," Uncle Louis added, reaching into his pocket, "but only if Kenzie gives you a ticket." He handed the tickets to Kenzie.

"Free lunch and dinner?" Damien repeated, pulling his blond, messy hair out of his eyes. Once his face could be seen, there was a pleasant look of surprise on it.

"Yes." Uncle Louis smiled. He didn't try to explain again that this was the bartering method used in Paradise. He just hoped that once the boys got used to working for their food, instead of stealing it, they might realise the trade system worked well.

"By the way," he said to Damien and Franz. "You both need a haircut. Talk to the girls. They have scissors."

"How come you don't ever need a haircut?" Damien asked.

"I've learned how to do it myself," Uncle Louis smiled, as he walked away.

The Stylists

Chapter Seventeen

The Professor and Evan were greatly dismayed when they heard about the violence that had erupted in Paradise. Louis had sent them a text. Seeing Charley with a white cast on his arm was very disconcerting for the Professor.

"*Ça alors!* A robbery and a broken arm," the Professor lamented that afternoon, as he and Evan looked in on the Tinys. "How can this be?"

"They will be teenagers in two weeks," Evan reminded him.

"But where is this aggression and sneakiness coming from?" the Professor bemoaned. "They don't play violent video games. They haven't witnessed violence in any shape or form. They have a loving uncle and everything they need. Why are they acting like this?"

"Do you feel they would have to see it to do it?" Evan questioned.

"I would have expected so," Jacques Lemans replied. "I am astonished. I'm glad that Louis has doled out some consequences. We must deter such behaviour, or Paradise won't be the safe, happy place that I intended it to be."

"They are kids – sometimes they will be selfish. It's just natural."

"But selfishness leads to... suffering. I don't understand why they are feeling selfish."

"Doesn't everyone feel selfish sometimes?" Evan pondered uneasily. He hoped it wasn't just him!

"In our world, perhaps," the Professor reasoned. "We don't always have enough. We aren't assured that we always will have enough, and we see selfish behaviour all around us. But the Tinys have everything they need."

"There weren't enough mangoes..."

"True, we'll have to work on that."

As they stood by the glass dome, watching the Tinys finish their dinner and begin taking their dirty plates into the kitchen, Aimee walked out of the store with the scissors in her hand.

"Haircuts," she called out cheerfully.

The Professor noticed the three chairs sitting on the grass near the store.

Uncle Louis brought out a mirror, which he gave to Sanaa to hold.

"Look at the sign," Evan chuckled.

Vinitha had walked out of the store with a large sign that said, "Haircuts. Bring one flat rock for the road."

Kenzie, Charley and Franz were the first to check in with rocks for the road. Kenzie had two good-sized rocks, one for himself and one for Charley. Franz had a small one. The other boys, who weren't entirely sure they wanted their long locks cut off, stood at a safe distance to watch what would happen. Most of the girls stayed close by as well, eager to watch the show.

"I'm with Aimee," Kenzie called out, sitting down in the chair in front of her.

Charley sat in Vinitha's chair and Franz sat down in front of Georgia.

"So, how do you want it to look?" Aimee asked nervously.

Sanaa walked in front of Kenzie with the mirror and held it up so they both could see.

Kenzie looked at his brown curly locks which framed his white, freckled face. "I really have no idea," he smiled. "I just want this hair out of my eyes."

"You mean the hair in front?"

"Yes."

Aimee picked up the hair in front and did a quick snip, not wanting to cut it too short, but just enough to be out of his eyes. "Is that good?" she asked.

One person laughed and then they all began laughing. Even the Professor and Evan had to restrain themselves.

"He looks like a pretty girl," Damien mocked. And poor Kenzie did look quite pretty with short bangs and long hair hanging down each side.

Outside Paradise, Evan whispered. "He sure does! She's got to go shorter."

Inside Paradise, Lema was of the same opinion. "If you're going to cut it - you've got to go short all over!" he quipped. With his tidy afro, he looked the most masculine of anyone.

"Lema's right," Kenzie agreed. "Just cut it really short everywhere."

Aimee plunged into Kenzie's curls. Everyone cheered her on. Sanaa held the mirror up so that Kenzie could see the progress. Kenzie watched nervously but didn't say a word.

Vinitha and Georgia waited, observing the process before beginning any cuts of their own.

Finally, Aimee stepped back as though she were done. There were a few calls for 'a little more on the left' and one suggestion to cut it shorter around the ears. After those minor adjustments, everyone clapped, and Kenzie stood up and bowed. Aimee smiled. The short cut looked good on Kenzie.

In a low voice, Evan remarked. "So much better! I'm glad those scissors finally came."

"It took a while," the Professor agreed quietly. "It was hard to find anyone who would custom-make scissors that small."

Vinitha and Georgia started on the boys sitting in their chairs.

"Any more customers?" Aimee asked with a smile.

"I guess I'll get mine cut," Damien shrugged. "I'll be back with a stone." And with that he ran off to fetch a rock. A number of other boys followed him to the hill, and so did Tina.

Damien's blond hair was thicker than Kenzie's, and very matted from all the swimming he'd done in the lake. It was challenging for Aimee to get a uniform look.

"I look too fluffy," Damien protested, when he glanced in Sanaa's mirror.

Peering at his reflection, Aimee had to agree. "Okay, I'll try to even it out," she told him. Working carefully, and cutting more off, she got it very even. The only trouble was, it was evenly slanted from left to right. Damien was not pleased.

"Oh dear," she said. "I'll try some more."

Watching carefully, the Professor smiled. "This may not be her thing," he whispered.

Evan chuckled.

Before long, Damien had the shortest hair of anyone, but at least it was even.

"I like it," Aimee told him. "You look quite dashing."

Damien smiled proudly into the mirror that Sanaa was sharing around. He ran his fingers over his stubby hair and nodded his thanks. "I guess I'll wash off in the lake," he said, heading toward the beach.

Uncle Louis stepped in front of him, shaking his head. "No lake for three weeks," he said.

"How can I get clean?" Damien demanded. "I need to go for a swim."

"Use the shower down by the outhouse," Uncle Louis reminded him. "You can clean off there."

Damien grudgingly headed to the shower.

The Professor shook his head. "I don't know how Louis will keep those boys out of the lake," he said quietly to Evan. "I agree with the road project, but he's asking too much to keep them out of the lake. I think I'd better say something."

Evan shrugged. "Louis may have overreacted a little," he surmised softly, "but he's got a tough job in there dealing with teen attitudes. We need to support him in whatever he decides." Imagining what his own reaction to the incident might be, Evan surmised, "I'm guessing we might have overreacted too, had we witnessed the fight and heard Charley screaming in pain."

"True," the Professor admitted. "He is trying to do his best, but I'm sure those boys didn't intend to break Charley's arm."

Speaking softly, Evan recalled, "Whether they did or didn't, you want to allow Louis to make his own decisions and learn from them, right? We are observing and helping this experiment along, but not directly governing?"

There was a long pause, and then Jacques Lemans said, "You're right, Evan. Louis must feel free to make his own decisions."

They watched as the boys admired their new looks. Vinitha had given Charley a creative cut, with the top hair a little longer than the closely trimmed sides. Franz was happy with his straight, stringy brown hair cut in a longer style, just above his eyes.

Vahid and Zahir lined up for Georgia. Milan and Ponce were asking for Vinitha.

The two dogs, Freddo and Maxi, laid close by, watching from the sidelines and nuzzling anyone who came within nuzzling distance, hoping for a few pats.

Tina was next in line for Aimee. "Please just off to my shoulders," she requested. "I don't want it too short."

Aimee carefully took her time doing Tina's thin hair. When she was done, the shoulder-length cut was a little crooked, but it still looked great on Tina.

One by one, many of the Tinys had either a trim or a cut. A pile of sixteen rocks lay around the chairs.

There was no doubt, however, when they were all done, that Vinitha and Georgia had a special knack for cutting hair.

"It's not really Aimee's thing," the Professor reflected softly.

Evan agreed.

"You're my haircutter from now on," they heard Zahir tell Georgia, as he admired his new look one more time in Sanaa's mirror.

Georgia smiled. "Thank you," she said with a pleased giggle.

The Professor looked in with surprise. Zahir had always preferred Aimee for almost everything. However, Georgia's stylish cuts looked great on Zahir, Vahid and Charley. Vinitha had shown great skill as well.

Aimee stood with her arms folded, looking in Zahir and Georgia's direction.

"They all have their different gifts," Professor Lemans told himself.

Teenagers

Chapter Eighteen

With black notebooks in hand, the two scientists stood at the south-east side of Paradise. "They are now teenagers," the Professor remarked to Evan quietly. Classes were over for the day. In fact, the first semester was nearly over.

Outside the Biosphere, trees were bare, snow was falling softly, and the sky was a gloomy grey. Evan and the Professor had met to spend an hour observing the Tinys. In his journal, which was nearly full, Evan entered, '13 months', at the top of a new page.

He examined the orchards. "Productivity has been exceptional for most of the fruit and vegetables," he remarked quietly, jotting similar words in his book.

"Yes," the Professor replied. "Everything pollinated by the bees has been successful. I'm not sure what to do about the mangoes."

"They aren't pollinated by bees?" Evan asked.

"They can be, but a Lesser long-nosed bat might do better. Only, I hesitate to introduce bats. They aren't exactly cute..." he smiled. "They might frighten the girls."

"Do you think we'd need many? Chances are, they won't be seen."

"It's not only that," the Professor contemplated quietly, "but what would they eat? We decided to avoid the annoying insects that are part of their food source."

"What about the fireflies?"

"They have a foul taste, apparently."

"Bees?"

"No, I checked into it. Bees are active in the day and bats come out at night. Besides, we don't want bats eating all our bees."

"The mangoes are a valuable commodity."

With a wry smile, the Professor whispered, "Ah yes, and their scarcity led to an outbreak of selfishness!"

Googling what long-nosed bats eat, Evan scrolled through a few articles and smiled. "Looks like we would need to miniaturize some cactus, and send in the fruit, but we can do that easily enough. Why don't we release two bats when the mango trees are in flower and see how they do?"

The Professor nodded and scribbled in his book, "Miniaturize two Lesser Long-Nosed bats and cactus."

"Building the road has gone well," Evan noted in his book. "There hasn't been any stealing or acts of aggression since the beach boys were assigned to work. Louis says they have occasionally been sick to their stomachs, which is unusual for them, but on the good days they've worked hard."

Standing close by, the Professor read Evan's entry, and then wrote his own. "I'm impressed by the quality of the roadwork. Kenzie is a good manager."

"Yes, he is," Evan whispered, comparing notes. "He and Damien have worked well together. I especially like the arched bridge. I know Louis helped them with ideas, but still, I'm impressed they chose to try something challenging."

"Oui. C'est fabuleux and well thought-out. They've made good use of the flat rocks that we buried in the hill."

Evan agreed. "Yes, once they figured out how to mix cement."

Suddenly the Professor pointed to the road. "It must be dinnertime," he whispered. "Here comes Aimee with the carrycart."

They both smiled, watching Aimee as she followed the newly laid stone road, happily pushing the cart ahead of her and making up little songs along the way. From a distance, she waved merrily to the group of kids planting new seeds in the garden. Vinitha, Vahid and Zahir waved back.

"She's such a happy one," the Professor said proudly.

"Wait," Evan whispered, cocking his head towards the speaker. "Do you hear what she's singing?"

"Oh, that she loves everything?"

"She might be using a particular name."

"Really?"

"Listen."

"I love the way you smile at me," Aimee was singing, very softly.

They strained to hear the next line, but Aimee was not singing to be heard. However, there was no doubt she had a dreamy look.

"She might have a crush on Kenzie," Evan suggested quietly. "They've been working together for two weeks on this project."

"You haven't noticed any special interactions till now?"

"Not really. They seem like good friends and all, but I haven't noticed any special attraction," Evan relayed, noting down the incident. "However, I've certainly seen improvement in the beach boys. When they started this project, they were lazy and trying to cut corners and get everything done as fast as possible. Now, they seem to have taken a real interest in making the road look good. Louis said it was also their suggestion to build the retaining wall around the drop-off into Rainy River."

"Really?" the Professor noted the fact in his journal. "I like that retaining wall," he added in a low voice. "The rock colours are well-balanced, and it should withstand a raging river." He chuckled softly.

"If we ever had to worry about raging rivers!" Evan laughed, muffling the accidental noise with his arm.

The road workers looked around suddenly as though they had heard the laugh. The Professor and Evan glanced uneasily at one another.

The dinner bell rang. "Time to eat," Vahid called out, standing up in the garden.

"Wash your hands, everyone," Zahir piped up, dashing toward the outhouse with the others following behind. As they ran across the newly laid road right in front of Aimee, Zahir looked at all the food in her carrycart. He stopped. "Is that for the road workers again?" he asked.

With a smile, Aimee nodded. "They are working really hard," she said proudly.

"What about the farmers?" he asked.

Aimee's face coloured. She didn't have a ready answer. "But you always go to the store," she explained.

"So could they."

"I guess," she faltered.

"Who's holding up the food?" Damien called out.

Zahir shrugged and ran off to wash his hands.

The Professor and Evan exchanged glances. "It's not really fair," Jacques remarked very quietly. "If she's going to take food to some, she should really do it for all."

Evan agreed and whispered, "Aimee started bringing just orange juice and snacks. It's grown from there."

"I suppose..."

Seeing that Aimee had reached the road workers, the Professor and Evan watched with smiles of approval as she reminded them to wash their hands. Grumbling just a little, the boys ran to the lake and quickly washed the dirt off their hands.

"I see why they've been sick a few times," the Professor remarked quietly to Evan. "They've been working in dirt – which must still contain trace amounts of bacteria, even though we attempted to purge it out," he sighed, "and they don't recognise the importance of soap."

146

"Do they wash at all without a reminder?" Evan questioned, raising his eyebrows. He picked up his phone. "I'll send Louis a message to give another lesson on the importance of washing with soap."

Aimee handed out the dinner. The hungry boys were very appreciative of the fresh bread, soup and salads that Aimee had helped Nancy prepare.

"Best bread ever," Damien complimented her. "I bet you made it this time."

"Look, she's blushing," Evan pointed out softly.

Aimee indeed had turned pink, and she nodded, looking down at the ground quickly.

"*Oh là là!* She can't be falling for a beach boy," the Professor moaned.

"Kenzie would be a far better choice," Evan agreed, quietly, "but Damien is a good-looking guy."

"Surely, Aimee isn't falling for looks. She's got so much to offer..."

"You sound like a dad."

"He'll break her heart!"

"You do sound like a dad."

"I feel like a dad!"

With compassion, Evan reached over and affectionately patted the Professor's back. "A dad with twenty-one children!" he teased, keeping his voice low, "and you're not emotionally attached?"

Reluctantly, the Professor had to admit that he was. "But my goal is still to remain as objective as possible," he whispered.

Evan just nodded and jotted a few words in his journal, "The Professor admits he has lost objectivity. ☺"

When Aimee gave out the desserts, the 'dads' standing outside the dome were still watching carefully.

All the boys looked up at her with gratitude. Flustered, Aimee dropped Damien's bowl of strawberries on the ground before she reached him.

147

"Don't worry," Damien reassured her, as Aimee glanced up in dismay. "I'll clean it up."

They both went to pick up the strawberries at the same time, hit heads and ended up sitting on the ground looking at each other. The other boys laughed out loud.

Standing up, Damien reached out to help Aimee to her feet. "Look after the other guys," he told her kindly. "I'll clean up the mess."

Lema offered to share his strawberries with Damien, and all the others agreed to do the same.

"I can wash these off," Damien said, loading the strawberries back into the bowl. "Mind if I use some of your water?" he asked Aimee.

"Of course," she offered, bringing it over to him.

"He's rather charming," Evan observed.

"He'd better be reformed," the Professor remarked grudgingly. In his thoughts, he assured himself that early crushes often fade away.

Once the dinner merriment was over, Aimee made her way back to the store, pulling her little cart and singing softly. The Professor sighed deeply.

"Are you okay?" Evan asked.

"Yes... yes, just not ready for them to start growing up. They've only lived just over a year!"

For a moment they watched in silence, pondering how quickly thirteen months had flown by. Then the Professor whispered, "Well, this road project has been quite successful in developing a good work ethic and building relationships. Now that all the houses are done and food production is going well, I think we need to introduce another project to keep everyone busy."

"I thought you wanted to let them discover materials and develop their own creativity."

"That was my original plan, but time is short. They don't have a hundred years to figure things out on their own. Plus, in such an ideal world, without any major adversity, wars, suffering, sickness, bad weather - you name it, there is no necessity driving human creativity."

Evan looked up in surprise. He thought it was interesting the Professor had admitted that adversity sometimes led to good inventions. He jotted it down.

"Necessity is often the 'Mother of Invention'," he agreed quietly. "So, what do you have in mind, Sir?"

"I'm going to suggest that Louis has a Build-a-Boat contest," the Professor announced, keeping his voice low. "There will be categories for the fastest, the most attractive, and the strongest."

"What kind of materials will you give them?"

"I looked it up online the other day, and there were suggestions for tin foil, wax from specialty cheese wrappers, corks, wooden sticks, balloons and even birch bark."

"Wow. But of course," Evan whispered, running one hand through his spiky blond hair, "those would be great materials! And there's always building boards and the glue gun down by the store. Sounds fun!"

For one delightful moment, Evan imagined shrinking himself down to Louis' size and leading the challenge. If only he could go back and forth between the two worlds! This was exactly the kind of competition he'd loved as a kid.

"Will you offer prizes?" he asked.

"I'd rather not," the Professor mused, stroking his graying goatee. "I'd just like everyone to enjoy the challenge for the sake of a challenge. It will be enjoyment enough if they manage to make a boat that floats."

Evan nodded in agreement, writing down the contest details.

Suddenly, the Professor leaned in to observe something more carefully. "Hey," he pointed out quietly. "What are Ponce and Odin doing with that large jar?"

Looking in the direction of the Professor's pointing finger, Evan observed the two lads pushing a wide carrycart holding the clear jar of vinegar that Louis had ordered for his science experiments. They were heading into the North Forest. "Interesting," he smiled. "Why don't we walk over there and see what's going on?"

Quickly making their way around the dome to the north side where they rarely looked in, the two scientists came to a forested area, where Odin and Ponce had built a small rickety shack. In front of the shack was one large, dark blue flag with gold writing. Dangling on a string from the roof of the shack was a large, black object with eight skinny legs.

"Is that a spider hanging there?" the Professor marvelled quietly, straining to see.

"They are proud of their victory," Evan remarked. "Guess I would be too."

Nodding, the Professor acknowledged, "Yes, I hate to think what would have happened if that black widow had bitten those girls. Odin and Ponce did save their lives."

"Did you ever determine how it got on the train?"

The Professor shrugged. "The box of wheels that I sent in that day had been stored in my garden shed. I assume the spider was hiding in the box, and sadly I didn't check carefully." He shook his head regretfully. "I won't make that mistake again!" Walking a little further towards the train tunnel, the Professor leaned in closer to watch where Odin and Ponce were taking the jar of vinegar.

The two spider heroes dragged the jar deep inside the forest and then clapped hands in the air. Evan noticed they had also captured the box of baking soda. It was sitting on a carrycart.

"I sure hope they traded well for those commodities," Evan remarked.

"I'm sure Nancy wouldn't let them away with anything less," the Professor nodded, rather pleased to see that Odin and Ponce were intrigued by chemical reactions.

The boys were far enough away from the store microphone that their voices came through rather faintly.

"And now to try doubling the soda!" Odin cheered.

Ponce picked up a mug and dipped into the box. He began ladling it into an empty jar beside him.

"Scientists in the making," Evan smiled. "They may find a new passion."

"Other than brooding about all the things they don't like?"

"Exactly!"

For a few minutes the two watched Odin and Ponce as they poured a cup of vinegar quickly on top of the soda and then used a lid to contain the mixture for as long as possible in the jar. When it burst out and sprayed all over them, the boys were delighted for about one second, and then the vinegar began to sting.

The scientists outside the dome tried hard to muffle their laughter as the amateurs raced at top speed to the lake and dove into the water.

Walking back around to the front, in full view of the lake with the lovely orchards surrounding it, Evan and the Professor commented on the heavily loaded banana plants.

"Plant reproduction has been quite normal," the Professor stated, "aside from the mango trees. In fact, it has been even more abundant than in our world. However, it's disappointing that we aren't getting any animal reproduction. Birds lay eggs but they never hatch. I would have thought there might be baby ducks, or rabbits, or puppies by now, or even a fawn or two. I think we should get the incubators going again and develop more baby animals."

"Just animal babies? No more humans?"

"The kids aren't ready to become parents."

Evan agreed with great relief.

Pondering the matter, the Professor added, "I do believe we should wait to gauge the public reaction to this project. Perhaps, if it all goes well, some may be eager to donate reproductive cells specifically for Paradise. There may be those who would prefer to see their children grow up in such a wonderful, safe environment!"

Evan considered the idea. "If we can develop a way for parents to interact with their children," he said thoughtfully, "Paradise might be a popular option. It might even become in high demand..."

"So much more could be developed if we gain public support," the Professor agreed. "For now, just animals and birds are required... and definitely more fish. I might try a few more plants... maybe some different varieties of roses and shrubs. The orchard girls need plants for their new gardens."

"And ferns... ferns for the waterfall," Evan reminded him, fully aware of the enormous task now ahead of him. With a smile he thought, "The semester is nearly over and Christmas holidays will soon be here. I was wondering what I'd do with all my time."

A Strange Event

Chapter Nineteen

The boys were coming. "Quickly," Aimee whispered to Zahir. "Are you ready, Georgia? Sanaa?"

Hearing Damien's laughter, Georgia stepped forward with the others on the new road and raised her shaker. As soon as the beach boys came around the corner, they all took their cue.

"Hey, guys," Aimee sang out, "we love the road!"

Zahir was next, with the simple little song that they had only put together that morning. "It runs through fields... that are hoed."

Georgia kept beat with her shakers, while Sanaa clapped her hands and added a harmonic, background melody.

"And meanders through cows that graze," Aimee added, joining in clapping.

"You've worked hard for many days," Zahir added, smiling at Aimee's enthusiasm.

"Your road goes for a long, long ways."

"Our world is better thanks to you," Aimee concluded, pointing to all the boys. "We love you for all that you do."

The last line surprised Zahir and he looked over, wide-eyed. His mouth dropped open when Aimee ran forward and gave Damien a hug. Damien was even more surprised! The beach boys warmly thanked the musicians for the song and all of them insisted on hugs.

Aimee happily complied, but the other musicians did not.

When the beach boys were well out of sight, Zahir mumbled, "I didn't know you were going to do that!"

"Do what?" Aimee asked, tying her long hair into a bun.

"Give them hugs! Since when do the beach boys deserve hugs?"

"I thought you agreed that we should sing them a song of thanks," Aimee replied. "They worked really hard."

"Everyone works hard in Paradise," Zahir put in defensively, as colour rose in his dark olive skin. "Does everyone need a hug for what they do?"

"Wouldn't it be nice?" Aimee smiled, humming the song. If there was anything that she felt was lacking in Paradise, it was hugs. Without mothers and fathers, and only one uncle for twenty children, physical affection hadn't been lavishly doled out. Some yearned for it more than others.

Sanaa and Georgia exchanged amused glances.

"Maybe Zahir wants a hug for helping you write the song?" Sanaa suggested merrily, clapping her hands and doing her wiggle dance.

"Of course!" Aimee laughed, reaching over to give her friend a hug.

Zahir turned bright red, but he stopped complaining.

"Time for school," Uncle Louis was calling. The kids ran across the orchard toward the schoolhouse. Uncle Louis was standing on the grass, holding a large book open, with some unusual looking materials behind him. When everyone had gathered and found a place to sit on the stairs, Uncle Louis made an announcement.

"We have a very special contest for everyone," he told them excitedly. "This contest will be the focus of our schooling for the next few weeks. We are going to design boats to sail on the lake."

There were loud cheers from everyone.

The beach boys weren't as enthusiastic, however. Having just finished two weeks of working on the road, with lake privileges resumed, they had been looking forward to many peaceful days of surfing.

155

"I would like to see who can make the strongest boat; one that can hold the most people," Uncle Louis told them. "I am also interested in the most attractive boat and the fastest boat. Those are your categories - strength, appearance and speed."

"Can we work in groups?" Charley asked, hopefully. He still had a cast on his right arm and was carrying Maxi in his left.

"Yes, up to four in a group." Uncle Louis replied. He showed them the instructions in the book and then turned to the materials sitting behind him. He picked up the shiny, silver sheets that sat in a pile. "This is tin foil," he said. "It is easily pliable, strong, lightweight and fairly waterproof."

Uncle Louis went on to tell them about the red wax, the corks and the rubber balloons of all sizes. Picking up each one, he explained the strengths and weaknesses of the various materials and the way to use them.

Aimee could hardly wait to get started. She looked over at Damien, hoping to catch his eye and motion that he should be in her group. However, he and the beach boys were already making plans.

Someone tugged playfully at her hair. She turned around.

"I'll work with you," Zahir suggested.

"Oh, okay," she said.

"Should we invite Rosa as well?"

Aimee didn't think twice. "No, not Rosa. Maybe Sanaa, or Georgia?" She looked over, but Georgia, Vinitha, Yu Yan and Tina were already forming a group. Nancy and Milan were beckoning to Sanaa.

Zahir was looking around too. Odin was standing all by himself and he didn't look very happy. His long messy hair stuck out all around him. He was the only boy who still had long hair. "Maybe we should ask Odin to be in our group?"

"Odin?" Aimee whispered in disbelief. "That would be awful. Why would you even think of asking him?"

"Because he's sitting all alone. Wouldn't you feel badly if no one wanted you in their group?"

Aimee looked over at Odin with a small spark of compassion. After all, he had rescued the girls and bravely fought the scary creature, but she couldn't imagine trying to work with him in a group. However, at that very moment, Rosa, Lily and Ponce approached Odin to ask him to join with them. He was still a mighty hero in their eyes.

"What about just you and me?" Aimee suggested, seeing that everyone else had now formed groups.

"Oh... okay," he said. "Well, what do you want to make? The fastest? The strongest? Or the most attractive?"

With a sparkle in her eye, Aimee replied, "How about we try for all three?"

Considering the options, Zahir hesitated, "But if we go for the fastest, we will need something lightweight. Then it may not be the strongest. If we go for the strongest, then it might not be attractive."

"Let's get the instructions for all of them," Aimee whispered secretively in his ear. "We'll read everything and see if we can do something better than all the rest."

Laughing, Zahir nodded. "We can certainly try."

The instructions were piled on the deck. Taking the sheets of paper for all three categories, Aimee and Zahir ran out to the nearby orchard to peruse the information privately. Most of the other children were helping themselves to the supplies first and already beginning to experiment with the materials.

Out in the orchard, Aimee and Zahir leaned against Charley's shed. Freddo saw them and came bounding over. He wanted to lie with his head on Zahir's lap. Zahir tried to hold the instruction papers up so that they could read them, but the papers were as tall as he was. Little did they know that the Professor cut every sheet of his own printer paper into eighths for the Tinys!

"Let's lay these on the ground," Aimee suggested. They had to get on to their hands and knees to read. Freddo groaned when he had to give up the warm lap he was resting on. Aimee patted Freddo's head while Zahir began reading aloud. Little lorikeets flitted noisily from tree to tree and Aimee wished they would come down and sit on her shoulder. Ripple sauntered over and tried to curl up on top of the pages. Zahir picked up the purring cat and placed her on top of his sleepy dog, but Ripple wasn't happy with that arrangement. With a nasty hiss at Freddo, the cat ran off.

As Zahir was explaining the benefits of using tin foil, Aimee suddenly noticed that one of the sunflowers was far taller than the others. She thought she could even see it moving upwards. Plants rarely moved in Paradise because there was never a wind, only a very gentle breeze from the air-filtration system.

"Hey, look at that sunflower," she notified Zahir. "You can almost see it grow. It's huge!"

Zahir stopped reading and looked in the direction she was pointing. "It is growing," he pondered. "Let's go check it out."

Leaving the papers on the ground, the two made their way to the flower garden. Ten sunflower plants stood in a neat row. The first nine plants reached only to their waists, but the one furthest away was three times their height! Yet, all of the plants, even the huge plant, had only their first four leaves.

They ran over to the gigantic sunflower. Maxi saw them approaching Charley's garden and came running over, barking. Aimee patted Maxi's brown and white fur, and told her that everything was okay.

"These leaves actually look big enough to sit on," Zahir laughed. Reaching up, he tried to climb onto the lowest leaf. The first time he slipped off, but the next time he managed to wriggle on. With a happy smile, he laid back with his arms behind his head. "Ah, this is nice!" he told Aimee.

"I'm going to try," Aimee said, choosing a leaf on the other side of the stem. Her first few attempts were unsuccessful. Finally, she spotted the cow grazing in the field. "I'm going to get Brownie," she said, "then I can climb on her!"

Brownie was very compliant, as long as she had grass in her mouth to chew. With Aimee's arm draped over her back, Brownie tripped happily along. Aimee positioned her underneath the sunflower leaves and hoisted herself up on the cow. However, just at that very moment, a rabbit hopped into the garden and the two dogs assumed guard duty. The commotion startled the cow, who lurched forward, throwing Aimee off her back.

Zahir slid off his leaf and jumped to the ground. He extended a hand to Aimee. "Are you okay?" he asked.

With a groan, Aimee took his hand and stood up. "I'm okay," she sighed. "I guess that was a dumb idea."

"I'll help you get on," Zahir offered. When Aimee agreed, he gave her a boost up to the leaf and helped her get on. The leaf was big enough for her to stretch out completely, and it almost seemed to be getting bigger by the moment.

"Thank you!" Aimee said with delight, as she lay back and breathed a happy sigh. Her long copper-brown curls hung over the edge of the leaf, mingling with the pale blue ribbons of her sundress. "Ooh, I love this!" she sighed.

Aware that it was still school time and they were supposed to be focused on their project, Aimee's mind went back to the project at hand. "So, we should really discuss which materials we want to use," she reminded Zahir, before he tried to remount his leaf. "I really like the wax because it's such a pretty red. I think it will be just as strong as the foil, if not stronger, and I just love the colour."

"Let me get the instruction sheets," Zahir said, running back over to the shed to collect them. When he returned with the large sheets in his arms, he passed them up to Aimee. Then he reached up to grab hold of the branch extending out to his leaf. "It's prickly," he remarked.

It was quite a struggle, but eventually Zahir pulled himself back up and brushed off the prickles from his arms and hands. "This plant is getting taller," he remarked, looking down at the ground. "I wonder how tall it will grow. This could be fun!"

Enjoying their soft, reclining leaves, neither one of them considered that their situation could be in any way precarious. The two dogs settled down for a snooze in the shade.

"I have an idea," Zahir smiled. "Why don't we try a small piece of each type of material? We can dig some rocks out of Mining Hill and weigh each material down in the water with the same-sized rock. Then we'll know for sure which one floats better."

"So, we'll try the cork as well?"

"Sure."

"It's rather ugly."

"We can mold the wax around it to add some colour and shape."

"True!"

"What was the other material that Uncle Louis mentioned?"

"Hmm," Aimee considered. "Maybe we should read these sheets and then we'll have all the details."

"Great plan," Zahir agreed. He placed his arms behind his head and got ready to listen.

For the next hour, Aimee read the sheets and they discussed the information. Finally, they felt educated enough to begin experimentation.

"Let's go dig up some rocks," Aimee cheered.

However, when Aimee tried to get down, she realized she was now almost twice her height from the ground.

Nervously, she said, "We're up really high."

"Whoa," Zahir said, sitting upright. "This plant is growing fast — very fast! We'd better tell Uncle Louis about this."

With that, Zahir shuffled himself to the edge of the leaf, took hold of the branch and slid down the stem. However, the prickles on the stem were even harder and longer now. There were many 'ouches' on the way down. Aimee didn't feel that she wanted to follow his lead.

"I'm scared," she said.

"I'll get the ladder," Zahir told her, running off to the store with Maxi and Freddo at his heels. When he returned, he set the ladder against the plant's prickly stem, but it wasn't tall enough.

"I'd better call Uncle Louis," Zahir said, pulling a piece of prickle out from his shirt. "There's something very strange about this plant. It's already way taller than the trees."

"Please hurry," Aimee pleaded, no longer enjoying the comfortable recline in the ever-expanding leaf.

Zahir dashed over to Uncle Louis, who was explaining things to Rosa and Lily.

"There is a huge plant growing really fast in the garden," Zahir shouted.

Everyone turned to look. Charley and Sanaa jumped to their feet.

"We'll deal with it when school is over," Uncle Louis replied, unfazed.

"But Aimee is sitting on it and she's way up in the air!"

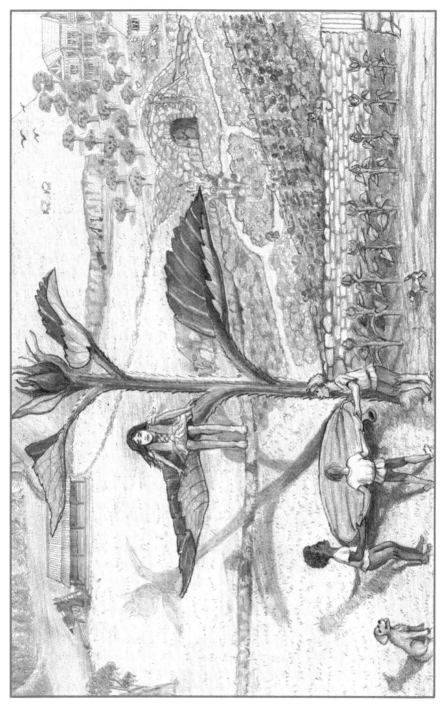

"Seriously?" Uncle Louis ran over to where he could see the garden, followed by all the other Tinys. Sure enough, one sunflower was six times the size of all the others. On a large leaf, Aimee sat perched near the edge, looking down nervously. Maxi and Freddo were chasing each other around the garden.

"We need to get Aimee down," Uncle Louis called out. "Someone, find something tall to stand on."

Damien picked up the strong balloon that he and his buddies had been experimenting with. "Hey guys, come on," he muttered.

While the others scurried around trying to find anything that might be tall enough to reach Aimee, Damien and his friends rushed to the plant. Uncle Louis was right behind them.

"Stretch it out," Damien told his friends. They all took an edge of the balloon and backed away from each other. "You've got to jump," he told Aimee. "We'll catch you."

"It's so far down," she cried.

"It's only going to get farther down," he told her. "Jump, Aimee!"

Closing her eyes and screwing up her face tightly, Aimee jumped.

Uncle Louis watched anxiously as she fell. Thankfully, she landed right in the middle of the balloon, stretching it almost all the way to the ground and then she bounced on the surface. The boys hung on to the edges and kept her safe. She was very relieved.

Aimee's knees were shaking, so Damien picked her up in his lanky arms and carried her back to the schoolhouse. All the Tinys followed, pestering Aimee with questions. No one noticed that Uncle Louis had suddenly disappeared.

Nor did it seem strange to anyone that after Uncle Louis returned and was helping them again with their boats, that the train came in for a second time that day.

School was immediately dismissed. The giant sunflower was now ten times the size of the others which still only reached up to the Tinys' waists. Taking all the Tinys with him, Uncle Louis opened the first train door. There were only two things inside - some rope and a big saw.

Taking the long, dangerous-looking instrument out, Uncle Louis told them all it was a bow saw. Some of the boys wanted to touch the grooved, serrated edges, and marvelled at how sharp it felt. They had used little kitchen knives occasionally and small skill saws on the building boards, but they had never seen a saw so long and with so many sharp spikes.

"Ouch!" Odin yelled as his hasty investigation of the blade drew blood on his finger.

"Do you need a bandage?" Tina inquired anxiously.

The cut was only skin deep. Odin shook his head and put his finger in his mouth. All the other boys pulled their hands back.

"Yes, it's very sharp," Uncle Louis affirmed. "This saw is the one we need to cut down the giant sunflower, but we have to be careful. It can do damage to us if we don't use it properly."

"So, it's a dangerous tool?" Franz asked with a sly look.

Uncle Louis saw Franz and Odin exchange crafty glances. "Yes," he agreed warily. "Anything that can be used for good purposes can also be used for bad. Always choose to use things for good if you want Paradise to stay safe and beautiful."

Franz and Odin lagged behind, while the other children followed Uncle Louis out to the garden with much excitement and apprehension.

Looking around for the best place to bring the giant down, Uncle Louis explained, "We need to make sure that when we cut this sunflower down that it doesn't fall on anyone, or wreck any plants in the garden."

Everyone's eyes grew wide. While some were fearful, others loved the drama. The sunflower was the tallest plant they had ever seen. It was now four times the size of Uncle Louis.

Eyeing the distance to the school roof carefully, Uncle Louis asked Damien to rope the plant, tying it tightly, and then the beach boys were told to carry the other end of the rope towards the meadow. Kenzie and Vahid were given the task of sawing through the stem, while everyone else was told to stand near the schoolhouse.

Several girls huddled under the school roof, hoping the plant wouldn't land on them. Most of the boys stood as far from the school and as close to the plant as they deemed to be courageously 'safe.'

Kenzie and Vahid began pulling the saw back and forth across the overgrown plant.

"Keep a tight hold on that rope," Uncle Louis demanded sharply, looking towards the beach boys.

Sawing with all their might, Kenzie and Vahid took frequent breaks to mop their sweaty foreheads. Suddenly, there was a loud crack and the whole plant began toppling towards the school!

"Pull hard," Uncle Louis yelled.

The beach boys yanked on the rope just in time. The tall plant changed direction and came down with a loud thud. Its top two leaves nearly reached the dry riverbed.

All of Paradise erupted into loud cheers. The garden was saved!

Uncle Louis directed all the boys to take a turn cutting up the plant. It took quite some time for all the pieces to be carried across the meadow and jammed into the train. When they were finished, Uncle Louis went back for the bow saw, but it wasn't where he had last seen it.

"Hey, guys, has anyone seen the saw?"

But no one seemed to know.

"I need the saw back now," he said firmly. "No dinner for anyone until it is back in my possession."

Damien, Franz and Odin exchanged glances.

"We'll bring it right back if we see it anywhere," Damien promised.

165

Uncle Louis nodded knowingly. While there were other small, useful saws and knives in Paradise for regular needs, none were so sharp and potentially destructive as the bow saw. He knew the Professor didn't want to see any living trees chopped down.

In five minutes, the boys were back with the saw, claiming they had found it in the forest.

"Thank you for finding and bringing the bow saw back," Uncle Louis said, wishing he could fully believe their story.

He put the saw into the first car on the train and waited until the train had backed out of Paradise. He hoped they wouldn't need such a hazardous tool again.

Stealing Again

Chapter Twenty

*E*van was in the supply room, when the train came through the secure entrance and backed into the loading dock. He could see it was full of sunflower pieces.

The Professor was walking down the long corridor. He had been checking on the new baby animals in the laboratory incubators. With a pleased smile, he was happy that his miniaturization process was improving with each new attempt. From the valuable banks of frozen embryos that were available for university research, this time he'd lost only one percent.

"The deer and calves are growing well," the Professor told Evan, as he entered the supply room corridor. "If we get the other animals started next week, they will all be ready to come out at the same time."

"I have three viable puppy embryos which can go into incubation today," Evan relayed. "I still need to finish testing the kitten embryos. I think we might have five or six."

"Excellent," the Professor nodded. He looked into the windows of the electric train and pressed a button to open the doors.

Watching the Professor take out a few of the crisply hewn pieces of plant, Evan imagined a worst-case scenario. "What if this sunflower had reached the top of the dome!" he remarked. "What would we have done?"

"I guess we'd have to send everyone back into the nursery so that we could re-open the dome and take it out," Jacques surmised. "That would be a major ordeal!"

"Especially if Aimee was still sitting on it!"

"True," the Professor contemplated with a shudder, picking up the growing tip for investigation. "We'd have had to send in an oxygen mask to keep her alive," he pondered. "She would have had the opportunity to see what goes on beyond her glass world... and then she'd tell all the others and our secret would be over! I'm glad we were both alerted quickly this time."

Evan was collecting the pieces of sunflower and laying them out end to end on the counter to measure.

Watching his assistant put the pieces in a line, the Professor remarked, "I'd like to know what caused such rapid growth."

"True. It didn't even grow normally," Evan pondered. "A normal sunflower would not grow that fast!"

Bringing over a long ruler, the Professor added his growth tip piece to the line and measured the overall length. "Hmm," he considered. "It did indeed demonstrate a very fast growth rate. Whatever mutation occurred affected the entire organism; it must have been initiated at the germ line."

"We'll have to look into it," Evan nodded thoughtfully.

"Should we see how the boat competition is coming along first?" Jacques suggested.

The two scientists put the sunflower pieces down in the lab, placing them in a moist container. Then they headed back up to the Paradise Room.

As they stood watching the various groups experiment and build, they noticed Damien, Franz and Lema sneaking off behind the schoolhouse. Louis was helping Lily, Rosa, Odin and Ponce. Between Rosa's wails that nothing was working out, and Odin's outbursts of frustration, Louis was quite distracted.

"Hey, what are they up to?" Evan questioned.

Walking around the outside of the dome, Professor Lemans followed the boys. They were sneaking through the thick forest of Rainbow Hill.

"How many pipe cleaners do you figure we'll need?" Lema asked.

"At least five," Franz answered.

"We really should trade something, guys," Damien protested.

"Us – trade?" Lema replied disdainfully.

"Do you want to be assigned to build another road?" Damien asked wearily.

"They won't catch us this time. No one is at the store," Franz replied.

"What if they see us using them? Then they'll ask how we got them?"

"We'll work on it at night and cover them over with the foil. No one will know."

The Professor looked over at Evan with disappointment. "When will these guys learn?" he whispered, shaking his head.

"Maybe Damien is learning," Evan replied.

"If he was smart, he'd turn and walk the other way!"

Evan didn't respond. He and the Professor watched with heavy hearts as the boys came to the store and tried to break in. Evan hoped Damien would have the courage to stop the others and find a right way to get what they needed.

"I'm not doing this," Damien said flatly.

"Then stand outside and at least let us know if anyone is coming," Lema ordered.

Damien agreed, much to the dismay of the Professor and Evan, who were hoping he would refuse altogether.

Franz tried the front door and laughed. "It's not even locked! This is a cinch."

In a moment, he and Lema were out with the five pipe cleaners and three bananas.

"You took bananas as well?" Damien frowned.

"Of course. I'm hungry," Franz smiled, handing one to Damien.

With a shrug, Damien took the fruit and pulled down the peel.

"How sad," the Professor remarked, shaking his head.

"Well, at least he's beginning to think it through," Evan advocated.

"I believe we should support Louis' desire for consequences," Professor Lemans decided. "Persuasion isn't always enough. Some people respond to reasoning better than others. I'll suggest to him that from now on, if anyone steals, they should pay back double for what they took."

"That's a good rule," Evan agreed.

"It's not... a rule," Professor Lemans told him firmly. "This is a consequence. It's just good common sense."

Evan didn't argue.

The boys were enjoying their bananas as they made their way back through the forest. Franz stopped suddenly and pointed to a place where the pine trees nestled together. "Here's a great place to hide the pipe cleaners until dark."

Lema laid the fuzzy cleaners down, well out of sight.

The Professor picked up his phone and began texting a message to Louis, letting him know what the boys had done and where the pipe cleaners could be found. He also suggested the new consequence if anyone was caught stealing. Knowing that Louis was unlikely to see the message until he checked the phone late at night, the Professor and Evan headed back down to the lab, hoping to investigate the genetics of the wayward sunflower.

The Boat Competition

Chapter Twenty-One

*A*imee's slim arms were folded across her chest. "I can't believe you were caught stealing again," she said icily.

"It was dumb. I know," Damien shrugged.

Aimee looked at him sceptically. Their friendship had been slowly developing. Weeks ago, she had thought Damien only cared about surfing, but gradually as he worked on the road, she had come to see diligence, creativity and a caring heart. However, Nancy had told Georgia, who had just told Aimee, that the three beach boys had stolen from the store again. "I don't know if I can trust you," she protested.

Turning away to go work on his boat, Damien mumbled, "You probably shouldn't."

It wasn't quite the answer Aimee was hoping for. She was looking for a reason to keep trusting, not to stop.

Walking over, whistling a cheerful tune, Zahir asked, "Ready to try out the boat?"

Aimee would have rather continued the discussion with Damien, but she saw her opportunity had vanished. Damien was running toward Franz. "Coming," she replied.

As she helped Zahir take their boat to the water, Aimee thought about Damien's response. She felt sorry for him. According to Georgia, Uncle Louis had made the beach boys dig enough supplies out of Mining Hill to do a fair trade for ten pipe cleaners and six bananas. It didn't take them long to fulfil the consequence, but all the respect the beach boys had earned by working so diligently on the road had been eroded. Still, Aimee wished she hadn't been so hard on Damien.

"What are you thinking about?" Zahir asked her curiously.

Coming back to reality, Aimee shook her head, "Oh, nothing important."

Smiling, Zahir said, "I was asking if you wanted to ride in the boat or not."

"Oh, really? Umm, is our boat ready for someone to ride in?"

Cocking his head to one side, Zahir looked at her curiously. "Well, yesterday we tried all those stones in it, and it floated fine."

"Sure then," Aimee replied hesitantly. Still unable to swim, as were the majority of the Tinys, she was afraid of deep water. "If you're sure it's safe."

Zahir slowly put his weight in the boat. For the last week everyone had worked on their boats during school hours and Zahir was confident theirs was now ready. It wobbled slightly from side to side, but it floated easily. "We have a great boat!" Zahir boasted.

Looking at it with pride, Aimee agreed. Corks, neatly tied together, formed the base. A thick layer of tin foil wrapped around the base and up the sides. Molded, red wax stripes decorated the sides and gave the base of the boat extra strength.

Seeing that it was floating well, Aimee mustered her courage to step in. The wobbles were a little unnerving at first, but once she was sitting, she realised the boat would hold them well above water level. Relaxing, she began to feel safe.

Picking up one of the wooden boards, Zahir dipped it in the lake and pushed the boat along. Aimee picked up the other stick and tried to do the same. Instantly, they began spinning in circles.

"Hey, this is fun," Zahir laughed. "Maybe we should call it 'Spinner.'"

172

For a few minutes they were content to spin, but then Zahir decided there must be some way to go straight. As the other Tinys finished up their boats, Zahir and Aimee tried to find out how to propel the boat forward. Finally, they discovered that they needed to paddle on opposite sides. Once they had coordinated their efforts, they had a great time gliding around the lake.

"Let's call it 'The Red Bird,'" Aimee suggested as the boat surged forward with the strokes of their boards. "It flies across the water!"

They made it all the way out to the floating surfboard that Damien had anchored far from shore that morning. It was the turn-around point for the race.

There was only an hour left for everyone to try their boats before Uncle Louis planned to announce the winners. The competition needed to be over before lunch while the lake was still calm. Once the waves came in it would be too dangerous. As Aimee and Zahir paddled around the shoreline, they observed their competition.

Rosa, Lily, Odin and Ponce were actually pulling their boat apart for the third time. Odin was yelling at Ponce. Rosa and Lily were crying and, once again, Uncle Louis was trying to mediate the situation.

There was no doubt that Georgia, Yu Yan, Tina and Vinitha had the most attractive boat. It was molded from tin foil with very fancy loops and swirls. A big arched canopy on top had several colourful balloons stretched across it. While it was floating well, and the balloons provided shade from the sun, the girls had still not discovered the way to avoid going in circles.

As Aimee and Zahir steered The Red Bird back to shore, Aimee noticed the beach boys were bringing their invention down to the water. She watched curiously. The last time the beach boys had tried to sail their boat it had tipped over, throwing them into the water - which they all thought was hilarious. "They must work on their boat at night," Aimee said to Zahir. "It always looks different every morning."

The beach boys' boat seemed to be made entirely from red wax on the outside and was very slim and sleek. Aimee was curious about the strange apparatus that was attached to the back of the boat. The stolen pipe cleaners, which now legitimately belonged to the boys, rose out of the back of the boat and circled around. No one had been able to figure out what they were for, and no one had seen the boat float successfully.

"Only a short time left, everyone," Uncle Louis announced loudly. "I'm going to count to one hundred, then regardless of whether or not your boat is ready, I want to see you give it your best attempt."

"It's a dumb boat," Odin snarled. "I should have had a better team!" He kicked the boat in frustration, frightening Rosa and Lily once again. The way the girls hugged each other timidly only made him madder.

"You're the dumb one," Ponce yelled back. "You keep wrecking everything we make!"

Uncle Louis had spent most of his time helping this group. Returning to their side, he asked, "What's going on?"

Red with anger, his pale blue eyes glaring, Odin complained, "It still doesn't float!"

"Odin put holes in the bottom," Ponce stated matter-of-factly, with his hands on his hips, "and now the water seeps in."

"It was to attach the corks," Odin yelled. "How else could we have attached them?"

"I would have figured something out," Ponce argued.

"It's okay," Uncle Louis told them both. "The whole purpose of this project was to learn about building boats. You've now learned that water quickly finds its way into any tiny crack or hole - so you've learned a valuable lesson. You're welcome to make a new group and build another boat anytime you want."

"I'll never build another boat!" Odin hollered.

Uncle Louis breathed deeply. "Go sit down, Odin," he ordered sharply, "and no more outbursts, or you'll miss lunch."

The no-lunch threat was about the only warning that had an impact on Odin. He plopped down on the sand and mumbled grumpily to himself.

Charley, Vahid and Kenzie - the farmer boys - had only used corks and building boards. They had worked for a long time to make an angular front on their boat so that it could cut through the water, but it was very plain-looking. There was no place to sit, or sides to hold onto. Aimee thought it looked more like a giant surfboard than a boat.

Working next to the giant surfboard, Sanaa was trying her best to get her boat stable, adding more corks to one side. She had partnered with Diya, Nancy and Milan. While Diya had plenty of ideas about how she wanted the boat to look, she wasn't inclined to create the results, but only to give the orders. Nancy and Milan had worked hard following their own ideas but had struggled to make their ideas fit in with Diya's orders or Sanaa's leadership.

"I hope it won't flip over this time," Sanaa laughed merrily, climbing into the boat. But within two seconds, Sanaa went headfirst into the water. Nancy and Milan looked at each other and shrugged.

Sitting in The Red Bird on the shoreline, Aimee watched the beach boys get ready. With only a few minutes left until launch time, they were carefully attaching a huge round balloon to the pipe cleaners on the back of their boat. She was amazed to see that the stretchy balloon which had saved her from a bad fall could become so round and big.

"How did they do that?" she asked Zahir.

"I don't know," he replied. "They've been experimenting at night, I guess. I don't even know what it's for. Does that balloon help the boat to float?"

Everyone was waiting for Uncle Louis to begin the contest. Finally, he counted down, "Five, four, three, two, one, Go!"

Digging in with their paddles, Aimee and Zahir were off to a furious start. Looking back, she saw that a few Tinys were still trying to figure out how to paddle forward. Sanaa's boat looked like it was ready to capsize. Odin's team was sitting on the beach dejectedly with the leaky boat pulled up next to them. A loud noise caught Aimee's attention as suddenly the beach boys blew noisily past The Red Bird. She felt the air in her face, as the large balloon at the back of the boys' boat quickly diminished in size.

"That's what it's for!" she exclaimed.

"Who would have thought?" Zahir replied.

The beach boys had blasted into the lead and doubled the distance between themselves and The Red Bird until the balloon ran out of air. Then they pulled out their paddles and easily glided around the surfboard marker.

Zahir and Aimee pulled hard on their paddles, but they were only halfway to the turn-around point. The farmer boys were in last place, standing on their cork surface and paddling with all their might. By the time Zahir and Aimee reached the surfboard and navigated a tight turn, the beach boys were breezing into shore.

Still paddling as fast as they could for second place, Aimee and Zahir could now see all the others. Georgia, Vinitha, Yu Yan and Tina were laughing hard as they turned in hopeless circles, having hardly begun the race. Sanaa, Nancy and Milan were completely drenched, dragging their overturned boat back to beach, while Diya unhappily sloshed through the water behind them. Rosa and Lily stood up to cheer for the beach boys as they slid into the beach.

There was no doubt about who had the fastest boat. Uncle Louis lavished praise on the beach boys' creative invention. Aimee and Zahir won for strength and durability. Georgia, Vinitha and Lily won for the most attractive. And then Uncle Louis gave out secondary prizes for 'Persistence', 'Team Co-operation', and such-like. Surprisingly, even Odin's team got a prize for 'Working Through Challenges.'

Without being asked, Damien and Lema began carrying the boats to an area beside the school. They positioned the boats neatly under the trees, but still close to shore.

"Thank you," Uncle Louis said with surprise.

Damien smiled, "The shoreline is the most important place."

"We want to keep it clear," Lema agreed.

"That was so fun watching you fly across the lake," Vinitha exclaimed shyly, as Damien walked past. "You guys should put on another show sometime."

It suddenly occurred to Aimee that here was a unique way for the beach boys to trade, which was a very novel idea for Paradise.

"We could all trade you for a show!" she burst out.

Damien looked up with interest.

With a frown, Lema asked, "What do you mean?"

"You can practice your cool tricks," she explained brightly, "and put on a show for us to watch. Anyone who wants to watch the show has to bring something that you need."

For a moment, everyone thought it over.

"That's a great idea," Nancy praised. "I'd be willing to bring fresh bread for a good show."

"I can help make some dinners," Aimee put in.

"I'll bring some fruit," Charley added.

"I'll use the shakers to let everyone know when the show will start," Georgia offered.

"Me too," said Kenzie.

With a very thankful expression, Damien said, "That would be amazing!" He looked over at Aimee. "Thanks."

Aimee smiled and nodded.

"What do you say, guys," Damien asked, looking at his friends. "Think we could pull off a show in a week?"

"Sure," they said, still a little surprised by the whole idea.

"And maybe we can make a place to tie the boats up in the water," Damien offered. "Then everyone can come to the lake and go boating when they want."

The other beach boys looked at him with astonishment.

"That sounds like work," Lema frowned.

Uncle Louis was quick to praise the idea. "Excellent suggestion!" he said. "If you boys work on that, your time will count for trade in the store, just like when you made the road."

"Let's do it, guys," Damien encouraged. "It will clean up the shoreline and keep things organized."

"And it will be a great place to watch your shows!" Georgia raved.

Franz and Lema weren't as enthused by the idea, but with Damien's prodding, they finally agreed.

Go-karts and Strange Animals

Chapter Twenty-Two

*I*n less than two weeks the boat dock was completed. The beach boys directed the project and many of the strong, young teenagers had been eager to help. Uncle Louis had designed the long pier that extended into the water. Zahir, Vahid, Kenzie and Milan had mined rocks every afternoon for an underwater foundation. The Professor had sent in the needed elements for submersed cement and with Uncle Louis' printed instructions, the beach boys had learned the right way to mix it.

Rocks now formed a tall foundation that stuck out of the water and went far enough out to tie up the five boats that floated next to it. All along the flat wooden surface of the pier, they had nailed in brass pins to attach ropes to anchor the boats. The pier also gave everyone a great platform from which they could dive into the lake or catch fish. It would also be, as Georgia had suggested, the perfect place to watch the beach boys when the shows began.

The new pier and the boats were a welcome addition for everyone, except Odin and Ponce, who had been spending a lot of time at the north end, hidden in the forest. Apparently, they had built a new shack in the forest, as it was too hard climbing the cliff every day. Occasionally, they were seen racing to the lake when their chemical concoctions reacted unpredictably. If ever anyone needed a carrycart, there were always several stashed away on their side of Paradise. They were always first in line for lunch and dinner, but they refused to come to come to school in the mornings, choosing instead to sleep in.

Generally, they were willing to trade rocks and cart loads of dirt for anyone who wanted to put in their own garden, and the Orchard girls were their best customer. From the Orchard girls they would get pottery or baskets of fruit to trade at the store with Nancy. At Louis' request, the Professor continued sending in more reactive supplies, glad to see Odin and Ponce occupied with some form of experimentation. Resigned to the fact that Odin and Ponce weren't going to be studious individuals, the Professor assured Louis, "They may not be going to school, but they are learning something."

One morning during their science lesson, Kenzie begged, "Can we please do another competition?"

They had learned a lot about problem solving in math, and had improved their writing skills, but after building boats, roads and piers, many were eager for another 'hands-on' project.

"Who would enjoy another interactive activity?" Uncle Louis asked.

Only five Tinys didn't put up their hands. Lily, Diya and Rosa preferred to just sit and listen, and Odin and Ponce didn't hear the question as they were still sleeping in.

"All right, we will do another project," Uncle Louis agreed, "but this time I will choose the groups."

There were sighs of relief and groans of disappointment.

"What will we build this time?" Vahid asked curiously.

Uncle Louis stroked his white beard thoughtfully. "I think it's time to experiment a little more with wheels and transportation," he considered. "We are done building houses and don't need so many carrycarts." He clapped his hands together remembering an idea he had seen online. "I think our one unnamed hill would be perfect for go-karts."

Almost everyone was excited to know what a 'go-kart' was. Uncle Louis walked over to the sand and drew a picture of the idea. "I'll get some instructions for you tomorrow," he said, "and we'll get to work."

For the next week, the Tinys kept busy with go-kart production. Ponce heard about the project and began showing up to take part. Uncle Louis put him in a group with Damien and Franz. Uncle Louis' choice of groups worked well, and since they had instructions to guide them, the new project went much more smoothly than the boat competition had gone.

Ponce and Franz fooled around with the small saws for building boards and accidentally cut each other before they even began to work on the carts. Tina came to their rescue with the First Aid kit, but Ponce and Franz lost their saw privileges for the extent of the project.

Aimee, Rosa and Georgia were in a group together, which they enjoyed, aside from Rosa's tendency to whine and give up whenever she didn't understand something. Since this wasn't a competition and they were all simply following instructions, Damien was quite willing to help the young ladies beside him, as well as his reckless partners. As they used the saws to cut the sticks to the right size, Damien did all the cutting for his group and often helped the girls. Sometimes all three boys helped the girls glue their pieces together, and the girls would help the boys. Of course, sometimes the boys also swiped the girls' pieces and a big chase ensued. And occasionally, Georgia or Aimee would hide the guys' wheels and watch with great amusement as they searched for them.

One day, as they were trying to attach the wheels to long metal bars that the Professor had sent in, Damien said, "Hey, Aimee and Georgia, you should try surfing. I'll give you lessons."

Aimee stopped trying to force the wheel onto the bar. "Do you really think I could do it?"

"With some lessons you could," he encouraged.

The thought of swimming out to the big waves was intimidating to Aimee. Uncle Louis had taught them enough to keep afloat for a few minutes, but she didn't feel confident in deep water. However, she was intrigued. "I'll try to get brave enough," she told him.

Damien laughed, his brown eyes merry. "I'll be right beside you," he said. "You'll have the board to float on. It's fun!"

It did sound fun, but Aimee wasn't fully convinced, and Georgia was fearful.

Franz looked up from under his stringy brown hair. "Girls are so scared of everything," he remarked with a disdainful laugh.

"Not everything!" Georgia and Aimee answered defensively.

Rosa spoke up timidly, "No... just scary black creatures and... drowning."

Ponce confessed in a low voice, "I'm not really a fan of drowning, either."

With a smile in his direction, Rosa giggled. "But you aren't afraid of spiders!" she praised.

Noticing that Aimee was really struggling to get the wheel on her metal bar, Damien offered to help.

She passed it to him gratefully. With his big hands he clamped it on with two pushes.

"Thanks," Aimee and Georgia both said in unison, impressed by his show of strength.

"Did you hear that strange animal last night?" Franz asked as he marked lines on a wooden board for Damien to cut.

Damien and the young ladies looked over at Franz in surprise.

"Strange animal?" Aimee frowned, working on the frame of her cart. "How can there be a strange animal in Paradise?"

"Remember the spider," Franz smiled, waggling his eyebrows mysteriously. "No one knows how that got in."

Rosa's bottom lip started to tremble. "I need to use the outhouse," she mumbled, rising to her feet. "I'll be back." And with that, she ran off.

Georgia was looking carefully from one young man to the other. "What did this animal sound like?" she asked with a nervous giggle.

Franz made a screeching noise followed by a low growl in his throat.

"I've never heard that," Aimee stated confidently.

"Down by the water, we hear a lot more during the night than anyone else," Franz told her. "But then, we're outside in the open, not shut-up in a big, safe house."

"I think I heard it the other night," Ponce remarked thoughtfully, as he held the board for Damien to cut. "It sounded huge! Even bigger than Freddo. I'm glad I'm not in a hammock. I wouldn't be able to sleep."

Looking skeptically from Damien to Franz and then to Ponce, Aimee asked, "Are you just trying to scare us?"

"Warn you, is more like it," Damien put in, speaking seriously. There was not even a hint of a smile on his face. "You're pretty safe in that mansion on the hill, but if you ever hear that screech at night, just make sure it's not something trying to get in."

"And if it is?"

"Then yell for us," Damien told her earnestly. "We aren't far away. We'll come track it down."

Georgia and Aimee looked at each other with lots of skepticism.

When school was over that day, Aimee went with Georgia to help Vinitha cut hair. Almost all the guys were in line for a cut. Kenzie, who didn't really care what his hair looked like as long as it was out of his eyes, was quite happy to give his two bananas to Aimee for a trim. Everyone else wanted Georgia or Vinitha. But even though Kenzie was Aimee's only customer, she did feel that she was getting better. Most of her cuts were even, she just lacked artistic flair.

Watching her friends, Aimee took careful note of what all the guys liked. Damien wasn't so keen on close cuts; he liked his blond curls. Franz kept his stringy brown hair on the longer side, just above his eyes. Charley always wanted a clean, close trim. Zahir liked to keep a few dark curls on top, with a close trim around the sides. Milan liked his blond hair to have a layered look, and Vahid kept his dark brown hair short and tidy. Odin had still not been convinced to cut his long, blond hair, and preferred to keep his wild, disheveled appearance. Ponce didn't really care what happened to his hair, as long as it wasn't too short.

After watching the others get a new look, Lema decided his afro needed a trim. Since Georgia and Vinitha were still working on Ponce and Vahid, he walked over to Aimee. "See what you can do," he said. "Just give me a trim and I promise I'll dig up whatever you want from Mining Hill."

"I would love a big, flat stone for the patio we want to put in front of the mansion," she said, picking up the scissors.

"Sure. I'll find you a good one," he promised.

With all good intentions, Aimee tried to give Lema a stylish haircut, but his hair was very tangled and matted. She struggled to make it all smooth. It became shorter and shorter, until Lema begged, "Just cut it all off."

"I'm so sorry," Aimee apologized.

Georgia was sweeping all the strands of cut hair into a pile. "You look good with a really close cut," she encouraged Lema.

Lema shrugged. "My head looks so small," he moaned, "but that's okay. I won't need another cut for a long, long time."

After the haircutting, the girls watched the surfers practice for a while until it was time for dinner. It was fun sitting on the pier, dangling their legs in the warm water and chatting about stuff, even laughing about Franz's wild tale of the strange animal.

"They are just teasing us," Georgia stated disdainfully. "I saw Franz wink at Ponce."

"Naughty boys," Aimee smiled with a shake of her head.

"Oh look," Vinitha called out. "Damien is riding inside that wave!"

184

All the girls looked and for a moment they couldn't see the tall, strong Tiny anywhere. Then, all of a sudden, he popped out from under the curling white water.

Clapping and cheering, the girls caught Damien's attention and he spun around on his board, which impressed them even more.

As they watched him swim back out to catch the next wave, Vinitha asked the girls, "What colour will you paint your go-kart?"

The young ladies launched into a discussion on which colours went best with which, and whether to decorate their go-kart with a swirl or stripes. Eventually, they heard the dinner bell ring. Twilight was falling as they raced to the store for the evening meal. Nancy and Milan had prepared a delicious fish chowder with lots of vegetables and bread.

Since darkness was falling earlier and earlier after dinner, everyone headed to their homes as soon as they had finished eating. It was already getting quite dark. There were no moon or stars to be seen above.

On the pathway up Rainbow Hill, Georgia and Aimee found themselves glancing sideways nervously.

Anxiously, Aimee reminded her, "They were just teasing us."

"I know," Georgia replied confidently. "The Professor would never let a strange animal get in."

"Well... aside from the spider," Aimee qualified.

"True, but that was an accident. I'm sure it won't happen again... ever."

Even though the girls were talking bravely to each other in the darkness, the mere thought of a strange animal in the woods sent shivers up their spines. As they approached the top of the hill, they remembered the solar twinkle lights. The switch was close by.

"Let's turn on the lights," Georgia said eagerly. "Then we can see better."

"The beach boys hate them," Aimee reminded her.

185

"They can turn them off, if they don't like them," Georgia stated, undeterred.

"Okay. It would be nice to see."

Carefully they made their way along the well-worn path to the clearing. They were within twenty footsteps of the light switch, when they heard rustling in the forest.

Immediately stopping in their tracks, they looked around.

It was dark. There wasn't any moonlight.

"It's just a squirrel," Aimee said dismissively.

The rustling started again, and there was a loud thud. It was much louder than a squirrel would make.

Georgia reached over and took Aimee's hand. "Is it a deer?" she asked in a high, wavering voice.

"Let's run home," Aimee whispered.

And then, they heard it. It began with a screech and became a low growl. The noise was exactly like Franz had described. Hugging each other, the young ladies weren't sure which way to run.

There was another loud thud, and then the screech was closer. The growl was louder. In fact, it sounded close enough to grab... or to grab them!

Both girls began screaming. They were too frightened to move. It was too dark to see anything clearly. And then the huge thing landed on them! The girls tried to fight it off, punching and kicking and screaming as loudly as they could.

A familiar laugh made Aimee look up, and she realized they were punching and kicking Damien and Franz!

Damien held Aimee's arms against her sides. He was laughing so hard; he could barely speak. "Whew... you girls... are tough!" he howled. "What fighters!"

Aimee's heart was beating very fast and her mouth was dry, but she was relieved that the strange animal was just two boys playing a prank.

"Don't ever do that again," she scolded, breaking free.

"We scared you, didn't we?" Damien teased, still laughing. "I'm sure everyone in Paradise heard you scream."

Aimee looked over at Georgia who had broken free from Franz and was dusting off her pink sundress.

"I was terrified," Aimee admitted, "and I'm glad I got some good kicks in. You deserved it!"

At that moment, Zahir and Milan came running up the hill. "Is everything okay?" Zahir asked, looking at Aimee in alarm. "We heard someone screaming. It sounded like they were being hurt!"

"The guys played a mean trick on us," Aimee told him with a smile. "We thought we were being attacked by a strange animal that screeched and growled."

"A strange animal?" Zahir questioned, unamused.

Damien tried to explain the conversation that had taken place earlier that day, only he thought the whole thing was so funny that he could hardly tell the story without doubling over in laughter. Franz had to fill in the details.

Zahir didn't seem to see the funny side.

"Why are you looking so serious?" Damien retorted. "It was just a joke!"

Then Uncle Louis arrived, a little out of breath, and the story had to be explained once again. Finally, everyone parted ways for another quiet, peaceful night in Paradise. Although... it wasn't all that quiet or peaceful. Vengeful, silly pranks were being discussed in the girl's mansion and the occasional growl and peals of laughter were frequently heard coming from the lake.

Probable or Impossible?

Chapter Twenty-Three

*E*van made his way to the Arctic Biome in twilight. He was meeting Seth McGeorge in the research library located off the main entrance. It was a much quieter study centre than the library in the Rainforest Biome, and therefore the one he preferred. Outside, just to the right of the glass structure which housed the winter-hardy animals, a large waterfall cascaded down a series of rocks, rushing away in a torrent of water that ran under a bridge. Canadian tundra gardens lined the winding pathway leading up to the main glass doors. In the spring and summer, the gardens were filled with small, unusual flowers, a few woody shrubs and a variety of grasses. Now that it was fall, the flowers were gone, but the grasses had turned various colours of green, rust and beige. Evan thought they were impressive to look at. Next to the gardens in a fancy black iron and glass enclosure, a few little white foxes were finishing off their fish dinner, and a large caribou was quietly chewing his cud. Above the black iron enclosure was a giant banner that read, "The Arctic Biome. Come Explore the North. Marvel at Your Evolving World."

Opening up the tall, blue-tinted doors, Evan breathed in the salty-sea aroma. Floor to ceiling glass windows allowed him to see the polar bear and the seals swimming on their well-separated sides of the large pool, which was surrounded by man-made snow and ice. The polar bear was the main attraction of the Arctic Biome, especially at feeding time. She had perfected the art of catching fish in her mouth as they were tossed to her by her trainer, and she was very big. The seals on the other side of the tall glass enclosure could do the same trick, but they didn't have the same commanding presence.

Seth was already sitting inside the library at the desk they always used. With a pile of heavy textbooks beside him, his red head was studiously bent over his notebook and calculator. He was punching in an equation.

"Good evening, young man," Evan said to him in a friendly fashion. "Which exam do you have tomorrow?"

"Biochemistry," Seth replied wearily. "It's going to be tough."

"I agree," Evan said. "It will be tough. I remember that one."

Sitting down across from Seth, Evan quizzed him for a couple of hours on various formulas, the components of a cell, methods of communication between the cells and the steps to ward off disease and mutations. He showed Seth the diagrams in the textbooks which he needed to memorize and had him draw a few from memory.

"So, any more questions?" Evan asked, noticing that it was now past eight o'clock.

"I do have one," Seth admitted, "but it won't be on the exam tomorrow."

"That's okay," Evan assured him. "What is it?"

Seth hesitated. "You've studied science for many years," he began. Pointing to the starry sky which could be clearly seen through the glass greenhouse structure, Seth asked, "Have you ever looked up into the sky at night, and wondered where it all began?"

"You mean like, 'the Universe'?" Evan frowned.

Seth nodded.

"Well, I guess the simplest answer is that it all began at the Big Bang."

With a shrug, Seth replied, "That's perhaps the most accepted answer at the moment, but how can you be sure it's true?"

"Physics and cosmology aren't my areas of specialty," Evan admitted, "but most scientists would affirm this theory correlates with the evidence we have available. I trust the scientific community – there are a lot of brilliant minds at work."

Seth prodded a little more. "But the way knowledge and understanding develop," he said, "theories change based on new discoveries." He pointed to his textbooks, adding, "What I'm studying right now wasn't known one hundred years ago, and some of it would have been considered preposterous."

"Fair enough," Evan conceded, "but what does that have to do with the Big Bang?"

"Well, take Einstein for example," Seth elaborated. "He had a brilliant mind, yet he struggled to remain unbiased by accepted scientific understanding, even when the evidence challenged it. His own cosmological model in 1917 showed the Universe was expanding, not static. But, because he accepted scientific belief at the time, which stated that the Universe was 'static', he altered his own model to fit the scientific beliefs of the day."

"True, I had heard that," Evan considered, "and only fifteen years later, when the discoveries by Hubbel and his colleagues showed that the Universe was expanding, Einstein had to admit he'd been wrong to doubt his original cosmological model, adding that his 'cosmological constant' had obscured the truth. He'd made a major breakthrough but doubted it!"

With a nod, Seth agreed. "So, if a brilliant mind like Einstein could be biased by the prevailing mode of scientific thought," he reasoned, "who's to say the scientists of today aren't biased in their interpretation of the Big Bang?"

Shaking his head, Evan smiled. "The theory will likely be fine-tuned as new information becomes available," he admitted, "but that's what we scientists do! Science is all about asking hard questions and searching for answers. It's through the process of experimentation, calculations, and trial and error that we discover and map out better theories. I find it exhilarating! We're like explorers discovering new lands!"

"I love it too!" Seth agreed with a chuckle. "And I do believe that following the true scientific method can lead to the discovery of truth. But if we are explorers, the 'maps' we inherit from earlier generations may sometimes turn out to be off track, leading everyone in the wrong direction."

"That's a bleak outlook, Seth," Evan frowned.

Seth paused before responding. "Solomon, the wisest man in the Old Testament, said in Ecclesiastes three that God has "made everything beautiful in its time. He has also set eternity in the hearts of men; yet they cannot fathom what God has done from beginning to end."

"Seth!" Evan rebuffed with a laugh. "You're at University now. You're in high-level lectures, reading from the best textbooks, learning from some of the most intelligent humans that have ever lived. Most readily dismiss any notion of a 'God.'"

"'Many scientists dismiss God – but not all," Seth reminded him.

"But it's so unlikely!" Evan argued earnestly, even though he privately toyed with a small possibility that God might be real. "There's just no proof, or evidence of a 'God,'" he stated harshly. "The Universe began with the Big Bang and physics shows the theory is the most plausible explanation. My best advice for you, as one budding scientist to another, is to go where the evidence leads."

"But what if the evidence we think demonstrates a 'Big Bang' is actually pointing to the beginning of God's creative act?" Seth reasoned.

"No way!" Evan retorted with a laugh, having never considered this possibility. "That's just trying to force 'God' into modern scientific discoveries. You won't make accurate discoveries if you are biased like that. You need to open your mind and read what other intelligent scientists have written. Have you read Professor Leman's book – 'Faith or Fact – An End to Delusion'?"

"Yes," Seth nodded. "It's pretty hard hitting. It threw me for a loop initially. I had to take a few days off school to recover."

"I'm sorry to hear that," Evan commiserated, "but, it's better to know the truth, right?" Then he frowned, "And you're still arguing for a God?"

"It wasn't the only book I read," Seth assured him. "Scientists always gather sufficient data before making final conclusions, right?"

"Okay," Evan shrugged. "So, then what?"

"I searched everything that had been written in response to his book. There are numerous articles both for and against his book, and even some online debates and public lectures that critique and challenge his claims."

"But how convincing were any of those challenges?" Evan prodded. "Who was giving them? You've got to be unbiased, Seth, if you really want honest answers. Of course, faith-based communities aren't going to agree with Professor Lemans."

"There are excellent critiques from scientific researchers, physicists, mathematicians and scientific philosophers," Seth told him. "The best debate was between a physicist and Professor Lemans. I'll send you the link," he said, picking up his phone and Googling the debate online. "It took place ten years ago, shortly after his book was released. The physicist – Dr. Mason - clearly shows that 'Faith or Fact' has a lot of slickly worded arguments and suppositions, but not much in the way of hard evidence or data."

"No way!" Evan argued. "There have been rave reviews in the scientific community for his book. Professor Lemans must have based his book on hard evidence, or he would never have gained such tremendous support."

"Have you looked at anything that critiques his work?"

"Well, no," Evan admitted hesitantly, taken off guard.

"Have you considered any arguments from those who were once atheists and now follow the evidence that leads them to admit that a highly intelligent Creator, like the God that many believe in, is the more probable explanation for the existence of such a perfectly well-tuned Universe?"

With surprise, Evan clarified, "You're telling me that there are respected scientists who believe in the possibility of a God based on *actual evidence?* No one I know has ever mentioned this... Really?"

"Many," Seth assured him. "And their writings, debates and lectures are all available online." He sent the debate link to Evan's phone, and Evan's phone beeped in response. "If you recognize the way in which bias can skew an investigation, then you should also consider the arguments on both sides and then decide where the weight of evidence lies."

With a shrug, Evan replied, "I'm sure the Big Bang explains everything better than a Creator God."

"Even the best theories attempting to explain how the Big Bang could have worked still require *pre-existing matter* and a specific, purposeful cause for the Universe to begin at that moment," Seth argued. "Up until the 1930's scientists – including Einstein – did not believe or accept that the Universe had a starting point like they do today, but the Bible has always stated that there was a specific moment in time when it all began. The very first verse in the Bible states, 'In the beginning, God created the heaven and the earth.' God prepared the matter, He was the cause, He spoke a word and it happened."

"Given enough time and opportunity, anything could happen *without Him,*" Evan reiterated.

With a thoughtful look on his face, Seth continued, "If you were to go out one wintery morning and see a well-sculpted snowdrift, would you assume your neighbour had spent weeks planning its design, and a whole day carving the shape?"

"No," Evan frowned, wondering what Seth was setting him up for. "Any Canadian knows what wind does to snow."

"Right," Seth nodded, "and when you examined the snowdrift carefully, you would find that it was a pile of intricate snowflakes – but nothing more than that."

"Of course," Evan agreed.

Seth smiled. "But let's say, the next morning you went out and discovered an elaborate ice image – a totally perfect representation of Professor Lemans. It was sculpted with all the white hairs of his goatee defined, the wrinkles in just the right places, even a cell phone sticking out of his right lab coat pocket!"

Evan had to laugh as he imagined the scenario.

"And not only that," Seth continued dramatically, "inside the ice sculpture there was a system of lights that perfectly illuminated the Professor's image at night, and a tiny electronic speaker that played a recording of his last lesson on Biochemistry, ending with 'This is your world- get out and solve the problems'. Would you assume the wind had been at work again?"

Evan chuckled and rolled his eyes. "I see where you are going with this, Seth," he told him unappreciatively. "Of course, I wouldn't. The wind doesn't do exact images and insert lights and recordings. Where would it even get them from?"

"Exactly," Seth agreed, "but neither can blind chance. If you look carefully at any living creature, you don't discover a well-sculptured pile of snowflakes- or 'dirt', in our case. Instead, you find something that is increasingly complex the more carefully you investigate. It's not a matter of one helpful mutation at a time, there are millions of intricate, perfectly functioning parts all fully interconnected and completely necessary for life to be possible. Even if we gave it millions or trillions of years, the wind could not make a perfect replica of Professor Lemans...*ever!*"

Evan sighed deeply.

"Consider the complexity of a simple cell," Seth prodded further. "There are two basic molecules required for the cell to function: the *amino acids*, that combine to form proteins; and the *nucleotides*, that combine to hold the information of our genes - instructions to create proteins. These molecules are composed of base elements, which when combined together make more complex structures. The DNA, or genes, provide instruction on how the amino acids must be assembled into a protein structure."

Evan frowned, "Given enough time, anything is possible..."

Seth shook his head and pressed his point further, "But the beauty of the complexity increases when you see that the proteins are necessary to replicate and assemble the DNA. You see, *both* the amino acids and the DNA are necessary *together*. This shows the *impossibility* of life springing into existence through mere 'Chance'- because neither amino acids nor DNA can exist without the other! *Both* must have come into existence together, which could only have happened if a Designer was creating life intentionally."

Seeing that his friend still looked doubtful, Seth added, "Taking this one step further, protein structures - amino acids - are also needed to read the DNA instructions, which then are needed to assemble proteins from these instructions. It's not just a matter of time, opportunity, or *probability* – it's actually *impossible*. And as human beings we can't even create one simple, fully-functioning living cell..."

"Oh yes we can," Evan interjected, a little overwhelmed by his friend's lengthy outburst. "You may not be aware of it, but cell therapies are being created for cancer treatments. And in IVF research, scientists design genetically healthy embryos."

"Can anyone create a cell from 'scratch' using only the base elements?"

"No," Evan admitted, rather deflated. This fact had already caused him much anguish when the Professor spoke of 'creating' Paradise.

195

"We still require existing, functional cells with the genetics already available." He sighed, "Only life can produce life."

Closing up the textbooks on the table, Evan got ready to leave. However, Seth was tightly wound up and he wasn't quite finished. Laying his hand on Evan's arm, he asked gently, "Evan, how do you think a great designer would feel if someone closely examined his ingenious craftsmanship, and then told everyone that it had all just happened by chance?"

Evan rose from his chair. His face was flushed. "All the best on your exam tomorrow, Seth," he said firmly. "Get those diagrams memorized tonight."

"I will," Seth promised, sighing heavily.

Without another word, Evan headed home to his small basement apartment, a dinner of eggs and ham, and... his own niggling thoughts.

The Bump in the Hill

Chapter Twenty-Four

Once the go-karts had been fully assembled and painted, they were finally ready for use. For the first hour that morning, Uncle Louis allowed the teenagers to push each other around on level ground. Then they advanced to rolling down the slope from the store. They could get all the way to the dry Rainy Riverbed. With some fine-tuning, everyone's go-kart worked well, even Ponce's and Lema's. The two dogs loved chasing the karts.

After lunch, Uncle Louis said, "Does everyone feel ready for the big hill?"

There were loud cheers.

"Alright then," he said. "Let's head to the hill."

Just to be sure they were all ready for the new adventure, Uncle Louis started them out only half-way up the hill. "And stay away from the bump," he said. "When you get really good at handling your go-kart, the bump will be a lot of fun. But for now, I want you to just get used to steering and managing your speed."

"Ah, we can handle the whole hill," Lema complained.

"I want everyone to wait a little longer before you try from the top," Uncle Louis cautioned.

"What's he so worried about?" Odin grumbled to no one in particular.

Ponce, Damien and Franz complained about avoiding the bump, but Uncle Louis wasn't backing down.

However, even with the restrictions, the ride was so fast and fun that the grumbling gave way to lots of laughter, happy shouts and delighted screams. Two Tinys fit comfortably in one go-kart, but it was possible for three to ride together if they hung on tightly. Odin hadn't made a go-kart, but he joined Ponce for several rides. Aimee overheard him admit that he wished he'd made one too.

As the day wore on and the sun began to set, Uncle Louis called out, "I think it's time to take a break for dinner."

Several Tinys were already halfway up the hill.

"Just one last ride all the way from the top," Kenzie begged. "This is so, so fun!"

The Tinys had learned well and were demonstrating good control of their karts. "All right then. One last ride from the top," Uncle Louis agreed.

Everyone below eagerly grabbed their karts and began pulling them up the hill. Freddo and Maxi bounded after them.

"Can I ride in the kart on the way up?" Rosa begged Aimee, as they began to trudge upwards. "My legs are so tired of climbing."

Aimee stopped and considered her request. Rosa wasn't tall but she was quite round and heavy. "Can we push her up, girls?"

"We can try," Georgia said, unenthusiastically. She turned to Rosa, "If you're so tired, why don't you just stay back this time?"

"But I love the ride down," Rosa moaned. "I just don't like walking up."

Damien was already half-way up the hill with Ponce and Franz, but he overheard the girls' conversation. "I'll help push," he offered, running back to give his assistance.

"Oh good!" Rosa said with relief, climbing into the kart.

Aimee smiled gratefully. "Thank you," she said to Damien. She grabbed the rope tighter and began pulling hard. Georgia and Damien

199

pushed from behind and the kart went up the hill at a good speed. By the time they reached the top, they were last in line to go down.

Charley, Sanaa and Milan had a big, clunky go-kart, but once it picked up speed it went quite fast. Maxi chased it all the way down, barking as she ran, and Sanaa whooped and hollered.

Zahir, Vinitha and Lily had the most attractive go-kart. Vinitha had painted flashy blue swirls all over it. Zahir steered well, even though he had coerced Freddo to sit on his lap. Crowded into the back, the two girls screamed with delight as they zipped along.

Next, the girls watched Damien, Ponce and Franz fly down the hill, carefully avoiding the bump in the middle, and swerving skillfully past the trees on the edge of the forest. Everyone cheered when they made it all the way to the train tracks. They had gone farther than anyone else.

"Let's beat them," Aimee said impishly, her blue eyes sparkling. "I'll steer."

She took the front seat, while Rosa climbed in behind her.

"Oh, don't go too fast," Rosa wailed. "And please tuck your hair and ribbons in so they don't hit me in the face."

Aimee didn't respond with words, but she frowned. A little irked, she tucked her ribbons inside her dress and tied her long, wavy hair into a bun.

"See if you can get over the train tracks," Georgia encouraged.

"I'm scared," Rosa pleaded. "Let's just enjoy a nice ride down the hill."

"Push us off," Aimee said to Georgia.

Georgia put her hands on the kart and ran, pushing the kart as fast as she could to the edge of the hill. Then she jumped in behind Rosa. They were off fast; faster than Aimee had ever gone before.

"Yes! We're going to beat them!" she yelled.

Aimee knew she needed to avoid the bump, but it came too quickly. For one glorious moment they were flying through the air, laughing and squealing. Then the kart landed hard, nose-first. With the impact at the front, the force pushed up the back end of the go-kart and it flipped completely over. As their vehicle continued to roll down the hill, the passengers rolled with it, colliding repeatedly with the hard ground, the wooden go-kart and each other. Finally, after what seemed like ages, the kart came to rest on top of its unmoving passengers at the bottom of the hill.

Everyone came running.

"Did you see that?" Odin laughed loudly.

Ponce was laughing too. "The go-kart landed right on top of them!"

But they were the only ones laughing. Uncle Louis knew the accident was serious.

Tragedy and Challenges
Chapter Twenty-Five

K neeling down beside them, Uncle Louis called out fearfully, "Girls, are you alright?"

Aimee opened her eyes. "Yes," she groaned, "but I hurt everywhere."

Georgia rolled off Rosa. "I'm okay... but I don't want to do that again." As she tried to push herself up, she grimaced and said, "My wrist hurts."

Rosa still hadn't moved. Her eyes were open with a strange glassy stare.

"Rosa," Uncle Louis called out sharply. "Rosa, are you okay?"

There was no response. He reached out and touched the top of Rosa's head and then drew back his blood-covered fingers in distress. "She's bleeding badly," he called out with great concern. "Someone, run for the First Aid kit."

Kenzie and Zahir took off towards the store.

Uncle Louis felt Rosa's neck for a pulse. Then he tried her wrist. He could tell she wasn't breathing. By this time, Georgia and Aimee were sitting upright, feeling his sense of panic. All the others crowded around to see what was going to happen. Blood was pooling around Rosa's head. Her eyes stared blankly without seeing.

"This can't be," Uncle Louis kept saying anxiously. "This can't be."

Uncle Louis felt terribly alone and unprepared for such a horrendous accident, even though he had done so well on the First Aid exam. He knew the theory; he had seen it performed in YouTube videos, but he had never practised the techniques. He also had a strong feeling that Rosa's injuries required more medical intervention than he could provide. He was almost certain that she must have fractured her skull. Frantically, he initiated CPR, much to the disgust of his teenaged onlookers, who were still waiting for Rosa to wake up. He could see her chest rise and fall just as it should – that was good. But as he alternated between chest compressions and mouth-to-mouth resuscitation, he was very concerned over the amount of blood she was losing. He anxiously debated in his mind whether he should run to the cave and call the Professor, or keep up the CPR and hope that Rosa would start breathing again.

The young lads returned with the First Aid kit rather quickly, but in Louis' mind, it had seemed to take forever. In a panic, he didn't explain anything to anyone, just hastily bound Rosa's head with one long piece of cloth and returned to his task, trying to bring her back to life. Without a watch, or a clock, he had no way of gauging how many minutes were passing by, but gradually he began to wear out and nothing had changed. Desperately weary, Uncle Louis knew he had to call the Professor, whatever risk there may be to disclose the secret cave.

"I just need to run," he panted, staggering to his feet, "and get help for Rosa. Stay... don't move her... I'll be right back."

Pushing himself as fast as he could, Uncle Louis ran to the cave. He fumbled frantically to open the lock on the door of the cave. Dashing in, he pressed the Professor's contact number. The phone rang over and over. Since the Professor was teaching a class it took a few tries before he answered.

"What is it, Louis?" he asked, standing outside the door of his room.

"We've had a terrible accident on the go-kart hill," he blurted out. "I think Rosa may be... dead." His words tumbled out as he struggled to catch his breath. "She has no pulse... none. There is blood coming out of her head. She's not conscious and her eyes are glazed over. I've done CPR..."

Jacques Lemans was horrified. Poking his head back into his room, he called out loudly, "Class is dismissed." Then he began running down the halls of the university, heading straight for the Rainforest Biome. "What happened, Louis?" he begged.

"The girls were coming down the hill... far too fast," Louis tried to explain, beginning to tremble from head to foot, "and they hit the bump. They were... were flung out of the kart and then it landed on them... while they all rolled down the hill."

"*Ça alors!* The bump!" Jacques cried out, bursting through the university doors and out into the cold. "Who was driving?" he queried, running and slipping along the snowy sidewalk in his dress shoes.

"Aimee," Louis blurted out anxiously, "and Georgia was the other passenger."

The Professor was seeing it all in his mind, the go-kart rolling down the hill, colliding with the girls over and over. How he regretted making the bump! "Is Aimee okay? How's Georgia?" he prodded, as his hands began to shake.

Louis suddenly realised he hadn't thoroughly examined the others; he had been completely focused on Rosa. "I think they are okay," he cried as tears welled up in his eyes, "but definitely bruised and shaken."

"I'm going to send in the train and take Rosa out!" the Professor said quickly, and then he fell hard as his shoes slipped on the icy snow at the front doors of the Biome. With the back of his pants covered in wet slush, the Professor picked himself back up franticly and pulled open the door.

Having seen him slip, Rachel was running to help him.

"I'm okay. I'm okay," he assured her quickly. Dashing past, he headed toward the mirrored hallway. Still holding the phone to his ear, he called out to Louis, "I need you to get Rosa to me as quickly as possible. If you think any of the others may be seriously injured, I'll send the train back in for them."

"But then they'll know about your side..." Louis began to sob. "I'm so sorry. I don't know what to do. I don't want to ruin your plan or lose a life. This is almost beyond me..."

Quickly looking around, the Professor saw that Rachel was watching him with bewilderment. He didn't have time to explain the crisis, and he certainly couldn't use the drop floor route. Racing around to his office door, he tried to give calm support and encouragement, appreciating that Louis was overwhelmed. "The train... will be heading in shortly," he assured him, breathing heavily as he unlocked his door and ensured it relocked behind him. "You did well to perform CPR," he praised, "that was very important, Louis. Do you remember how to recognize a medical emergency?"

"Yes," Louis sobbed.

Running through the viewing hall, Jacques relayed the warning signs to Louis once more, just to refresh his memory. Reaching the supply room, he grabbed a small stretcher from the First Aid shelf and put it on the train. From the ice machine, he grabbed some tiny cubes for the girls and placed them in a small pail. "I'm sending in a stretcher..." he told him, somewhat out of breath. "Get the young guys to help... immediately... and put Rosa on the train. Then check... Aimee and Georgia... thoroughly. If anything seems questionable... contact me and I'll send the train back in."

"Thank you," Louis replied with relief, wiping the tears from his eyes and face. "I will. I will. I hope you can do something for Rosa."

"I'll do my best," the Professor promised, reaching toward the train button on the wall. "I'm sending the train in now," he relayed urgently. "There's ice for the girls. Get back to them as quickly as you can. Goodbye, Louis... I love you! And thanks for trying your very best!"

By the time Louis raced back to the site of the accident, the train was pulling up to the store with its whistle blowing. Zahir, Charley and Vahid stood up uncertainly, looking in its direction.

"Run!" Louis called out to them. "Unload the train and bring all the supplies."

Reaching the sad little group gathered around Rosa, he saw that they were trying to engage her in conversation. Aimee was waving her hand frantically in front of Rosa's eyes, and saying, "Look at me, Rosa. I'm right here. Can you see me?"

Tears welled up in Louis' eyes. He hoped that his diagnosis was wrong and that the Professor could make Rosa better. He hated to think that such a fun experience could have gone so wrong – ending a precious life! While a few of the young teens had seen the dead spider, Zahir's fish and the occasional dead insect, nothing of such importance had ever died in Paradise. "I really haven't explained death to them," he thought anxiously, as the boys raced toward him with the supplies. "And while I've heard about it, I don't fully understand it either. What will I say if Rosa is actually dead?"

Ponce's bronzed face was turned in his direction. His dark eyes were troubled. "You said you were going to get something to help Rosa," he challenged. "Why don't you have anything with you?"

For a moment there was a fearful look on Uncle Louis' face. "I couldn't find it," he lied. Then he felt even worse. He glanced quickly at Odin and saw the suspicious gleam in his pale blue eyes. But there was no time to discuss the matter. Charley and Vahid had brought the stretcher and Zahir had the pail of ice.

Looking at the long apparatus he was carrying, Charley inquired, "What is this thing?"

"It's a stretcher," Uncle Louis mumbled. "This is how we are going to carefully pick up Rosa, so that we don't hurt her." Tears began running down his cheeks again.

None of the Tinys had ever seen Uncle Louis cry!

Odin ran over to help lift Rosa onto the stretcher. "I'll take it," he said brusquely to Charley, picking up the handles with Vahid.

"Let's get Rosa on the train," Uncle Louis said gently to everyone.

Quietly, everyone followed Odin and Vahid as they carried Rosa on the stretcher. Georgia and Aimee were limping a little and Georgia was holding her arm gingerly, but Louis observed that they were both interacting normally with the others, alert, and moving well without any serious grimaces of pain. Now that the Professor was nearby and aware of all that was going on, Louis didn't feel quite so overwhelmed. It wasn't all on him.

After Rosa had been put on the train, and the train began backing out, Uncle Louis called Aimee and Georgia over to the store deck. Everyone else followed quietly, unsure of what to do. Uncle Louis made sure that the two girls didn't have broken limbs or double vision, or severe pain in any places. Georgia had sprained her wrist but could still move her fingers freely, so he wrapped ice in a cloth and placed it on the swelling. He attended to their scratches and sores with antibiotic ointment, and Tina helped him to put on the bandages.

When he was done, he sat down with relief and weariness. All the anxious faces were looking at him for answers, but he didn't feel he had the mental presence of mind to talk about what had just happened. "I'm going to read everyone a story," he said. "We all need to just stay calm and see what will happen with Rosa."

"I'll get some books," Kenzie offered.

Uncle Louis nodded gratefully. Kenzie, Zahir and Vahid ran to the school to grab some stories off the deck. With his head in his hands Uncle Louis desperately hoped, "Maybe the train will come back soon, and Rosa will be alright."

Disconcerted and traumatized, the Tinys sat on the store deck waiting for the books. Odin suddenly challenged him. "Something's going on," he said, with a tremor in his voice. "You're always running to the outhouse for help. I've been there. You're not going to find any help in there. And how does this train know when to come and go, and what to bring? Something's up!"

Exhausted, Uncle Louis sighed heavily. He had expected that his sudden dash to the cave would ignite curiosity. Weary, very emotional, and disappointed that he had lied to the Tinys, he resolved to tell the truth. The Tinys were getting older and wiser and there was no way the cave could stay a secret forever. Thankfully, there was only one key!

"I guess it's about time I let you all in on a secret," Uncle Louis relayed in a serious manner just as the boys came back with the books. Thanking them, Uncle Louis suggested they sit down for a moment as he had something important to say.

When everyone was seated and looking up at him, Uncle Louis began, "In Rainbow Hill there is a cave with a locked door."

Some of the boys leaned forward to listen better. "This is a private place that none of you are allowed to enter," he warned wearily. "In this cave I can talk to the Professor. Just like you had a window in the nursery and could see Evan, I have a window to the Professor. He can hear me and I can hear him."

The Tinys were wide-eyed with wonder. Even Odin was impressed.

"So, there really is a Professor?" Lema remarked.

Franz rolled his eyes dubiously.

"Does he live in the cave?" Sanaa asked.

"Yes, he is real!" Uncle Louis frowned. "He doesn't live in the cave, he comes and goes, just like Evan did in the nursery."

Sanaa nodded slowly. Several Tinys looked at the hill as though they were wondering if it was tall enough to contain the Professor.

"How does he get in?" Franz asked.

"There is a way," Uncle Louis told him. "Communication between myself and the Professor is vital here in Paradise," he explained, "especially in emergencies. I tell him what we need, and the Professor or Evan will send it in on the train. But I am the only one who is allowed in the cave... for now. Does everyone understand?"

All heads nodded. There was a mischievous smile on Odin's face that Uncle Louis didn't trust.

"If anyone ever goes inside that cave without my permission," Uncle Louis warned sternly, "there will be serious consequences. They will completely lose their freedom in Paradise." He paused trying to think how best to explain 'loss of freedom.' "They will have to stay beside me all day and sleep on my couch at night," he said threateningly. "Don't try it!"

For a few minutes everyone sat in silence absorbing the new information and thinking through the instances when the train had come in at odd times. Uncle Louis stood up to read a story.

Aimee had been twisting her hands nervously the whole time. Before he could even walk one step forward, she asked, "Uncle Louis, what does it mean to be 'dead'?"

With a start, his face fell. Nineteen curious pairs of eyes were looking in his direction. He thought of telling Aimee that they didn't need to discuss this just yet, that hopefully Rosa would be fine, and that it would be better to read a story and calm down... but he could see that they all desperately needed to talk. "Come down to the beach with me," he encouraged everyone.

All the Tinys gathered around Uncle Louis on the beach, sitting in the warm, white sand. Above, the sky was overcast and darkening, but the surfing waves had ceased and were now gently lapping against the shore.

"This is a really hard thing to talk about," Uncle Louis began, looking at all the bewildered faces and feeling tears well up in his eyes. "Up until today, you've only known a fairly trouble-free existence. Yes, we've had one broken bone, some fights, scrapes and burns, a day of heat, and even a scary incident with the spider, but for the most part, life has been pretty good. Would you agree?"

Everyone nodded, aside from Odin and Franz. Diya and Ponce didn't seem completely sure and shrugged their shoulders.

Uncle Louis sighed. "But we won't live like this forever - none of us will."

"We won't?" Aimee questioned anxiously. "What do you mean?"

"The Professor can help us with a lot of hurts and damage - like when Charley hurt his arm. It's all better now, right Charley?"

Charley nodded and waved his arm around. "Sure is!" he said.

With a sad smile, Uncle Louis nodded at Charley, and then he continued, "There are some things that cause damage which can't always be repaired. We are alive right now, but if we stop breathing, or our hearts stop beating," he paused and swallowed hard, "sometimes they can be restarted, but sometimes they can't. If we are 'dead' that means we can't start breathing again... unless, the Professor finds a way... but it seems he hasn't found one just yet."

"He hasn't?" Aimee asked in a panic, turning very white.

"But the Professor is the Mastermind of Paradise," Zahir reasoned. "If he made us once, then why can't he just make us again?"

Uncle Louis took a deep breath, and then another as he pondered the question. "I'm going to have to ask him about that, Zahir," he said at last. "I don't know that I have all the answers on this. I do hope that maybe there is some way."

"There's got to be a way," Kenzie piped up. "Maybe he can do some experiments on Rosa and discover how to do it."

"True," Uncle Louis nodded. "I hope you're right. But in the meantime," he said, looking around at everyone, "be careful what you do. Your life is very precious."

"We will fix that bump on the hill before anyone else goes on it," Kenzie exclaimed. He looked around at the group. "Who's willing to help me tomorrow morning?"

Nearly everyone put up their hand.

"Well, we only have five shovels," Kenzie considered appreciatively, "but we can all take turns."

The Tinys waited for the train that evening until the darkness had descended. Some of the young teens were falling asleep on the beach. Finally, Uncle Louis encouraged them all to go to bed. "Let's hope there is good news in the morning," he said, desperate to get to the cave and talk to the Professor. "I'm sure the Professor is doing all that he can to fix Rosa back up."

With that hopeful thought in mind, the Tinys straggled off to their homes for the night.

Hope

Chapter Twenty-Six

*H*aving cancelled his classes for the rest of the day, the Professor messaged Evan with an urgent request to join him in the cryonics lab. Then he rushed Rosa from the train down into the laboratory. As fast as he could, he hooked her up to the miniature life-support machine and checked her carefully. There was no time to mourn. He had to act quickly if he wanted to preserve her body and brain for any future hope of life. Once he was certain that she was dead, he took her into the cryonics lab and began administering medications and antifreeze to cool her body as quickly as possible. Cryonics research had not yet discovered an effective way to restore a human back to life, but keeping Rosa frozen until an effective way was found was the only hope he had.

Evan came rushing into the lighted lab and began helping. They had performed this procedure before on a few miniaturized animals that had died, in preparation for such an emergency. In silence, they focused on the necessary, important steps until the tiny body was fully prepared. Finally, the Professor placed Rosa inside the special sleeping bag, donned protective gloves and lowered her into the vat of liquid nitrogen.

Sadly, he turned to Evan and they embraced. With their arms around each other, they mourned the loss of their first Tiny in a world where suffering was to be completely minimized.

"A death in Paradise?" Jacques questioned, as tears rolled down his cheeks. "Killed when they were just having fun? Oh, why did I put that bump on that hill?"

"What happened, Jacques?" Evan begged, knowing nothing of the circumstances and having restrained himself from asking until now.

The Professor told him the whole tragic story.

Evan was very distraught as tears ran down his face. "Poor little Rosa!" he cried. "She's so young to lose her life in a freak accident. How could this happen? And the Tinys witnessed all this?"

"Ça alors! They saw it all," Jacques lamented, shaking his head. "Who knows how they will deal with this trauma! How do we tell them that Rosa is dead? Even Louis is hopeful that I can fix her up and send her back in."

Many things were going through Evan's mind. The questions that Jacques was asking were deep and difficult. He wasn't sure how to answer, but there was one thing he thought they should do. "I think we should ban go-karting on the hill," he said.

"I've thought of that," Jacques Lemans replied dismally, "but if we discontinue go-karting, we'll have to stop them from swimming in the lake. They are both equally dangerous."

"That would take away a lot of their fun."

"It would. It would!" He sighed heavily, "But I do agree that losing one life is a tragedy!"

Regretfully, Evan said, "We should have made the fun hill smaller."

"Perhaps!" the Professor fretted, "Or I shouldn't have added the bump. We simply wanted everyone to enjoy our world and develop their skills, but adding exciting adventures increases the risk of danger and sadness."

"The greater the excitement, the greater the potential for disaster," Evan agreed.

The Professor's phone rang. Louis was making a video call. Picking it up, the sad look on Louis' face was terribly distressing to both scientists.

"Is there any hope for Rosa?" was his first question.

Agonized, the Professor replied, "Unfortunately, she is... dead."

Louis' face fell and he breathed heavily. "I can't believe this has happened," he confessed, "We are all in a lot of shock. This is the first time we have seen one of us die and we're all trying to understand what it means."

"It is a terrible tragedy!" the Professor agreed as tears welled up in his eyes once again. "We are in shock as well."

"Can you remake Rosa?" Louis begged. "One of the boys mentioned that if you gave Rosa life the first time, surely you can give her life again?"

Evan looked over at the Professor curiously. He felt this was the time to admit that they couldn't give life. They could only rework a life that was already in existence.

Rubbing his face with his hands, the Professor hesitated. "I've done everything I can," he assured Louis. "There is hope that with some more experimentation and research, we may eventually find a way to restore life to the cells. But it won't be soon. It's not simple, but there is hope. You can tell the children that there is hope that Rosa will come back to life one day."

Evan wasn't so sure that cryonics was a substantial hope, but he didn't voice his skepticism with Louis still on the phone.

The Professor talked to Louis about how to counsel the Tinys through this tragedy. The three of them grieved together. Jacques admonished Louis that it was important to not suppress his sadness, or that of the children. "Keeping it bottled inside will only lead to more hurt later," he said. "They've got to talk it through whenever they feel like talking."

When the Professor had finished his conversation and put down his phone, Evan murmured, "I will be more convinced of the merits of cryonics when they actually bring someone back to life."

"I know. I know," the Professor agreed thoughtfully, "but it's all we can offer for now, and it may prove viable at some point in the future. What we are discovering in science today would have seemed preposterous a hundred years ago... or less. Perhaps you and I will discover the way to bring life back to the cells," he said, looking up with a smile. "In the meantime," he reasoned, "a false hope is better than no hope at all. It will help them all feel better."

Evan had picked up on the words, 'bring life back.' He frowned. "But we didn't give life in the first place," he pointed out warily; "that is beyond the ability of any scientist!"

"True, true," the Professor agreed, "but I do believe that science will discover a way. It's just a matter of time."

After his conversation in the library with Seth and the online debate that he had watched, Evan was no longer sure what he believed. If Seth and the physicist were right, and there really was hard evidence to believe in a supernatural, all-powerful God, then life was a gift that only He could give. He shuddered at the thought of humans finding a way to generate life. It sounded like a plot for a scary sci-fi movie. "Would it be wise," he pondered privately, "for such incredible power to be in the hands of those who might use it for good but... may well use it for evil?"

Excusing himself from the lab to check on the Tinys, Evan walked past the incubators below with tiny new puppies and kittens developing inside. He was thankful they had decided not to create any more human beings. "I must discourage Jacques from developing anymore humans," Evan told himself anxiously. "This has been a fabulous experiment, but if there is even a remote chance that there is a 'great designer', what does He think of us modifying His creation and offering hope that we can't give?" Agitated and distressed, Evan rode the elevator up to the Paradise Room. "Does Seth's God offer any hope for life after death?" he pondered, walking into the dark greenhouse structure. "And if He does, is there any evidence to believe it is possible? Or do Christians just hope for something, because it's better than no hope at all?" As he walked across the room, he was surprised to see the dome was glowing softly.

Gazing inside, he noticed that the solar twinkle lights had been turned on. The beach boys were not in their hammocks. Sad, muffled voices came over the speakers, but the voices didn't seem to be coming from the houses. He could see Uncle Louis walking across the shadowy meadow.

A loud wail caught his attention. It sounded like it came from the meadow. "We can't sleep, Uncle Louis," Aimee was crying. "Is Rosa okay?"

Gazing across the field in the direction of her voice, Evan noticed that a large group of Tinys were huddled together on Louis' cabin deck. He could only see shadowy figures, but it seemed that perhaps all of Paradise had decided they couldn't sleep on their own.

Uncle Louis reached his cabin and sat down beside them. A tall girl plunked herself in his lap and threw her arms around his neck. He could hear crying. There was movement on the deck as the others piled in close and soon Louis was surrounded by all the distraught young teenagers. He could hear many of the girls sobbing. Lily was wailing. Uncle Louis seemed to be hugging them all. Other voices inquired about Rosa.

Eventually, Uncle Louis replied, his voice trembling, "Rosa is... isn't okay. She won't be coming back... for a long time."

"Is she dead?"

"Yes," he replied softly.

There were many sorrowful cries, even from the boys. When they had quietened back down, Louis continued kindly. "The Professor hopes that with some more research he will find a way to bring Rosa back to life. But it will take time."

Gazing at the grief-stricken scene, Evan's heart bled compassion. "Regardless of whether it's right or wrong, I'm in this so deep, I have to stay," he thought. "These Tinys are real people. I can't leave this project, especially not when things are going wrong."

For a long while, Evan stood listening to Louis comforting the Tinys. Gradually, the noises subsided, but no one left his cabin.

When the Professor joined him after cleaning up the lab, it was peaceful and quiet in Paradise with only the odd snore here and there.

"I think they've all fallen asleep on Louis' deck," Evan whispered.

The Professor peered into the dark shadows and smiled sadly. "Louis is bearing the brunt of this once again," he admitted. "I hope he gets some sleep tonight."

"I hope he can bear up," Evan agreed. "What would we do without Louis?"

They both looked at each other and swallowed hard. There was no comforting answer to that question.

"We'd better go get some sleep too," the Professor said sadly. "There's not much left of the night."

Grieving

Chapter Twenty-Seven

That night, the Professor lay awake for ages trying to think of something special he could send in to comfort the Tinys. Finally, it came to him at three a.m.. Satisfied, he drifted off to sleep. He woke up four hours later and headed back to the Rainforest Biome. Taking the drop floor entrance, he strode quickly to the greenhouse and picked up a newly germinated rose. It wasn't much more than a seedling, with only five leaves. In the supply room, he made a small card and wrote a short message in his best writing. Tucking it in carefully with the requested supplies of bird food, pet food, oil, yeast and flour, he also stuffed in a bag of Wonderdrink to fill the formula machine. He knew Nancy had been too distraught to make any bread. Sending the train in, he walked down the long corridor and through the elevator entrances to the Paradise Room. Evan was already there, peering inside. They nodded to one another.

The Tinys had also woken early, having had a restless night on the uncomfortable deck. Evan and the Professor could see some of the young men were bringing big rocks from Mining Hill. With the widest carrycarts, Odin, Ponce and Vahid were leading the group, pushing their loads along the stone road. All the other Tinys stood by the school.

Together, the two scientists watched quietly as the young teens reached the schoolhouse and took out the stones to build a large pillar equidistant between the school and the shoreline. Then all the Tinys stood in a circle around it, with their arms around each other. Zahir led the group in a goodbye song to Rosa; a simple, heartfelt lament that he must have composed during the night. Evan noticed that Aimee didn't sing. Instead, she looked down at the ground the whole time obviously trying to choke back sobs. She was in tears when he finished the song.

"Rosa is dead because of me!" she burst out crying. "I went too fast. I hit the bump. It's all my fault!"

"Me too," Georgia wailed, coming over to put her arms around Aimee. "I rolled on top of her, over and over!"

Damien came over as well. "I pushed her up the hill," he admitted with deep distress, putting his arms around the two sorrowful young ladies. "I should have told her, that if she couldn't climb, then she couldn't ride!"

"I shouldn't have asked to go from the top," Kenzie lamented.

For a few moments, Uncle Louis let them all comfort each other. He knew how important it was to show empathy and help the group heal. Finally, he gently asked, "Did anyone intend to hurt Rosa?"

"No, not at all," Aimee protested tearfully. "I was upset by her complaining, but I never planned to hurt her!"

"Did you plan to roll on her?" Uncle Louis asked Georgia.

"No, I couldn't stop myself."

Uncle Louis looked at Damien.

"I was just trying to help her out," he said.

Kenzie didn't wait for a look. "I just wanted more fun."

"I believe you all," Uncle Louis told them. "What happened on that hill was an accident. It wasn't planned by anyone. It was a mistake, a mishap, and certainly a tragedy, but it wasn't intentional. Sometimes bad things happen by accident. We can't blame ourselves as though we planned to hurt her. Rosa made a choice to go down the hill, just like you all did," he continued. "Life will be full of choices and sometimes our choices may have disastrous consequences... and there will be no one to blame."

"We can blame the Professor for the dumb bump on the hill," Odin burst out sorrowfully, with uncharacteristic emotion.

"Yeah, why was there a bump?" Ponce agreed.

Hearing the boys' accusatory questions, the Professor was crushed. Evan reached over and put his arm around him.

"Did the Professor put the bump there to hurt people?" Uncle Louis asked.

"Well, it was sure a dumb mistake, if it wasn't intended," Odin argued, almost crying himself.

On the other side of the glass, the Professor agreed with Odin. "Yes, it was," he whispered sadly. "I made a very dumb mistake."

Down beside the shore, Uncle Louis walked over and put his arm around Odin. "We know it wasn't intended for harm," he assured him, "because the Professor has shown his love in so many ways. Look how wonderful Paradise is; look all around you."

All the Tinys gazed sadly around at their wonderful world - the huge sparkling lake stocked with fish, the long, white sandy beach, the prosperous gardens, the fruitful orchards and the forested hills.

"Would someone who has been so kind, and done so much good for us, and who sends us everything we need on a daily basis - would he put things in Paradise only to hurt us?"

Unprepared to concede the point, Odin just shrugged and pulled away from Uncle Louis.

Looking at all the glum-faced teenagers, Uncle Louis reasoned, "The bump could have added a lot of fun and increased our skill level once we were more experienced driving. It wasn't placed to harm us but to give us pleasure. However, due to what happened yesterday, we will go ahead and remove that bump tomorrow."

Wearily and with forced optimism, Uncle Louis announced, "I want you to all hold on to this little ray of hope – a little ray of hope for

Rosa and for all of us. The Professor is going to do all that he can to bring Rosa back to life. He says there is a way; it just takes time."

Everyone cheered and clapped their hands.

Outside the dome, Evan glanced quickly at the Professor. "There is? You will?" he whispered.

"I didn't say it exactly like that," the Professor frowned, keeping his eyes on the Tinys, "but I will definitely do some research."

Shaking his head in disbelief, Evan glanced at his phone and mumbled. "I should get going. I've got a group meeting this morning." But then he saw Aimee put up her hand.

"Yes, Aimee?" Uncle Louis acknowledged.

"Do you think we could call that hill, Rosa's Hill?" she pleaded, her voice full of emotion. "Then it will always have a special memory of her."

There were nods of approval all around.

"Rosa's Hill!" some of the girls shouted.

"I think that is a lovely idea, Aimee," Uncle Louis agreed.

"But what happens when the next person dies?" Franz queried. "There aren't any more hills needing names."

"We will all be much more careful in the future," Uncle Louis said.

"Oh, and being more careful will save us from anything bad?" Odin sneered angrily. "If we were more careful, it wouldn't have been so hot that one day. If we were more careful, a giant spider wouldn't have crept in..."

Uncle Louis knew Odin was hurting, but he was also weary and worn out from the devastating ordeal. Nothing he had said or done seemed to help Odin, and Uncle Louis felt he might respond angrily himself. "The train came in," he replied bluntly. "Let's go see what gifts we were sent today."

Zahir stood up and replied directly to Odin. "Being careful will help a great deal," he argued. "If we're careful to wash our hands, we won't get sick. If we're careful when we use sharp knives and saws, we won't hurt ourselves or others. If we're careful to listen to the advice Uncle Louis gives us, we can avoid situations that he knows could cause harm... he knows more than us. We have to do our part to keep Paradise safe."

Odin retorted fiercely, "Oh yeah, well, being careful wouldn't have saved the girls from the spider, would it? You would have been too careful to help out! You likely would have run off and hid in the store."

There were a few snickers among the beach boys

Not wanting to pursue an argument, Zahir turned away.

Ponce called out, "Come on, Odin. Let's go see if there's any food in the store. I'm starving!"

The mention of food sent many of the Tinys hurrying towards the store. They had missed dinner the night before and no one had made breakfast that morning.

Still reeling from Odin's taunt, Zahir looked around for his dog who was following a rabbit trail in the forest. Freddo hadn't eaten breakfast either. He called for him and waited for his dog to come.

Uncle Louis walked over and put his arm around the young lad's shoulders. "Thank you, Zahir," he said with relief. "Thanks for speaking up."

Zahir nodded. His dark skin was quite flushed. "I believe you, Uncle Louis," he said. "And I believe the Professor will remake Rosa. We'll see her again... likely soon."

On the other side of the glass, Evan turned to the Professor with alarm.

"I didn't say when," the Professor whispered. Looking down at Zahir with deep affection, he demurred, "What a special young man Zahir is becoming! He has real leadership potential. Let him have a little hope to hold onto."

Again, Evan turned to leave.

"I sent in some Wonderdrink," the Professor told his assistant as most of the Tinys ran toward the store, "and a note and gift."

Evan's phone was vibrating with messages, but he left it in his pocket and stayed to see what would happen next.

Kenzie reached the train first and discovered the special note. He opened it, skimmed through the message and called out in astonishment, "It's a card from the Professor!"

Everyone hurried forward to see what the card would say.

"Please read it," Uncle Louis requested.

Kenzie read,

"My dearest Tinys, I am so grieved that you have lost a precious friend in Paradise. I am so sorry that the hill which I made for you to enjoy, and the bump that I put in to give you some excitement, has resulted in Rosa's death. This was never my intention. I love you all and only want the best for everyone. If I can find a way to keep you all alive forever, I will do whatever it takes for that to happen.

You will find a little rose in a container. It's a rose for Rosa. Please plant it in a special place for her.

With much love and sorrow,

The Professor"

All the Tinys were comforted by the loving message. Vinitha and Yu Yan looked in the train and pulled out the container. "We'll plant it," they offered. "We'll put it right by Rosa's pillar."

"I'll bring some good dirt," Odin offered, much to everyone's surprise. "As much as you need."

Turning to look at each other sadly, the Professor and Evan understood that Odin, in his own unique way, was heartbroken over Rosa's death.

"Louis will need to give him some counselling," the Professor mused.

Evan agreed, watching Louis and Nancy unload the Wonderdrink. "They all need counselling," he mused. "We could use a whole team of counsellors right now..."

"Or Rachel Khalid," the Professor added regretfully. "If we can just get through a few more months..."

"You'd really like her to be a part of this, wouldn't you?" Evan smiled.

"I'm sure she'd have great insights," the Professor nodded. "She came from a family of eight."

As much as they could see that all the Tinys needed counselling, and as much as they told themselves that they loved all the Tinys equally, there were some that tugged at their heartstrings more than others. Foremost in the Professor's heart were the Tinys who felt they had caused the accident and were openly displaying their grief. They were also the Tinys most responsive to reason and affection. As Evan pulled out his phone to check his messages, the Professor said, "Maybe it's time to release the baby animals."

"But they've only just come out of the incubators. They are still so fragile," Evan reminded him.

"I believe caring for baby animals will help the Tinys heal and distract their minds from what has happened. We'll tell them what they need to do and send in the formula machines. It will also develop their nurturing potential and generate tamer animals."

"I suggest we give the babies one more week in the nursery," Evan stated, feeling the plan was rather risky. "You don't want there to be more accidental deaths. We can tell Louis to let all the Tinys know that the babies are coming. They can do some research during school hours and those who want pets can get busy preparing for their care, which will distract their minds. Any that don't get adopted, we'll nurture here in the nursery."

Considering the matter carefully, the Professor agreed. "You're right, Evan. One more week is wise. I'll collect some helpful information and send it in on the train tomorrow. Even the anticipation of new pets will be helpful to take their minds off this great heartbreak."

Evan's phone began ringing, and this time he rushed off to his meeting.

A Ping

Chapter Twenty-Eight

Aimee and Georgia were ecstatic when Uncle Louis told his class about the new adoption plan. "Babies?" they blurted out happily, hugging each other on the school stairs.

"Who gets them?" Charley wanted to know.

"You can sign up right here," Uncle Louis said, holding up a piece of paper. "These baby animals are so little that they will require a couple weeks of intensive care. You will need to feed them every two to three hours, change their bedding, and give them lots of love. Don't sign up unless you're prepared to dedicate yourself to the task."

Almost every young lady rushed to the sign-up sheet. Lema and Franz had no interest, Odin and Ponce were still asleep in bed, but the other guys were eager to be involved. While many of the young teens signed up for puppies or kittens, Charley and Vahid wanted a calf and were willing to look after forty more chickens for the farm as eggs were an important food source in Paradise. Kenzie was eager to look after the lambs, Zahir chose the squirrels, Nancy picked rabbits, and Aimee, Georgia and Lily wanted pet birds.

"What kind of a bird?" Damien asked, as they left school that day to trade for lunch at the store.

"A lorikeet," Aimee said. "They are so pretty! I'm hoping it will want to sit on my shoulder."

"Cool!" he replied. "I'm getting a puppy. A golden puppy. I hope it will be just like Zahir's."

The rest of that week, school focused on animal care and training. Charley brought Maxi to all the lessons, and Zahir brought Freddo. Nancy would have liked her cat to join in, but Ripple kept returning to the forest; she preferred to spend her time stalking the squirrels.

"Cats aren't quite as co-operative as dogs," Nancy had to concede.

Uncle Louis was feeling quite tired that week, as almost every night, a group of Tinys would come to his cabin, unable to sleep. Sitting with them in the dark on his couch, talking through the accident and the images they struggled to forget was helpful counselling, but it was only a help for those who sought it out. Odin and a few of the others didn't seek help and Uncle Louis was too weary to impose it upon them. Often, the Tinys would go back to their homes, but Aimee, Georgia, Yu Yan and Lily often fell asleep cuddled up to him on the couch. Uncle Louis didn't sleep so well sitting up.

With all the ongoing drama at night, it was helpful that the morning classes were on the easy topic of pet care and handling. He taught them how to train an animal to come when it was called, to praise it for good behaviour and let it know when it had misbehaved. They practised on Charley and Zahir's dogs. Time after time, Freddo responded much more quickly than Maxi. Freddo loved attention and would do anything for a little praise and tasty treats - especially Nancy's bread. Maxi was very distracted by smells and noises, and not nearly so eager to please.

On the last day of animal care classes, the beach boys invited everyone to come watch the first surfing show. They rushed off right after school was over to set up with Georgia and Kenzie. All the others followed Zahir and Vahid to wash their hands by the outhouse, and then they went to the store to trade for lunch.

Lunch was a surprise!

"Look, it's a little kitty!" Vinitha cried out with delight, coming out of the store with her bread roll.

Sure enough, Nancy had made the bread rolls look like a kitten face, pinching the dough to look like pointed ears, with bits of fruit embedded for eyes, and grass for whiskers.

"That's so dumb," Ponce complained, when he and Odin showed up, yawning. He handed in three, small, pretty rocks that he'd mined for his kitty bun. Odin had a flat rock. Everyone else was delighted with the cute faces.

As usual, the teens found a place to sit on the store deck stairs to enjoy the bread. Water was always free, but those with extra supplies to trade often picked up Aimee's freshly squeezed orange juice instead. While everyone was still enjoying their kitty rolls, the cymbal clanged and the shakers could be heard, an indication that the beach boys were ready.

"Show time!" Vinitha called out to the other Tinys. Charley quickly passed around some fresh bananas to all the teenagers who had given an hour to help him weed the grass out of the garden. "I'm bringing the rest of the bananas to the show," he told Sanaa, picking up his half-full basket. "The trees are loaded!"

Aimee had spent her lunchtime making soup in the store kitchen to give the beach boys. It was squash soup, and she had added apple to it for extra sweetness. She thought it was delicious! Putting it into a big glass jar, she screwed on the lid.

Nancy dashed out ahead of her with three fresh kitty buns.

Aside from Odin and Ponce, all of Paradise turned out for the first surfing demonstration. The Tinys placed their offerings in the bin that Zahir had built to hold the goods they received and then sat down on the long pier. Dangling their legs in the cool water, they finished off their lunches.

Aimee sat down beside Georgia and Vahid. Zahir arrived soon after, but he didn't put anything in the bin. Uncle Louis had given him and Kenzie free passes to everything that week since they had both worked hard to remove the bump on the hill. It had taken five afternoons, but finally the job was done.

Damien, Franz and Lema sat on the end of the pier ready to begin.

"Look at the balloon," Aimee said, pointing in Damien's direction. "I wonder what he will do with it this time."

Damien had attached a large round balloon to his surfboard using the fuzzy pipe cleaners. The bright red balloon was big and round, filled with air and he was holding the closed end of it tightly.

"Those guys are always coming up with something new," Zahir replied, "and I know how they blow it up so big."

"Really?" Aimee asked, very attentive.

"I'll show you sometime," Zahir told her. "I saw them holding a balloon over the breeze holes at the edge of Paradise."

Damien signalled it was time to begin.

Kenzie clanged his cymbals together and Georgia shook the shakers extra hard, and the show began. While Lema and Franz plunged into the water on their boards to swim out to the waves, Damien stood up on his and loosened his hold on the end of the balloon. Immediately, with a sharp spluttering noise, the balloon propelled him across the water far ahead of his friends. He zipped across the lake as though he was riding a go-kart down the hill. When the balloon fizzled out, Damien caught a wave and rode it into shore.

Everyone was clapping and cheering for Damien as he picked up his board and ran back into the water. He began swimming out to the big waves while Lema and Franz stood up on their boards. Far out in the deep water, they had something new to perform as well. Instead of just riding waves like they normally did, they pulled off a few flips. Franz was only able to do one, and then went face-first into the water, but the audience enjoyed the mistakes almost as much as the perfectly performed flips. Lema managed to do two!

As the boys were setting up for one more demonstration, Aimee heard a distant ping. She and Charley turned to look toward the North Forest.

"It's just Odin and Ponce fooling around," Kenzie muttered.

"I've never heard a ping before," Aimee worried.

Zahir agreed. "Want to go investigate?" he asked.

"Okay," she nodded, "as soon as the show is over."

Everyone stayed till the end of the surfing show and clapped enthusiastically when it was done. The beach boys were getting better and better at their stunts.

When the applause began to die down, Aimee and Zahir raced off in the direction of the noise. It wasn't often that Aimee or any of the other Tinys ventured near Odin and Ponce's hideout. Aimee stopped quickly when she saw a big round object dangling from a tree. It had eight skinny legs. She let out a cry of surprise.

Zahir laughed and poked it with his finger. Made from black pipe cleaners, it twirled around on a string but had no other reaction. He reached out and slapped it hard.

"Don't worry," he smiled, as it swung back and forth. "It's just a fake spider."

They could hear Odin and Ponce discussing how to make the pebble shoot further. Zahir ran through the woods and Aimee followed him slowly, trying to avoid the black dangling creatures. Fake or not, they were creepy looking.

"What are you guys up to?" she heard Zahir ask.

"Did you hear that last one?" Odin laughed. "That was our best yet!"

Aimee caught up to Zahir. "Did you hit something?" she questioned the gloating experimenters.

"Maybe," Ponce chuckled. "If we did, it was something up there." He pointed in a sideways, upward fashion.

Aimee looked at the pot the young teens were using. They had given Vinitha rocks for her garden in exchange for a custom-ordered pot. The large clay jar in front of Ponce was very wide at the bottom with only a small opening at the top. Ponce was holding a lid on the jar.

Zahir tried to get closer to see what exactly the guys were blasting into the air, but Odin stopped him. "Top secret stuff going on here," he said. "No one is allowed to see what we're doing."

"Does Uncle Louis know about this?" Aimee asked.

"He's the one that taught us about chemical combinations," Ponce smirked, his bronze face glowing. "We're just doing our own science experiments. The Professor keeps sending in the supplies."

"Now get yourselves somewhere else," Odin demanded. "This is private property."

"Paradise doesn't have private property," Zahir reminded him.

"Well, I do," Odin told him.

"We don't want to endanger anyone else," Ponce piped up with a comical grin. "We're doing some testing here, and it could be dangerous to other Tinys." He spoke firmly, "So, we're going to have to ask you to leave before we let the next one off."

"Uncle Louis is going to know about this," Aimee frowned.

"See if I care," Odin taunted.

Zahir took Aimee's hand and pulled her away.

No sooner were they out of the trees, when they heard laughter and another ping. Turning around quickly, Aimee whispered to Zahir, "Let's go see if something fell." Running back into the woods they scoured the ground for unusual objects, keeping a safe distance away from Odin and Ponce's worksite.

As they diligently searched the forest for anything that might explain the noise, they could hear Odin and Ponce boasting about their experiments.

"Those pebbles work great!" Odin said.

"We are definitely hitting something," Ponce agreed. "I love the p-i-n-g!"

"If there really is a Professor, we'll see if he hears it," Odin chuckled. "Maybe he'll show his face!"

"I doubt we'll see him," Ponce argued. "Evan maybe, but not the Professor."

"Let's try and do one more before Louis comes to shut us down," Odin urged. "Got to do as much damage as we can, while we still have a chance. If we do some real damage, the Professor will have to come and fix it!"

"Heh, heh," Ponce snickered. "Then we'll see if he's real or not." He held up a handful of stones. "We have five more pebbles. Want to put in three at once?"

"Nah, let's do all five. Louis will be here any minute."

With a look of alarm, Aimee glanced up at Zahir. He looked back with concern. "Let's go," he mouthed.

Trying to escape from the forest without a noise, Aimee and Zahir slid under the trees and high-tailed it towards Uncle Louis' house. They hoped Uncle Louis would be there.

Banging on the door of his single-story, wooden house, they soon determined no one was home. They raced to the store, but Nancy and Milan didn't know where he was, and were busy preparing spinach and tomato quiche for everyone's dinner that night. Following the stone road down to the lake, they came across Charley, Sanaa and Kenzie who were working in the garden picking fruit. But no one had seen Uncle Louis. They checked the beach, without success. They even checked the outhouse. Finally, Aimee suggested climbing Rainbow Hill, where they could see all around Paradise. Uncle Louis was coming down the pathway as they came up.

"You both look worried," he observed. "Is everything okay?"

"Have you heard the pings?" Aimee asked.

"No," he said, frowning. "Are Odin and Ponce at it again?"

Aimee nodded frantically.

"They are planning to do another one with five pebbles this time," Zahir relayed.

"Five pebbles? Is that what they are using?" Without another word, Uncle Louis started running towards the forest.

Aimee and Zahir followed.

"They want to do damage!" Aimee called out as they dashed down the hill and across the meadow. "I heard them say that. They want to see if the Professor will come and fix it!"

"This is more serious than I thought," Uncle Louis exclaimed. "We have to stop them!"

As the three of them came around Rosa's Hill, they heard a succession of pings.

"They are hitting something for sure," Uncle Louis stated angrily. "What are they thinking?"

Marching into the woods, Uncle Louis met the boys as they were quickly closing up their jars of supplies. "Do you have any idea of what you're doing?" he confronted them angrily.

No one had never seen Uncle Louis so angry before.

"We're just experimenting," Odin said proudly.

Suddenly, Aimee spotted a pebble lying nearby. She picked it up. "With these?" she asked.

"We want to see just how far we can shoot the pebbles," Ponce smiled. "When we hear one hit something, we know we've had good success!"

Uncle Louis was furious, but he didn't want to say or do anything that might betray the Professor's ideals for Paradise. He decided he needed time to think and confer with the Professor. "Both of you are coming with me," he fumed. "I'm not sure what to do with either of you, but for now you have lost your freedom. You will be kept under my supervision."

As they walked out of the forest, Uncle Louis wasn't sure how he would keep an eye on the reckless young men and manage to get to the control cave to talk to the Professor, but somehow, he knew he was going to have to pull it off.

Rain began falling from the sky. It wasn't abnormal for rain to fall in the afternoon, but there was a strange, muffled, beeping sound that echoed in the distance.

All of them looked up in surprise. Uncle Louis had never heard the noise before, but at the moment his attention was fully on the troublemakers.

"Zahir," Uncle Louis said, turning to him with a red face, "can you please gather all these supplies and take them back to the store? Tell Nancy she is not allowed to trade these chemicals for anything, or to anyone, unless she asks my permission first." Then he added sharply, "Have them locked away in a secret place!"

Aimee and Zahir exchanged anxious glances as they ran to get carrycarts to transport the supplies. They knew the situation must be serious for Uncle Louis to take away freedom and lock up supplies!

Something is not Right

Chapter Twenty-Nine

Uncle Louis kept the troublemakers busy for the next hour until the sun went down. He had not been planning to put a rock patio around his house, but it seemed the perfect 'make-work' project for two foolish young men, even if it was raining hard. Never allowing Odin or Ponce out of his sight, Uncle Louis followed them as they dug for rocks in the hill and marched behind them as they wheeled the cart back to his house by the store. He talked to them about responsibility, thinking of others and that the greatest joy in life is found in serving others, not in being served. While he was working with Odin and Ponce, the other Tinys enjoyed the steady rain. Daytime rain was always a welcome novelty, as it only happened once a week. Cascading Mountain was sending down a fabulous waterfall and many had discovered that if they put their boats in the river, right near the falls, they could get a fast ride to the lake. It was a little bit dangerous as they had to duck down to get under the bridge, but it was fun. Water was beginning to pool in the low-lying areas and Zahir, Kenzie and Vahid were racing their go-karts down Rosa's Hill. Large puddles sprayed in all directions when they zipped through. Uncle Louis was pleased to see the other Tinys were enjoying themselves.

"No fair," Odin complained. "They get to have fun in this rain, and we have to work in it."

"There are consequences to acting irresponsibly," Uncle Louis stated firmly. "This is what it's like to lose the freedom to do as you please."

Dinner time came and went, the rain continued, and the muffled noise was a steady annoyance. Now that it was dark, an odd red glow blinked on and off in the hazy, glazed horizons of Paradise.

"I really must ask the Professor about that noise," Louis said to himself. "It seems rather strange. Maybe the Professor is doing something unusual on the other side."

Once it was dark, and the go-karting was over, Uncle Louis allowed the troublemakers to have dinner. Nancy and Milan were busy cleaning up the kitchen. He asked Zahir, Kenzie and Vahid to supervise the reckless teenagers while they ate, and then Uncle Louis excused himself. "I must talk to the Professor about that noise," he said. "I will be right back."

The river was too swollen to cross, so Uncle Louis ran around the mountain. Behind the mountain, he saw something he'd never seen before. Attached to the perimeter of the dome, little fountains of water were spraying out in every direction. It was a forceful spray that hurt when it hit him.

"Does this happen every time it rains?" he wondered. He had never walked in behind the hills when it rained, as generally he was sound asleep in bed. Ducking under the fountains and sloshing through the water, Uncle Louis' concern grew exponentially.

When he got to the cave, he had to cross a stream to reach the door. "If this rain doesn't stop soon," he thought, "the cave will be flooded." Knowing a little about electricity, Uncle Louis was certain that would be a big problem.

Quickly, he ducked inside and closed the door. He tried to video call the Professor, but with no success. He tried three times in a row but there was no answer. "He must be busy," he thought. "After all, it is dinner time." Deciding to text the message, he typed in, "Ponce and Odin were experimenting with baking soda and vinegar again. Only they've now discovered they can restrict the reaction and project pebbles into the air. We all heard numerous pings. Apparently, they were hoping to cause damage to see if you would appear to fix the problem. Since then we have been getting heavy rain and I just noticed that fountains of water are spraying all around the perimeter. Is that normal? There is also a distant beeping noise that I've never heard before and a flashing red glow. The water is getting quite deep, and I'm worried the cave may soon be flooded. I would highly recommend turning off the rain. I hope you get this message soon. I am trying to keep a close eye on Odin and Ponce, so I may not have another chance to get back to the cave."

Trying one more video call, Louis was disappointed that there was still no answer. "He could be teaching, or at a conference, or maybe just talking to someone else," he speculated. Impatiently, he waited a few more minutes to see if there would be a reply to his text. But there was nothing. "Oh well," he thought. "I've got to get back and keep everyone safe. I'm sure the Professor will look at his phone soon enough."

When he opened the cave door, he stepped back quickly in alarm as a stream of water poured into his office. "This is not good," he thought, quickly exiting and slamming the door behind him. "We need this rain to stop!" Then it occurred to him that he could message Evan. Glancing down at the water which was now past his ankles, he decided not to open the door again. "The Professor will get my message," he assured himself. "Surely, he won't be distracted for much longer."

Ducking under the fountain sprayers and sloshing through waist deep puddles in the low-lying areas, Uncle Louis was well-drenched when he returned to the store. In the dark, he could faintly make out seven black figures sitting on the deck under the veranda.

In the dim moonlight, Zahir and Kenzie could tell that Uncle Louis was still worried.

"What's wrong?" they asked.

"There's been far too much rain!" Uncle Louis replied. "It needs to end soon."

"Did you talk to the Professor?" Odin taunted. "Was he there looking in the window?"

"Did he hear the pings?" Ponce giggled.

Not wanting to cause any concern about the Professor's absence, Uncle Louis didn't reply. He turned to Zahir, Kenzie and Vahid.

"Guys," he said calmly. "I think it would be a good idea to get the boats and bring them over to the farmland."

There was silence. In the dim lighting, Uncle Louis could see faintly their look of surprise.

"Won't the rain stop soon?" Nancy asked timidly.

"I hope so," Uncle Louis told her flatly. "The farmland is the lowest-lying area," he explained. "I'm concerned that if this rain continues, we may need to get everyone to higher ground."

"Why won't the Professor stop this rain when we've had enough?" Kenzie asked.

Odin chuckled. "Didn't you tell him that we have lakes and rivers everywhere?"

In anger, Uncle Louis said, "I'm not exactly sure what is going on. But, for some reason, the water levels are rising dangerously and it's continuing to rain."

"Could those pebbles have hit something important?" Zahir queried.

Uncle Louis frowned. He considered Zahir's suggestion. "This rain began after the last round of pebbles... didn't it?"

Odin chuckled. Ponce looked surprised. Kenzie and Vahid shared an anxious glance.

"Round of pebbles?" Nancy echoed. "Did you cause this, Odin?"

"Certainly didn't mean to," Odin waffled. "I don't know how to make it rain."

Standing on the deck, Uncle Louis turned and looked towards the swollen, raging river that was overflowing the gardens and running to the lake. The water was creeping up the small hill on which the store stood and had surrounded his cabin completely. He could still faintly hear the steady, annoying, beeping sound. He wondered how many Tinys were already asleep in bed.

"I think we may have an emergency," he announced fearfully. "I'm going to need all your help to keep everyone safe."

Zahir and Kenzie jumped to their feet. "What can we do?" they asked.

Taking charge, Uncle Louis planned their strategy. "You both run in behind Cascading Mountain and find your way to Rainbow Hill," he told them. "Turn on the twinkle lights. Being able to see will be of great assistance to everyone. Then make sure everyone is awake on the hill. Tell the girls to stay safe where they are. Run down to the lake and make sure all the beach boys are accounted for. Grab all the boats. We need at least three or four of you to bring the boats over to the farmland. We've got to get the animals and everyone in the low areas up on top of Mining Hill."

Dashing off, Kenzie and Zahir plowed through the water that was creeping up the small hill. They headed towards the backside of Cascading Mountain.

"Should I go as well?" Vahid offered.

"You come with me," Uncle Louis told him. "The rest of us will get over to the farmlands and begin the evacuation."

"But I'm so tired," Odin complained, stretching out on the deck. "This is bedtime."

"You wanted to cause damage," Uncle Louis reminded him angrily, "and you were hoping someone else would fix things up. Well, Odin, tonight you will be helping to minimize the damage! You are coming with me."

"I'll find Ripple," Nancy cried out, jumping to her feet. Milan jumped to his as well.

"Get the cat," Uncle Louis nodded, "and meet us on Mining Hill."

Ponce stood up. "How will we get over there?" he asked anxiously. "I can't swim."

Odin was still lying on the deck.

"Odin, get up now," Uncle Louis yelled loudly, "or you won't eat all day... or the next!"

Odin slowly sat up and looked around. With mounting fear, he moaned, "We could all drown! I don't know how to swim either!"

Shaking his head, Uncle Louis realised that he should have insisted that all the Tinys learned to swim, regardless of whether or not they enjoyed the lake. Watching the water rise and the river rage, he wished he had made the effort to become a confident swimmer himself. "We won't be crossing the river," he assured Odin and Ponce. "We can make it to the farmland," he encouraged. "It's not that far away."

There was no time for hesitancy and Vahid was already plunging in. Stepping into the standing water, Uncle Louis was relieved to find it was only up to his chest. "Come on, you can walk across," he begged. "We have to do this quickly."

Taking hold of the reluctant teens' hands, Uncle Louis dragged them across to the other side.

"I'll wake up the guys," Vahid called back as he headed to the farmhouse.

"Thanks," Uncle Louis yelled back. "We'll get the girls." Once they had crossed the deep troughs of water, they ran up the gentle slope to the girl's home. In the distance, Uncle Louis could hear Vahid calling out to all the farmers. Brownie, the cow, was mooing. The sheep were bleating pitifully and even the hens were cackling in distress.

Uncle Louis led Odin and Ponce to the door of the orchard girls' home. They knocked loudly and yelled out their names.

Vinitha came to the window. "What's the matter?" she asked sleepily.

"We're being flooded," Uncle Louis called out. "Everyone needs to get up on top of Mining Hill. And we need to fetch the animals."

240

Vinitha ran around waking up her friends. In a few moments, the girls came running out, dressed and yawning.

"Why isn't the Professor turning off the rain?" Tina inquired.

"Something has gone wrong," Uncle Louis informed her. "For now, we just need to get everyone to safety. Hopefully the rain will stop soon."

"Sometimes the Professor really doesn't know what's going on, does he?" Odin smirked. "Remember when we all had to sit in the lake because it got too hot?

"Yeah," Ponce agreed. "That took forever to fix!"

The girls looked over in distress. They remembered the hot day. "What if he doesn't notice till the morning?" Yu Yan called out.

Vinitha's large eyes opened wider. "We could all drown!" she cried out in dismay.

Yu Yan burst out in tears.

"We have high hills," Uncle Louis assured the girls, reaching out to give them hugs. "It would take days of rain before the hills would be covered." Yet, he wasn't entirely sure how long it would take. The water was rising fast.

Turning to the boys, he spoke sharply, "Odin and Ponce, go and find Brownie the cow. It's your job to get her up the hill. It might be helpful to put a rope around her neck, but you'll have to find one. When you get her up the hill, you can wait for the rest of us. Don't stop till your job is done!"

Grumbling and complaining, they wandered off to find the cow.

Suddenly the twinkle lights on Rainbow Hill lit up. Still holding the fearful girls close, Uncle Louis was thankful that someone had turned on the switch and that they could all see so much better. However, his relief was short-lived; he could now see the enormity of the situation. The amount of water rushing through the meadow to the lake was alarming. As he was glancing back towards the store, he saw his house lurch forward and quickly sail off to the river.

"This is very, very serious," he thought to himself. With all the challenges they had been through in the first four months, he had never felt more abandoned and alone. Never had he seen destruction on this level. All their lives were in danger. In his mind he pleaded silently, "Please, Professor, look at your phone!"

"What should we do?" Tina asked.

Turning to the girls in a state of shock, Uncle Louis encouraged them to get the sheep and herd them up Mining Hill. "There are enough farmers to handle the rest of the animals," he told them. "I want you to all be safe – just worry about the sheep."

Wanting to do their part, the girls ran to get the bleating sheep out of their fenced enclosure. Uncle Louis ran down towards the farmhouse. Water was pouring into the windows. It was past his waist.

Charley and the farm boys were already outside, struggling to open the henhouse as the water was halfway up the door.

"Let's rip off the roof," Uncle Louis said, reaching up, hoping to pull himself on top. Vahid pulled himself up easily, then he extended his hand to help Uncle Louis. Charley was holding on to the door handle, trying not to float away. Being shorter, the water came to his armpits. Vahid pulled Charley up.

Once they were all on top, the three of them worked together trying to pull off a chunk of the roof, but it was quite secure. Brownie the cow was huddled behind the henhouse, surrounded by water and mooing over and over. Odin and Ponce were not having any success in coaxing her to move. "How can we find a rope?" Odin yelled.

"There's one in the henhouse," Charley called out. "Help us get this roof off."

With Odin's help, a corner of the roof broke off. The others lowered Charley down into the gaping hole. "Everyone is floating in here!" he called out. "Poor little chickens!"

Charley handed up the rope which was passed on to Odin, and then they began hauling the chickens out of the house.

Ponce and Odin strained heavily to move Brownie. "Come on," Odin roared. "We're trying to help you, you stubborn, foolish animal!"

"Talk nicely to Brownie," Vahid called out. "She's scared."

Charley's dog swam through the water and nipped at Brownie's hindquarters, coaxing her to move.

It was then that Uncle Louis saw four young men coming across the water toward them. Damien was leading the way on his surfboard. Zahir and Kenzie were in The Red Bird and Lema was paddling the beach boys' boat.

"Just in time," Uncle Louis said with relief. "We're going to need those boats."

Odin and Ponce heaved and managed to pull Brownie away from the henhouse, as Maxi continued to nip at her rear end. No sooner had she moved away, when Uncle Louis felt the henhouse lurch forward.

"Oh no," he shouted, as he felt the house begin to move towards the river.

Vahid looked at him anxiously. The chickens began to squawk and flap around. Fearfully, Charley reached up, and the others pulled him onto the roof.

"Hang on," Damien encouraged, as the henhouse drifted towards the raging river. "Let's stop them, guys."

Damien and the others in the boats paddled as hard as they could, attempting to steer their vehicles toward the floating house.

"Get ready for a collision," Uncle Louis warned, as he held firmly to the hole in the roof.

The others did the same. When the house struck the boats, the chickens flew up into the air, but the young men held firm.

"Be quick," Uncle Louis yelled. "Charley first." Charley grabbed a chicken and Vahid lowered him into Zahir's boat. Then they tried to grab more chickens, while the house lurched back and forth, and they were all in great danger of falling off.

Maxi had come back for her master and was swimming near Zahir's boat. Damien grabbed her, while the others grabbed the chickens.

Then the house lurched forward again and Vahid was tossed into the water. Seeing that the house was heading for the river, Uncle Louis jumped in after him. Vahid wasn't a confident swimmer and began to panic. Uncle Louis could only do a basic dog paddle, but he managed to grab the back of Vahid's shirt and pull him toward Lema. The henhouse slammed into the stone bridge and was dashed to pieces.

Rowing hard against the currents with both arms, Lema wasn't able to extend a hand to help anyone get on board. There was a desperate look on his face as he tried to keep his boat near the swimmers. Zahir and Kenzie were rowing hard to get their passengers to the hill. Damien was struggling to hold on to Maxi and move his surfboard forward. Maxi wanted to be with her master.

With all his might, Uncle Louis dragged Vahid toward the boat. He was fearful that Lema would give up rowing and be swept to the lake. The bridge was now a dangerous obstacle that no one wanted to hit. Desperate to get out of the water, Vahid reached out for the boat. He caught the edge and pulled hard. Uncle Louis grabbed the boat as well. Both of them dragged themselves on board. There was no time to catch their breath. Lema needed help. Vahid grabbed the spare building board and began to paddle. Slowly, ever so slowly, they moved forward.

Suddenly, Maxi plunged into the water to swim to Charley. However, the current had become too strong and the little dog was immediately pulled in the opposite direction.

"Come back, Maxi," Damien yelled, paddling wildly with his arms to fight the raging water and race after the dog. The others watched in horror as the current overpowered Damien. Losing the fight, he and Maxi were quickly drawn towards the river and the dangerous bridge.

A Nightmare

Chapter Thirty

Tossing and turning, the Professor was having a nightmare. It was all too real - a dream that often haunted him in the middle of the night. He was watching planes take off into the sky. He saw the aircraft taxi down the runway and get ready for take-off. His pregnant wife, Wendy, was on board. She was heading out to visit her family in Newfoundland. The jet engines roared, then the plane whirred down the runway and rose smoothly into the air. With a smile he waved in the parking lot, even though he knew that his wife couldn't see him. He stood gazing upward... and then there was an explosion. Fire and thick black smoke belched out from the jet engine. The plane was thrown off course, nosediving towards the highway below. He heard screams from people nearby, brakes screeching on the road, crashes, more explosions and then the blackest cloud rose silently into the air.

Sweating, his heart pounding, and breathing quickly, the Professor sat up, calling, "Wendy! Wendy!"

But he wasn't at the airport. He wasn't even in his bed. He was alone in his living room, sitting up on the couch.

Jumping to his feet, he turned on a light and walked around the room, making sure he was fully awake. *"Ça alors!* Will I never stop having this nightmare?" he asked himself.

He didn't want the dream to reoccur. He looked for his phone, hoping there might be some messages that would provide a distraction. It wasn't on the coffee table. Mystified, he checked the couch, even lifting the cushions to see if it had slipped in behind. It wasn't there. "What have I done with my phone?" he fretted. Running over to the hall where his lab coat hung on the stand, he was greatly relieved to find the phone in his right coat pocket.

"Whew!" he said. "I can't be without this phone." He touched the side button, but it didn't turn on. He tried a few more times before he realised his phone was dead.

"*Oh là là!*" he exclaimed, and then he thought over his usage. "I guess I had a few video calls yesterday with the relatives... and there was that cryonics article I was trying to read! Maybe I just need a new battery! It's been running out too fast lately."

Walking into his bedroom, he plugged his phone into the charger. It took a few seconds before the battery icon showed up. It was at zero percent.

"This will take a while," he muttered, coming into the kitchen for a snack. Finding some potato chips, he sat down and turned on his TV. There wasn't much on at three in the morning of December 26th, but he scanned through the options. "No wonder I had such a quiet evening... no phone!" he grimaced. After attending a lovely Christmas Dinner for the Biosphere staff held in the Arctic Biome, he had come home late and viewed some old videos. He had watched his wedding video with tears in his eyes, reminisced about their trips to India, Africa and the Philippines, and even looked at the video they had shared with his in-laws announcing their first successful IVF pregnancy. It had all been a bit much, stirring up past memories of happier days, still, he wondered how he didn't realise his phone was missing. Flipping through the TV channels, he tried to recall the day's events. "I talked to Wendy's parents for nearly an hour, then Aunt Claudette, and I read that article as soon as I sat down at my desk," he remembered. "I did receive a message around ten, just before I headed out to the Arctic Biome... and... well, that's the last communication I think..."

A news flash caught his eye. A record-setting earthquake had struck California, triggering a massive tsunami. As he watched terrible scenes of boats and cars being smashed up against hotel resorts and people fleeing for their lives, he shuddered in horror. *"C'est affreux!* How can terrible things like this happen on Christmas Day?" he raged. "All those poor people were just trying to enjoy their family vacations!"

As the news reporters struggled to make sense of the catastrophe, agonizing over the estimated loss of life, they interviewed an Australian scientist. Professor Lemans was surprised when the expert attempted to portray plate tectonics as an essential element of a living planet, regulating the temperatures on earth and moderating levels of carbon dioxide. As the scientist delved into the life-sustaining benefits of subduction, the Professor shook his head angrily. "This is not the time to make a case for a senseless tragedy!" he exclaimed. Suddenly, he heard a strange noise coming from his phone.

Dashing back into his bedroom, he saw a warning light flashing on the phone screen and heard a piercing alarm. For a moment or two he was befuddled. He was certain he had never seen this particular alarm before. Looking carefully, he read the words, "PARADISE FIRE ALARM".

Aghast, the Professor reeled unsteadily on his feet. Swallowing hard, he turned a ghostly white, realising the emergency had to be taking place in the Paradise Room... or the dome! Immediately, he imagined terrifying scenes. "How long as this been going on?" he wondered fearfully. "Has Evan responded? He must be getting this same alarm!"

The fire alarm system in the dome was not linked to any public fire department. Since Paradise was still a secret operation, he hadn't wanted to alert the public over an emergency he was confident would never happen. He felt certain that he and Evan would be able to handle everything on their own.

"What has happened?" he asked himself over and over, as he grabbed his keys from the counter and rushed for his car. At the last minute, he dashed back in to pick up his phone. Without the phone app, he would be unable to use the drop floor, which was the fastest way in. "I'll charge it in the car," he thought.

Racing outside in the middle of a snowstorm, the Professor climbed into his cold Toyota SUV. He plugged in his phone. In the wee hours of the morning, on one of the most important holidays, there were very few vehicles on the road. He made it quickly to the Biosphere.

Racing into the parking lot, the Professor noticed that Evan's car wasn't there! He spun out in the freshly fallen snow. With no other cars to collide into, he pulled out of the spin, parked safely and dashed into the Biosphere. Swiping his security card, he entered the large glass doors and ran down the halls. He hit the green icon on his phone and dropped into the secret chamber. He fumbled the code in the dark tunnel - taking two tries before '0suffering66' was entered correctly. Then he sprinted between the locked doors. As he ran through the underground lab, he could hear the distant echo of the fire alarm, but he couldn't smell smoke. Riding the elevator up, the doors slid open. The red warning light was flashing on the wall and the alarm was blasting noisily.

"I sure hope there wasn't a fire," he fretted, dashing to the dome. "Please let it be a false alarm! Where is Evan?"

Tiny lights lit up Paradise. He peered inside and saw the heavy flooding. The rainmaker was running back and forth letting down a spray of water at the highest intensity. All the sprinklers were running full blast. The whole system was performing well in 'fire response' mode, but he didn't see any evidence of a fire. *"Ça alors!* This has been going on for a long while," he deduced, looking around anxiously for the Tinys. He saw small groups on the hills and hoped they were all accounted for. Then he dashed towards the wall and hit the black emergency reset button. The alarm ceased, the flashing light stopped, the sprinklers turned off, and the rainmaker slid down into place next to the oxygenator.

Even though it was the middle of the night, he picked up his phone, and called Evan. There was no answer. He called him a second time and left a message. Then he sent a text. "Are you getting the alarm? We've had a major flood in Paradise," he typed. "I think everyone is safe. Please come in as soon as you can!"

Breathing heavily, and afraid of what he might see, the Professor ran fearfully back over to the Dome. "Thank goodness they've turned on the twinkle lights," he said to himself. In the middle of the churning water, he could see the boats full of chickens and Tinys. The young men were straining to paddle towards the hills. Swift motion caught his eye, and he looked over to see Damien desperately holding onto his surfboard as he was swept through the torrents.

"He's reaching for something," the Professor said to himself. "What is it?"

Then he noticed the little beagle trying to keep her head above the water. "*Oh là là!* Poor Maxi!" he whispered.

Transfixed, he watched as Damien reached out to pull the dog back onto his board. He had almost grabbed her tail when she was pulled under by the rapids.

Suddenly, the Professor noticed the stone bridge was sticking up above the water. It was right in Damien's path. Before he had time to wonder what might happen, Damien hit the bridge and flew up into the air. His surfboard went one direction and Damien went the other.

There was a long pause as the Professor waited, desperately hoping the young surfer was okay. Finally, to his great relief, Damien popped back up. Stretching out his strong arms, he swam toward Uncle Louis' house which was floating in the lake. When he climbed aboard safely, the Professor gave a long sigh of relief. However, Charley's dog failed to resurface.

Seeing the two boats had made it safely to Mining Hill, the Professor looked around for the other Tinys. He counted everyone that he could see on both hills. Aside from Damien, they had all made it to land. The occupants of the boats were climbing out and straggling up to higher ground with all the chickens. "I am so thankful! I am so thankful!" he said, holding his hand to his heart. "If I hadn't woken up, this could have been far, far worse." Quickly surveying the flooded dome, he saw that the school and the store were completely submerged.

"I need to open the drain," he told himself. "Everyone is safe on the hills now, and Damien is floating in the lake. The drain will take the water down slowly in the farmland. He should be okay."

Running over to his desk, the Professor wiggled his mouse to wake up the computer. He entered his password and put in the code to open the drain under the cliff. A gurgling sound indicated the command had taken place.

Now that the rainmaker had stopped and everyone had reached a place of safety, the Tinys huddled together. Drenched and shivering they had no way to dry off.

"He figured it out finally," Odin was grumbling. "Sure took him long enough."

The Professor was pleased to hear Uncle Louis' response. "Your foolishness started this, Odin. I don't know what you guys hit, but you damaged something. We could have lost lives tonight. Don't ever assume that you will be saved out of every reckless action that you take. I don't want to hear anything but thankfulness from you!"

"They hit something?" the Professor pondered. "Louis must have told me about this," he realised in dismay, taking his phone out of his pocket. Finally, he could take the time to check his messages.

Sure enough, a descriptive text had come through around six-thirty in the evening. "*Oh là là!* That was almost ten hours ago!" he calculated. Clapping his hand to his forehead, he berated himself for being so distracted.

Evan came rushing through the door, just as the Professor had finished reading the message. The young man's face was filled with dread.

"Everyone is alive," the Professor assured him in a hushed tone. "Thanks for coming right away."

Peering into the dome, Evan was horrified. "It's a complete flood!" he whispered harshly. "This is terrible! They could have been killed! What happened?"

"Apparently, Ponce and Odin were experimenting with the baking soda and vinegar again. They discovered how to project pebbles into the air, and were hoping to cause some damage..."

"What fools!" Evan breathed angrily. "Why would they ever want to damage their world?"

"Apparently, they wanted to see what I would do."

Shaking his head, Evan was in shock.

"I'm guessing they must have hit a sensor and caused it to malfunction," the Professor deduced softly. "Something caused the sensor to set off the fire alarm system."

"But you would have heard the alarm?" Evan questioned, trying to put all the details together. "I should have... but my phone was on vibrate. I was at a party... anyway, no excuses! I can't believe I missed it!"

The Professor admitted his own neglect of the phone and the quiet evening he had enjoyed after the staff dinner.

Evan listened in disbelief as the Professor recalled the details, keeping his voice low. "We failed them tonight," he confessed bitterly. "Even though we were both linked in to our 'failproof' system... we let them down!"

"We're so human!" Evan agonized, covering his face with his hands. "I'm thankful I'm not in charge of the world!" Tossing his arms up in the air, he whispered loudly, "Paradise is an enormous responsibility!"

"Everyone is still alive," the Professor reminded him.

Turning his attention to the Tinys, Evan counted those he could see. "There are thirteen shivering Tinys on Mining Hill," he remarked anxiously. "One Tiny is floating on debris in the lake. Where are the others?"

The Professor looked in. Rainbow Hill was deserted. "Well, they were all standing on the clearing when I came in," he mused softly. "I suppose if I lived on the hill, I'd be very tempted to get out of wet clothes and go back to bed."

"I wish we could drop in some blankets on Mining Hill," Evan whispered. There were no houses on Mining Hill.

"I could turn up the heat," the Professor suggested, running over to his desk to fiddle with the controls.

Making his way around to the west side, Evan suddenly pointed to the lake. "Two Tinys are in a boat," he said softly. "I'd say they are heading out to rescue Damien."

"Really?" the Professor whispered, looking up with a pleased expression.

"I'd say it's Aimee and Sanaa."

Rushing over to have a look, the Professor smiled to see the young ladies' courage. Now that the rain and sprinklers had stopped, and the raging river had subsided, the lake was fairly calm. Using Georgia and Vinitha's boat, the two young teenagers were paddling with all their strength towards the floating house.

Damien was very relieved to be rescued and quickly climbed aboard. He took Aimee's board and helped Sanaa paddle back to dry land. When they reached the shore, the Professor could hear Damien thanking the girls over and over. He gave them each a hug.

"We'll need another courage ceremony," Evan reflected. "I'm guessing there were a number of brave Tinys who helped out tonight."

"Yes," the Professor agreed. "A ceremony to celebrate courage will be in order once everything has settled back down. There is so much to clean up. Although, I am pleased that the fire response system worked so well."

"Had there been a fire, it would have quenched it," Evan agreed, still shaken by the ordeal. "However, we nearly lost lives because our safety system malfunctioned."

"That doesn't mean our safety system was faulty," the Professor argued.

Evan didn't reply. The Professor had designed the system and regardless of its unnecessary response to impact – if that had indeed been the cause – it did appear it would function well in a fire.

"We need a timer," Evan suggested. "An hour or two of rain should put out any fire."

"Yes, a timer is required," the Professor agreed wearily. His limitations and oversights were stacking up; he no longer prided himself on creating a 'perfect' world. Walking back and forth in front of the dome, he began listing off an action plan. "We will have to send everyone back to the nursery," he said. "I suppose we'll have to wait until the water levels have dropped so that they can walk out safely."

"A few hours of draining should take it down."

Nodding, the Professor agreed. "The sensors will need to be checked and replaced if necessary," he added, "and everything needs an opportunity to dry out. It may take a couple of weeks to do all the repairs."

As the initial shock wore off, and Evan realised that the Tinys were going to be okay, he quietly pondered the mishaps that had occurred. "This is the second time we've let the Tinys down because we didn't know what was happening!" he chided himself silently. Then he considered the breaking news story that he had heard on his rushed journey to the Biome. "There was an earthquake and tsunami in California last night," he thought, "but it was much worse than this!

253

Many lives were lost!" Mystified, he pondered, "This is Professor Lemans' big grievance against any 'God' notion. Catastrophes happen in our world all the time on a much larger scale. Is this because Seth's God isn't aware of what is going on? But if He's so powerful – how would He not know? Does He not care? Or does He simply choose not to intervene? And if not, why not?"

Suddenly, a terrible, immediate, practical realisation dawned on Evan and he spoke out loud, "How will we communicate with Louis?"

The two scientists looked at one another. The cave was fully submerged and so were the train tracks. Anything electrical would have to be replaced.

Stroking his goatee anxiously, the Professor was dismayed. "I suppose we can't... at the moment," he admitted.

"Once the water levels drop," Evan suggested, "we could open the train entrance and push in a note."

"Odin spends a lot of time guarding the entrance," the Professor nodded, observing the slowly receding water levels. "I'm sure he'll notice from Mining Hill. We need to get them out as soon as possible. Some of the houses are completely water-logged; the store and kitchen are ruined, the outhouses overflowed, and most of the fruit trees are floating in the lake. I hope we can get the message through in the morning, perhaps?"

"That may be possible," Evan nodded. "Good thing you have all those baby animals ready for nurturing," he smiled. "The timing couldn't be better. It will all work out."

"Yes," the Professor sighed deeply. "It will all work out."

Leaving Paradise

Chapter Thirty-One

*A*imee wearily pulled on the rope that she and Damien had placed around the deer's head. Georgia was pulling on the other. The two deer had always lived furtively in the forest and weren't used to close contact, never mind ropes.

"Come on," she begged the frightened animals. "We have to leave Paradise."

"I'll take the ropes," Damien offered. "You girls try and coax them from behind."

All the Tinys were distraught, even the animals. After the dangerous flood they had survived, Ponce had woken everyone in the morning, saying that they had to leave Paradise. Even the animals had to leave. It had taken a long time to catch the deer. If Damien hadn't found ropes and apples in Zahir and Milan's house, they may never have found a way.

With the girls behind them, and Damien pulling strongly in front, the deer reluctantly trotted along. Freddo stayed close to Aimee's side, anxious to find his master. Sanaa tried to catch a rabbit but without success.

"What will happen to the animals if they don't come with us?" she blurted out. "We can't catch them all."

"What about the ducks and the loons?" Lily asked.

No one really knew what to say.

"What would happen if we decided to stay?" Diya moaned.

"I don't see why any of us have to leave," Damien muttered. "We can fix things up. I can't imagine living in the nursery again!"

Passing by Zahir's house, Damien called out angrily. "Get up, Franz," he said. "Everyone has to leave. We're heading down now."

They waited impatiently for Franz. He finally emerged in a dry pair of Milan's clothes. Everything was topsy-turvy. Many of the Tinys had been trapped on the other side of Paradise. Those who had bravely taken the rescue boats had spent the night on Mining Hill. Damien and Franz had spent the last few hours of the short night sleeping in Zahir and Milan's house. Aimee, Georgia, Sanaa, Diya and Lily had been safe in their mansion on Rainbow Hill, with their own dry beds and clothes.

Up on the forested hill, the Tinys hadn't suffered nearly as much as those in the valley. No trees had been uprooted, and the water hadn't pooled around their homes. As they reached the clearing and looked out on the rest of Paradise, they were horrified.

Standing on the hilltop, Aimee began to cry. "It's ruined!" she wailed. "Our beautiful world is ruined!"

Sanaa came close and put her arm around her. The deer tried to pull away to run into the forest, and the two young men did all they could to hang on.

Paradise was in ruins. Water lay on the devastated gardens. Many fruit trees were uprooted and now floated in the brown lake. All the low-lying houses were bobbing up and down in the dirty water. The store, which had a foundation, had been fully submerged and the walls were now covered in green scum. The outhouse was a mess. Only a few pillars remained upright on the remains of the school. The lower sections of the hills were scarred with deep water furrows and mud lay everywhere. And little did any of them know that all the electronic equipment hidden in the cave under Rainbow Hill had been completely destroyed.

Sadly, they began their descent. The deer bolted, pulling hard on the ropes. Damien and Franz began sliding down the hill after them. "Whoa," they called out as mud splattered everywhere. "Girls, help!"

Hitting a tree, Damien was finally able to gain some leverage and take control. Franz slipped and fell but didn't let go of his rope. Aimee, Georgia and Sanaa ran down, slipping and sliding on the soggy slope to help the guys. Once two Tinys were holding onto each rope, they were able to control the deer. Sanaa saw the rabbit again and tried to catch him. Unfortunately, she tripped and fell face first in the mud. She picked herself up with dismay.

Diya carefully stepped from tree to tree. "Everything is so wet and gross!" she called out.

Lily tried to help her friend.

Coming out of the forest, they could see the others across the muddy valley. Uncle Louis was slowly making his way down Mining Hill. Zahir, Odin and Ponce were ahead of him. Charley and Kenzie had their arms full of chickens. Brownie and the sheep were happily following Vahid. Nancy was holding Ripple and Tina had a rabbit in her arms.

"Watch out, this mud is slippery," Uncle Louis called out loudly, almost falling himself. Ponce sat down and slid all the way to the bottom. Cheering wildly, he stood up covered with mud. Impulsively, Zahir and Odin did the same.

"Well, that's a quicker way," Damien mused, watching enviously as they sloshed through the muddy field. "If there were no trees on that hill, I'd have been even faster behind the deer!"

"You sure swam fast last night," Georgia remarked.

"Super fast!" Aimee agreed, looking proudly back over her shoulder as she helped hold the rope. "We were all watching you and hoping you would be okay!" Then with an anxious expression, she added, "Especially when you hit that bridge."

"I almost wasn't... okay," Damien admitted quietly, pulling hard on the rope as the deer tried to bolt.

"What?" the two girls asked in unison, helping the boys reign in the deer. Even Franz looked up in surprise.

"I got pulled way down by the water," he admitted. "When I came back up, I just barely made it to Uncle Louis' house. I didn't have the strength to swim to shore." With a quick smile in Aimee's direction, he said, "I'm awfully glad I got rescued!"

Helping Damien hold onto the rope, Aimee swallowed hard. "I'm so thankful we all survived that flood!" she cried out. "I couldn't bear to lose anyone else!"

"I'm going to write a book!" Georgia stated suddenly, as she and Franz held tightly to the other rope. "What happened to us last night is a story that everyone would want to read."

"Hey, that's a great idea," Damien nodded. He laughed, "It would be way more interesting than, "Jake and Ellie go to a Farm."

Loving the idea, Aimee suggested, "And you could draw pictures too!"

Franz piped up, "Maybe you could write about the hot day..."

Georgia's eyes shone, "When I saw the rainbow! And we first felt rain."

"And you will have to do the spider encounter!" Aimee added. "You tell that story so well."

Georgia was elated. "We've had some very exciting adventures!" she said.

Freddo looked up to see Zahir standing in the orchard ruins. With a happy bark, he came bounding through the brown water to greet his master. He then proceeded to shake, sending muddy water in all directions. Everyone yelled and tried to get out of the way.

Finally, all the Tinys gathered together in the uprooted orchard. Uncle Louis was talking to the others about the nursery. Aimee noticed Charley run over to place a little stone marker next to Rosa's pillar.

The bedraggled rose was still green, but Maxi had gone missing. Charley was heartbroken. Aimee felt so sad!

"So, we will see our pets in the nursery?" Milan inquired.

"Yes," Uncle Louis smiled. "The baby animals will need lots of love and nurturing. Evan is going to put plenty of new books in the library and he has even ordered some very special art and craft supplies."

"Really?" Vinitha and Yu Yan responded with delight, clapping their hands together.

"I'll start on my new book!" Georgia said quietly.

"I hope there will be clean, dry clothes," Vinitha said wistfully.

"Me too!" Uncle Louis agreed, looking around at all the wet and muddy teens.

"I hate the nursery," Odin complained. "We're going to be all crammed together again in one big, boring room!"

Many glaring eyes turned on Odin.

"Okay, okay," he growled, throwing his hands up. "I didn't know it was so easy to ruin Paradise. Maybe if the..."

"Odin, that's enough," Uncle Louis said sharply.

"Maybe we could help to fix Paradise back up, rather than stay in the nursery," Zahir suggested eagerly. "If we all pitched in, we could probably clean everything up in a few weeks. It would be kind of fun rebuilding..."

Damien and Kenzie agreed.

"I appreciate your enthusiasm," Uncle Louis acknowledged, "but this disaster is beyond us. We'll rebuild our homes when we return. We have more experience now, so we can build even better ones than we did before."

"And we'll appreciate Paradise so much more," Aimee nodded.

"Hard to believe that a tiny pebble can create this much damage," Odin grumbled, "or maybe the Professor just needs to pay better attention to what's going on... if he's even real!"

259

Ponce placed his hands on his hips and looked up with narrowed eyes. "He didn't know what was happening – did he?"

"Evan didn't either!" Odin smirked.

Turning around in the devastated orchard, Uncle Louis faced the challengers. The cow mooed, the chickens cackled, and Freddo was rolling in the low-lying water. All the wet, weary Tinys were looking toward him and many eyes were full of fear. While Uncle Louis could empathize with the feelings of abandonment to a certain degree, he was not in any doubt about the Professor's love or intentions. He was very loyal to the big, kind scientist he spoke to regularly on the Smartphone. Yet, it wasn't easy to transfer his allegiance or explain a being who preferred to remain unseen. He was well aware that his relationship had developed through continual interactions over the last four years, while the rest of the Tinys had never met the Mastermind of Paradise. Somehow, he had to provide a satisfactory answer to what had just happened even though he hadn't completely worked it out in his own mind.

"It was an unfortunate oversight," Uncle Louis admitted slowly. "I don't know why it took so long for anyone to respond, but from now on we have to realise the Professor and Evan may not be paying attention all of the time. That is true. There may be more emergencies that we will face in the future where we will have to rely on our own ingenuity to stay alive just as we've done before. Thankfully, they've equipped us with everything they could think of to protect us from danger. The lake kept us safe from the heat. The hills helped us to escape the flood. Who knows what the next emergency will be, but maybe there are other things built into Paradise that will help us to survive?"

Some of the Tinys were nodding in agreement, but Odin, Ponce and Franz rolled their eyes at each other, and smirked in amusement.

With narrowed eyes, Uncle Louis focused on the three scoffers and said firmly, "Let's learn one lesson from this! From now on we need to be very careful how we treat our environment. Carefulness may not protect us from every emergency, but it will avoid some!"

Odin kicked a muddy apple, "So, are you saying we can't do anymore experimenting?" he grumbled.

Zahir frowned. "You intended to cause damage," he argued. "Why don't you experiment and find a way to make things better?"

"Do you think you're Uncle Louis the Second?" Odin retorted, but no one laughed.

Uncle Louis mustered what strength he could, despite his exhaustion, to put on a brave face. "We're going to look on the positive side," he replied. "We survived this flood. We haven't been left to clean the mess up all on our own. We have an important work to do, looking after the next group of animal babies. We will keep busy in the nursery and the time will go fast. When we return with all our new pets, Paradise will be ready for us to enjoy once again."

Most of the Tinys cheered. When the tunnel doors opened, the farm boys led the way through the hall and toward the ramp, herding the animals ahead of them.

Aimee hung back, intending to be last in line. She turned for a final look at the marred ruins of Paradise, where they had been so happy for over four months.

"I love you, dear little home," she sang wistfully, looking up at her forested hill. "No matter where I roam, No matter how long we're away, I'm coming back someday. You'll be green with a pretty view. Rainbows will rise over you. And when I see you again... "

Another voice joined hers - a deeper, richer voice, "I'll know just how lucky I am."

Turning around abruptly, she saw Zahir standing behind her. "Good ending," she said with a tearful smile.

Zahir held out his muddy hand, and she took it gratefully.

"It won't be long!" he assured her. "Come on. Let's go see our new pets."

261

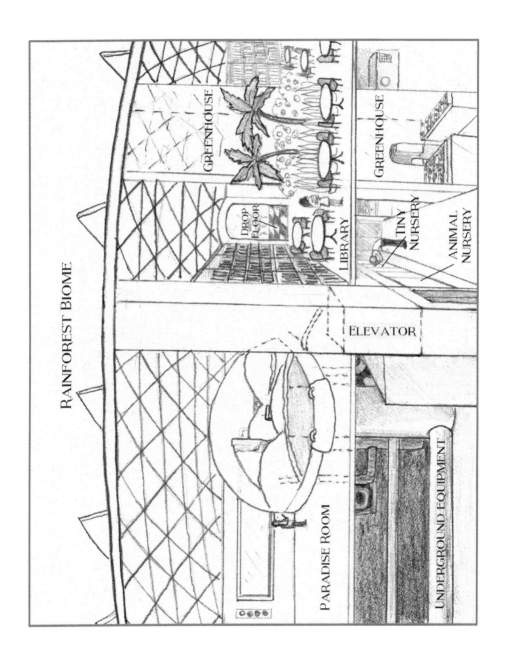

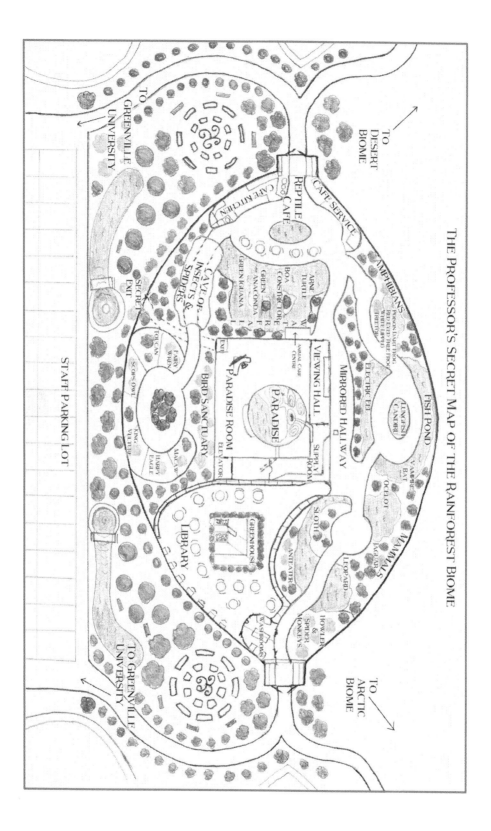

THE PROFESSOR'S SECRET MAP OF THE RAINFOREST BIOME

Next in THE ENORMOUS TINY EXPERIMENT series:

Pain in Paradise

Entering adolescence, the Tinys return to their beautiful, restored world only to discover that human shortcomings can undermine happiness and ruin friendships. Sadly, there is also a major problem the Professor can't overcome and tears begin to flow. Hoping to showcase Paradise to their colleagues, will the evidence of suffering turn the world against this project?

Within the Greenville University, a challenge from the Professor drives Seth to compile convincing evidence that God exists. A close friendship develops as the scientists discuss: Is there a purpose for suffering? Why does God allow natural disasters to occur? What is human nature and why did God make us the way that we are? And why were Christian scientists able to discover so many universal laws of nature?

After a reluctant interchange with Seth over human freewill the Professor begins to view God's justice in a new light, but nothing prepares him for the devasting choice a few Tinys make when Uncle Louis' back is turned.

Acknowledgements

All profits from "THE ENORMOUS TINY EXPERIMENT" series will be donated towards Agape in Action.

Agape in Action is a Christadelphian charitable organization helping underprivileged children, widows and families in Africa and India. Support to Agape in Action is provided through child sponsorship, project sponsorship and general donations.

Although the needs are enormous, Agape in Action aims to affect change one child at a time, one family at a time, one community at a time. The name Agape in Action reflects our intention of putting love ('agape') into action by responding compassionately to those who are in need. Providing wells for water, basic nutrition and hygiene programs, schools and scholarships, homes for orphans, help for widows, and in-depth Sunday School and Bible tuition, Agape in Action seeks to assist children and families living in extreme poverty.

http://www.agapeinaction.org/

I would like to express grateful thanks to our Heavenly Father for ideas, time and helpful supporters. Thanks to all who lovingly gave me your honest feedback and corrections.

An enormous thank you to Carrie and David Reynolds who with their combined scientific and psychological expertise were able to thoroughly edit this book, advise me on many matters and even write sections of "Probable or Improbable."

Thanks also to Andrew Bramhill who encouraged me to pick up the pen, and to those who added and refined many issues along the way: Frank and Dorothy Abel, Katie Stedman, Christina Lloyd, Olivia Badger, Heather Venton, Jed Snobelen, Lisa Mansfield, Becky, Joanna, Zoe and James Gore, Mary-Jane and Eden Styles, Jake Robinson, my very supportive husband Chris, and Josiah, Faith and Verity.

A special thanks to those who cheerfully modelled numerous times for the pictures - my son, my husband, my son-in-law, J. Jackson, and the Abel and Aback teens. ☺

Comments are always welcome: annatikvah@yahoo.ca

Bibliography

Many helpful ideas for this series have come from the Bible and my Christadelphian fellow believers. The following books and websites have also provided scientific insights and logical arguments to counter Postmodernism, Evolution and New Atheism:

David Burges. *"Wonders of Creation. The works of the Divine Designer"* (The Testimony, 2017; http://testimonymagazine.com)

Scott Hann and Benjamin Wiker. *Answering the New Atheism – Dismantling Dawkin's Case Against God.* (Emmaus Road Publishing, 2008)

Hillary Morgan Ferrer. *Mama Bear Apologetics.* (Harvest House Publishers, 2019)

Robert K. Greenleaf. *Servant Leadership.* (Paulist Press, 1977)

Dr. Robert Carter. Creation Ministries International. Creation.com

John Launchbury. Change us Not God – Bible Mediations on the Death of Jesus. (WCF Publishing, 2009 – wcfoundation.org)

The Purpose of Suffering

GOD'S PURPOSE WITH THE EARTH

1. What is God's eventual purpose with the earth?

_____

_____

"For the earth will be filled with the knowledge of the glory of the LORD as the waters cover the sea." Habakkuk 2:14; See also Psalm 72

"And I heard a loud voice from the throne saying, "Behold, the dwelling place of God is with man. He will dwell with them, and they will be his people, and God himself will be with them as their God. He will wipe away every tear from their eyes, and death shall be no more, neither shall there be mourning, nor crying, nor pain anymore, for the former things have passed away." Revelation 21:3-4

2. Consider God's description of His character. How do God's characteristics impact the world?

_____

_____

"The LORD, the LORD, a God merciful and gracious, slow to anger, and abounding in steadfast love and faithfulness, keeping steadfast love for thousands, forgiving iniquity and transgression and sin, but who will by no means clear the guilty, visiting the iniquity of the fathers on the children and the children's children, to the third and the fourth generation." Exodus 34:6-7

"But I say to you, Love your enemies and pray for those who persecute you, so that you may be sons of your Father who is in heaven. For he makes his sun rise on the evil and on the good, and sends rain on the just and on the unjust." Matthew 5:44-45

3. Does God ever forget about His Creation? _____

"Are not five sparrows sold for two farthings, and not one of them is forgotten before God? But even the very hairs of your head are all numbered. Fear not therefore: ye are of more value than many sparrows." Luke 12:6-7

4. If we lived in an ideal world without any sickness or disease, natural calamities, harmful insects and animals, would we all be happy and peaceful? Why or why not?_____

THE PURPOSE OF SUFFERING

1. Why did God bring suffering into our world? (see references)

_____

"Because you have listened to the voice of your wife and have eaten of the tree of which I commanded you, 'You shall not eat of it,' cursed is the ground because of you; in pain you shall eat of it all the days of your life; thorns and thistles it shall bring forth for you; and you shall eat the plants of the field. By the sweat of your face you shall eat bread; till you return to the ground, for out of it you were taken; for you are dust, and to dust you shall return." Genesis 3:17-19

"For the creation was subjected to futility, not willingly, but because of him who subjected it, in hope that the creation itself will be set free from its bondage to corruption and obtain the freedom of the glory of the children of God." Rom. 8:20-21

"Not only that, but we rejoice in our sufferings, knowing that suffering produces endurance, and endurance produces character, and character produces hope, and hope does not put us to shame, because God's love has been poured into our hearts through the Holy Spirit who has been given to us." Romans 5:3-5

2. What can we learn from suffering?

_____

_____

"Blessed be the God and Father of our Lord Jesus Christ, the Father of mercies and God of all comfort, who comforts us in all our affliction, so that we may be able to comfort those who are in any affliction, with the comfort with which we ourselves are comforted by God. For as we share abundantly in Christ's sufferings, so through Christ we share abundantly in comfort too. If we are afflicted, it is for your comfort and salvation; and if we are comforted, it is for your comfort, which you experience when you patiently endure the same sufferings that we suffer." 2 Corinthians 1:3-6

"It is better to go to the house of mourning than to go to the house of feasting, for this is the end of all mankind, and the living will lay it to heart. Sorrow is better than laughter, for by sadness of face the heart is made glad. The heart of the wise is in the house of mourning, but the heart of fools is in the house of mirth. It is better for a man to hear the rebuke of the wise than to hear the song of fools." Ecclesiastes 7:2-5

"For godly grief produces a repentance that leads to salvation without regret, whereas worldly grief produces death." 2 Corinthians 7:10

3.   What did Job learn from suffering?

"As an example of suffering and patience, brothers, take the prophets who spoke in the name of the Lord. Behold, we consider those blessed who remained steadfast. You have heard of the steadfastness of Job, and you have seen the purpose of the Lord, how the Lord is compassionate and merciful." James 5:10-11

"Then Job answered the LORD and said: "I know that you can do all things, and that no purpose of yours can be thwarted. Who is this that hides counsel without knowledge?' Therefore I have uttered what I did not understand, things too wonderful for me, which I did not know. 'Hear, and I will speak; I will question you, and you make it known to me.' I had heard of you by the hearing of the ear, but now my eye sees you; therefore I despise myself, and repent in dust and ashes." Job 42:1-6

4.   What did David learn by suffering?

(See Psalm 32 and Psalm 51)

5.   What did Jesus learn from suffering?

"In the days of his flesh, Jesus offered up prayers and supplications, with loud cries and tears, to him who was able to save him from death, and he was heard because of his reverence. Although he was a son, he learned obedience through what he suffered. And being made perfect, he became the source of eternal salvation to all who obey him," Hebrews 5:7-9

"Since then we have a great high priest who has passed through the heavens, Jesus, the Son of God, let us hold fast our confession. For we do not have a high priest who is unable to sympathize with our weaknesses, but one who in every respect has been tempted as we are, yet without sin. Let us then with confidence draw near to the throne of grace, that we may receive mercy and find grace to help in time of need." Hebrews 4:14-16

6.   Does suffering make people stronger or weaker? Explain:

"'My son, do not regard lightly the discipline of the Lord, nor be weary when reproved by him. For the Lord disciplines the one he loves, and chastises every son whom he receives.' It is for discipline that you have to endure. God is treating you as sons. For what son is there whom his father does not discipline?... Besides this, we have had

269

earthly fathers who disciplined us and we respected them. Shall we not much more be subject to the Father of spirits and live? For they disciplined us for a short time as it seemed best to them, but he disciplines us for our good, that we may share his holiness. For the moment all discipline seems painful rather than pleasant, but later it yields the peaceful fruit of righteousness to those who have been trained by it." Hebrews 12:5-11

"Therefore, as the Holy Spirit says, 'Today, if you hear his voice, do not harden your hearts as in the rebellion, on the day of testing in the wilderness, where your fathers put me to the test and saw my works for forty years. Therefore I was provoked with that generation, and said, 'They always go astray in their heart; they have not known my ways.' As I swore in my wrath, 'They shall not enter my rest.' Take care, brothers, lest there be in any of you an evil, unbelieving heart, leading you to fall away from the living God." Hebrews 3:7-13

7.   Does anything good come from enduring or battling dangerous situations? Explain:

_____

8.   In general, do people become more appreciative or less appreciative when they have everything they need? Explain:

_____

9.   Think generally about the attitudes of people in the 'First World' compared to those in the 'Third World:'

Generally speaking, in countries with corrupt governments:
  Who is blamed for the suffering?

_____

  Who is seen as the only hope for salvation?

_____

In countries where the government attempts to solve all the problems:
  Who are seen as the 'saviours'?

_____

  Who gets blamed for the world's woes? _____

10. How do people feel when they solve a problem, create or do something for the betterment of others? _____

11.   How do we feel if we've prayed to God for help and he rescues us from our troubles?_____

12.   When society is ideal and all needs provided for, are people inclined to invest money, time and finances into improving technology? Think of the common phrase "Necessity is the motherhood of invention." Explain:

_____

13.   Would you enjoy reading a book in which the characters never experienced danger or suffering? Why or why not?

_____

14.   Has God suffered in creating our world, experiencing our rebellion, and redeeming us from sin?

_____

"The LORD saw that the wickedness of man was great in the earth, and that every intention of the thoughts of his heart was only evil continually. And the LORD regretted that he had made man on the earth, and it grieved him to his heart." Genesis 6:5-6

"For he said, "Surely they are my people, children who will not deal falsely. And he became their Savior. In all their affliction he was afflicted, and the angel of his presence saved them; in his love and in his pity he redeemed them; he lifted them up and carried them all the days of old. But they rebelled and grieved his Holy Spirit; therefore he turned to be their enemy, and himself fought against them." Isaiah 63:8-10

"For God so loved the world, that he gave his only Son, that whoever believes in him should not perish but have eternal life. For God did not send his Son into the world to condemn the world, but in order that the world might be saved through him." John 3:16-17

"In this the love of God was made manifest among us, that God sent his only Son into the world, so that we might live through him. In this is love, not that we have loved God but that he loved us and sent his Son to be the propitiation for our sins. Beloved, if God so loved us, we also ought to love one another." 1 John 4:9-10

RESPONSIBILITY FOR SUFFERING

1. Does God expect us to take care of His earth? Explain:

_____

"The LORD God took the man and put him in the garden of Eden to work it and keep it." Genesis 2:15

"The nations raged, but your wrath came, and the time for the dead to be judged, and for rewarding your servants, the prophets and saints, and those who fear your name, both small and great, and for destroying the destroyers of the earth."" Revelation 11:18

2. When we care for things (tidy, clean, fix and make more beautiful) how do we feel about ourselves and our environment?

_____

3. When we litter, destroy, neglect or make mess for others – how do we feel about ourselves and our environment?

_____

4. Who is most responsible for the following problems? God or Man?
    _____Global warming
    _____Cancer
    _____Fear of nuclear warfare
    _____Deformity in people
    _____Poverty/Famine in countries where governments are corrupt
    _____Fires
    _____Rape and murder
    _____Increase in violence and harmful actions?
    _____Earthquakes and Natural Disasters
    _____Violence and Evil Actions
    _____Pestilence and Disease

5. What do we do to each other that causes pain and suffering?
    Small scale _____
    Large scale _____

6. What drives people to hurt each other?_____

7.   What man-made things can be used for good, but are very dangerous if used for evil? _____

9. What gifts has God given us that can be used for good purposes or evil?
_____

WILL IT ALWAYS BE THIS WAY?

1.   Is it possible for mankind to completely solve the problems of global warming and other environmental issues? Explain:
_____

2.   How can mankind reduce the loss of life in:
Earthquakes? _____
Floods? _____
Tsunamis? _____
Fires? _____
Disease? _____

3.   Will God always protect His followers from natural disasters? Why or why not? _____

4.   Consider the future promises God has made to rectify the problems we face in our world: (You may want to highlight them)

"Behold, the dwelling place of God is with man. He will dwell with them, and they will be his people, and God himself will be with them as their God. He will wipe away every tear from their eyes, and death shall be no more, neither shall there be mourning, nor crying, nor pain anymore, for the former things have passed away." Revelation 21:3-4

"There shall come forth a shoot from the stump of Jesse, and a branch from his roots shall bear fruit. And the Spirit of the LORD shall rest upon him, the Spirit of wisdom and understanding, the Spirit of counsel and might, the Spirit of knowledge and the fear of the LORD. And his delight shall be in the fear of the LORD. He shall not judge by what his eyes see, or decide disputes by what his ears hear, but with righteousness he shall judge the poor, and decide with equity for the meek of the earth; and he shall strike the

earth with the rod of his mouth, and with the breath of his lips he shall kill the wicked. Righteousness shall be the belt of his waist, and faithfulness the belt of his loins. The wolf shall dwell with the lamb, and the leopard shall lie down with the young goat, and the calf and the lion and the fattened calf together; and a little child shall lead them. The cow and the bear shall graze; their young shall lie down together; and the lion shall eat straw like the ox. The nursing child shall play over the hole of the cobra, and the weaned child shall put his hand on the adder's den. They shall not hurt or destroy in all my holy mountain; for the earth shall be full of the knowledge of the LORD as the waters cover the sea."

"Blessed are those who wash their robes, so that they may have the right to the tree of life and that they may enter the city by the gates. Outside are the dogs and sorcerers and the sexually immoral and murderers and idolaters, and everyone who loves and practices falsehood." Revelation 22:14-15
See also Psalm 72; Isaiah 35; Psalm 37

5.   While humans can extend life by better health care and research, and use their wisdom to overcome natural disasters, their skills to save others, ultimately what enemy cannot be defeated?

_____

6.   Does God have a way to defeat death? When? And How?

_____

–

"For the trumpet will sound, and the dead will be raised imperishable, and we shall be changed. For this perishable body must put on the imperishable, and this mortal body must put on immortality. When the perishable puts on the imperishable, and the mortal puts on immortality, then shall come to pass the saying that is written: "Death is swallowed up in victory. O death, where is your victory? O death, where is your sting? The sting of death is sin, and the power of sin is the law. But thanks be to God, who gives us the victory through our Lord Jesus Christ." 1 Corinthians 15:52-57

"The first man was from the earth, a man of dust; the second man is from heaven. As was the man of dust, so also are those who are of the dust, and as is the man of heaven, so also are those who are of heaven. Just as we have borne the image of the man of dust, we shall also bear the image of the man of heaven. I tell you this, brothers: flesh and blood cannot inherit the kingdom of God, nor does the perishable inherit the imperishable." 1 Corinthians 15:47-50

"But our citizenship is in heaven, and from it we await a Savior, the Lord Jesus Christ, who will transform our lowly body to be like his glorious body, by the power that enables him even to subject all things to himself." Philippians 3:20-21

See also John 11; Romans 8:29; 1 John 3:1-3; John 5:41; 6:40-44

7.   Assuming the Bible is inspired by God, has God given any evidence to prove His remedy is possible?

_____

8.   Can a 'mortal' being fully *enjoy* living in an ideal world with no suffering, danger or lack of provisions?

_____

9.   In order to fully enjoy a perfect world, what needs to happen to us?

_____

Printed in Great Britain
by Amazon

10274812R00163